"Get your wife out of here!"
Hawk yelled to the candidate.
"This is sorcerer's work!"

Adamant started to hurry Dannielle towards the front door,
and then stopped short as a dark shape began to materialise
between them and the door. The falling blood ran together,
drop joining with drop, to form the beginnings of a body.
In the space of a few minutes it grew arms and legs and a
hunched misshapen body. It stood something like a man,
but the proportions were all wrong. It had huge teeth and
claws, and swirling dark clots of blood where its eyes
should have been. It moved slowly towards its prey, its
body heaving and swelling with every movement.
Hawk and Fisher both cut at the figure, and it laughed
hideously at them . . .

Hawk & Fisher
Winner Takes All

HAWK & FISHER
WINNER TAKES ALL

SIMON R. GREEN

ACE BOOKS, NEW YORK

This book is an Ace original edition,
and has never been previously published.

WINNER TAKES ALL

An Ace Book/published by arrangement with
the author

PRINTING HISTORY
Ace edition/January 1991

ISBN: 0-441-14291-5

Ace Books are published by The Berkley Publishing Group,
200 Madison Avenue, New York, NY 10016.
The name ''ACE'' and the ''A'' logo
are trademarks belonging to Charter Communications, Inc.

PRINTED IN THE UNITED STATES OF AMERICA

10 9 8 7 6 5 4 3 2 1

1

The Hollow Men

Every city has its favourite blood sports. Some cities prefer the traditional cruelties of bearbaiting or cockfights, while others indulge their baser appetites with gladiators and arenas. The city port of Haven gets its thrills from the dirtiest, bloodiest sport of all: politics.

It was election time in Haven, and the shutters were going up all over town. It was a time for banners and parades, speeches, and festivities, and the occasional, good old-fashioned riot. The streets were packed with excited crowds, pickpockets and cutpurses were having the time of their lives, and the taverns were making money hand over fist. Work in the city slowed to a standstill as everyone got caught up in election fever. Everyone except the Guards, who were working double shifts in an increasingly vain attempt to keep Haven from turning into a war zone.

It was autumn in Haven, and the weather was at its most civilised. The days were comfortably warm, and the nights delightfully cool. There was a constant breeze from off the ocean, and it rained just often enough to make people grateful for the times when it didn't. Just the kind of weather to make a man dissatisfied with his lot, and determined to get out and enjoy the weather while it lasted. Which meant there were even more people out on the streets than was usual for an election. The smart money was betting on a complete breakdown of law and order by mid-afternoon. Luckily the city only allowed twenty-four hours for electioneering. Anything more than that was begging for trouble. Not to mention civil war.

Hawk and Fisher, husband and wife and Captains in the city Guard, strolled unhurriedly down Market Street, and the bustling crowds parted quickly before them. Patience tended to be in short supply and tempers flared quickly around election time, but no one in Haven, drunk or sober, was stupid enough to upset Hawk and Fisher. There were quicker and less painful ways to commit suicide.

Hawk was tall and dark, but no longer handsome. A series of old scars ran down the right side of his face, pale against the tanned skin, and a black silk patch covered his right eye. He wore a simple white cotton shirt and trousers, and the traditional black cloak of the Guards. Normally he didn't bother with the cloak. It got in the way during fights. But with so many strangers come to town for the election, the cloak served as a badge of authority, so he wore it all the time now, with little grace and even less style. Hawk always looked a little on the scruffy side, and his boots in particular were old and battered, but a keen eye might have noticed that they had once been of very superior quality and workmanship. There were many rumours about Hawk's background, usually to do with whether or not his parents had been married, but no one knew anything for sure. The man's past was a mystery, and he liked it that way.

On the whole, he didn't look like much. He was lean and wiry rather than muscular, and beginning to build a stomach. He wore his dark hair at shoulder length, in defiance of fashion, swept back from his forehead and tied with a silver clasp. He had only just turned thirty, but already there were thick streaks of grey in his hair. At first glance he looked like just another bravo, past his prime and going to seed. But few people stopped at the first glance. There was something about Hawk, something in the scarred face and single cold eye that gave even the drunkest hardcase pause for thought. On his right hip Hawk carried a short-handled axe instead of a sword.

He was very good with an axe. He'd had plenty of practice, down the years.

Isobel Fisher walked at Hawk's side, echoing his pace and stance with the naturalness of long companionship. She was tall, easily six feet in height, and her long blond hair fell to her waist in a single thick plait, weighted at the tip with a polished steel ball. She was in her mid- to late-twenties, and handsome rather than beautiful. There was a rawboned harshness to her face that contrasted strongly with her deep blue eyes and generous mouth. Somewhere in her past something had scoured all the human weaknesses out of her, and it showed. Like Hawk, she wore a white cotton shirt and trousers, and the regulation black cloak. The shirt was half unbuttoned to show a generous amount of bosom, and her shirt sleeves were rolled up above her elbows, revealing arms corded with muscle and lined with old scars. Her boots were battered and scuffed and looked as though they hadn't been cleaned in years. Fisher wore a sword on her left hip, and her hand rested comfortably on the pommel.

Hawk and Fisher were known throughout Haven. Firstly, they were honest, which was in itself enough to mark them as unusual amongst Haven's overworked and underpaid Guards. And secondly, they kept the peace; whatever it took. Hawk and Fisher brought in the bad guys, dead or alive. Mostly dead.

People tended to be very law-abiding while Hawk and Fisher were around.

They made their way unhurriedly down Market Street, enjoying the early morning warmth, and keeping an eye on the street traders. The election crowds meant good pickings for the fast-food sellers, souvenir stalls, and back-alley conjurers with their cheap charms and amulets. Stalls lined the streets from one end to the other without a gap, varying from tatty affairs of wood and canvas to established family concerns with padded silk and beaded awnings. The clamour of the merchants was deafening, and the more tawdry the goods, the louder and more extravagant were the claims made on their behalf.

There were drink stands everywhere, competing with the

taverns by offering cheap spirits with the traditional sign: DRUNK FOR A PENNY; DEAD DRUNK FOR TUPPENCE. There was beer as well, for the less adventurously minded. That came free, courtesy of the Conservatives. On the whole, they preferred the electorate to be well the worse for drink on polling day. That way, they were either grateful enough to vote Conservative in the hope of more free booze, or too drunk to raise any real opposition. And since the populace was also usually too drunk to riot, the Guards liked it that way too.

Everywhere Hawk and Fisher looked there were more traders' stalls, crowding the streets and spilling into the alleyways. There were flags and fireworks and masks and all kinds of novelties for sale, every one of them guaranteed to be worth a damn sight less than what you paid for it. If you wanted more upmarket souvenirs, like delicate china and glassware tastefully engraved with designs and slogans from the election, then you had to go uptown to find them. The Northside might have been upmarket once, but if so, it was so long ago that no one could remember when. These days the Northside was the harshest, poorest, and most dangerous area in Haven. Which was why Hawk and Fisher got the job of patrolling it. Partly because they were the best, and everyone knew it, but mainly because they'd made just as many enemies inside the Guard as out. It was possible to be too honest, in Haven.

Hawk looked wistfully at a stall offering spiced sausage meat on wooden skewers. It looked quite appetising, if you ignored the flies. Fisher noticed his interest, and pulled him firmly away.

"No, Hawk; we don't know what kind of meat went into those sausages. You can't afford to spend the rest of the day squatting in the jakes with your trousers round your ankles."

Hawk laughed. "You're probably right, Isobel. It doesn't matter; if I remember correctly, there's a tavern down here on the right that does an excellent lobster dinner for two."

"It's too early for dinner."

"All right; we'll have a lobster lunch, then."

"You're eating too many snacks these days," said Fisher sternly. "It's a wonder you can still do up your sword belt."

"Everyone's entitled to a hobby," said Hawk.

They walked on in silence for a while, just looking around them, seeing what there was to be seen. People in the crowds waved and smiled, or ostentatiously ignored them. Hawk and Fisher gave them all the same polite nod, and walked on. They couldn't trust the smiles, and the rest didn't matter. Hawk's attention began to drift away. He'd been in Haven for five years now, and some days it seemed like fifty. He missed his homeland. He felt it most of all at autumn. Back in the Forest Kingdom, the leaves would be turning bronze and gold, and the whole sight and sound and smell of the Forest would be changing as the great trees prepared for winter. Hawk sighed quietly and turned his attention once again to the grimy stone houses and filthy cobbled streets of Haven. For better or worse, he was a city boy now.

Explosions shook the air ahead, and Hawk's hand went to his axe before he realised it was just more fireworks. The Haven electors were great ones for fireworks; the louder and more extravagant the better. Bright splashes of magically augmented colors burst across the sky, staining the clouds contrasting shades until they looked like a rather messy artist's pallet. There were several attempts at sign-writing in the sky, but they all got entangled with each other, producing only broken lines of gibberish. The various factions quickly grew bored, and began using the fireworks as ammunition against each other. There were shouts and yells and the occasional scream, but luckily the fireworks weren't powerful enough to do any real damage. Hawk and Fisher just looked the other way and let them get on with it. It kept the crowds amused.

Sudden movement up ahead caught Hawk's eye, and he increased his pace slightly. The crowd at the end of the street had turned away from the fireworks to watch something more interesting. Already there were cheers and catcalls.

"Sounds like trouble," said Hawk resignedly, drawing his axe.

"It does, doesn't it?" said Fisher, drawing her sword. "Let's go and make a nuisance of ourselves."

They pressed forward, and the crowd parted unwillingly before them, giving ground only because of the naked steel in the Guards' hands. Hawk frowned as he saw what had drawn the crowd's attention. At the intersection of two streets two rival gangs of posterers were fighting each other with fists, clubs, and anything else they could get their hands on. The crowd cheered both sides impartially, and hurried to lay bets on the outcome.

Since most of the electorate was barely literate, the main political parties couldn't rely on pamphlets or interviews in Haven's newspapers to get their message across. Instead, they trusted to open-air gatherings, broadsheet singers, and lots of posters. The posters tended to be simple affairs, bearing slogans or insults in very large type. COUNCILLOR HARDCASTLE DOES IT WITH TRADESMEN was a popular one at the moment, though whether that was a slogan or an insult was open to interpretation.

Posters could appear anywhere; on walls, shopfronts, or slow-moving passersby. A gang of posterers moving at full speed could slap posters up all over Haven in under two hours. Assuming the paste held out. And also assuming no one got in their way. Unfortunately, most gangs of posterers spent half their time tearing down or defacing posters put up by rival gangs. So when two gangs met, as was bound to happen on occasion, political rivalry tended to express itself through spirited exchanges and open mayhem, to the delight of whatever onlookers happened to be around at the time. Haven liked its politics simple and direct, and preferably brutal.

Hawk and Fisher stood at the front of the crowd and watched interestedly as the fight spilled back and forth across the cobbles. It was fairly amateurish, as fights went, with more pushing and shoving than actual fisticuffs. Hawk was minded to just wander off and let them get on with it. They weren't causing anyone else any trouble, and the crowd was too busy placing bets to get involved themselves. Besides, a good punch-up helped to take some of the pressure off. But then he saw knives gleaming in some of the posterers' hands, and he sighed regretfully. Knives changed everything.

He stepped forward into the fight, grabbed the nearest posterer with a knife, and slammed him face first against the nearest wall. There was an echoing meaty thud, and the posterer slid unconscious to the ground. His erstwhile opponent rounded on Hawk, knife at the ready. Fisher knocked him cold with a single punch. Several of the fallen posterers' friends started forward, only to stop dead as they took in Hawk's nasty grin and the gleaming axe in his hand. Some turned to run, only to find Fisher had already moved to block their way, sword in hand. The few remaining fights quickly broke up as they realised something was wrong. The watching crowd began booing and catcalling at the Guards. Hawk glared at them, and they shut up. Hawk turned his attention back to the posterers.

"You know the rules," he said flatly. "No knives. Now, turn out your pockets, the lot of you. Come on, get on with it, or I'll have Fisher do it for you."

There was a sudden rush to see who could empty their pockets the quickest. A largish pile of knives, knuckledusters, and blackjacks formed on the cobbles. There were also a fair number of good-luck charms and trinkets, and one shrunken head on a string. Hawk looked at the posterers disgustedly.

"If you can't be trusted to play nicely, you won't be allowed to play at all. Understand? Now, get the hell out of here before I arrest the lot of you for loitering. One group goes North, the other goes South. And if I get any more trouble from any of you today, I'll send you home to your families in chutney jars. Now, move it!"

The posterers vanished, taking their wounded with them. Only a few crumpled posters scattered across the street remained to show they'd ever been there. Hawk kicked the pile of weapons into the gutter, and they disappeared down a storm drain. He and Fisher took turns glaring at the crowd until it broke up, and then they put away their weapons and continued their patrol.

"That was a nice punch of yours, Isobel."

"My strength is as the strength of ten, because my heart is pure."

"And because you wear a knuckle-duster under your glove."

Fisher shrugged. "On the whole, I thought we handled that very diplomatically."

Hawk raised an eyebrow. "Diplomatically?"

"Of course. We didn't kill anyone, did we?"

Hawk smiled sourly. Fisher sniffed. "Look, Hawk, if we hadn't stepped in when we did, the odds were that fight would have developed into a full-blown riot. And how many would we have had to kill to stop a riot in its tracks?" Fisher shook her head. "We've already had five riots since they announced the date of the election, and that was less than two days ago. Hawk, this city is going to the dogs."

"How can you tell?" said Hawk, and Fisher snorted with laughter. Hawk smiled too, but there wasn't much humour in it. "I don't think that bunch had it in them to riot. It was taking them all their time to work up to a disturbance of the peace. We didn't *have* to come down on them so hard."

"Yes, we did." Fisher gave Hawk a puzzled look. "This is Haven, remember? The most violent and uncivilised city in the Low Kingdoms. The only way we can hope to keep the lid on things here is by being harder than everyone else."

"I'm not sure I believe that anymore."

They walked a while in silence.

"This is to do with the Blackstone case, isn't it?" said Fisher eventually.

"Yeah. That witch Visage might be alive today if she and Dorimant had talked to us in time. But they didn't trust us. They kept their mouths shut because they were afraid of our reputation. Afraid of what we might do to them. We've spent too long in this city, Isobel. I don't like what it's done to us."

Fisher took his arm in hers. "It's not really that much different here than anywhere else, love. They're just more open about it in Haven."

Hawk sighed slowly. "Maybe you're right. If we had arrested those posterers, I don't know where we could have put them. The gaols are crammed full to bursting as it is."

"And there's still more than half a day to go before they

vote.'' Fisher shook her head slowly. ''I don't know why they don't just have a civil war and be done with it.''

Hawk smiled. ''About forty years ago they did. The Reformers won that one, and the result was universal suffrage throughout the Low Kingdoms. These days, the lead-up to the elections acts as a safety valve. People are allowed to go a little crazy for a while. They get to let off some steam, and the city avoids the buildup of pressures that leads to civil wars. After the voting's over, the winners declare a general amnesty, everyone goes back to work, and things get back to normal again.''

''Crazy,'' said Fisher. ''Absolutely bloody crazy.''

Hawk grinned. ''That's Haven for you.''

They walked on in companiable silence, pausing now and then to intimidate some would-be pickpocket, or caution a drunk who was getting too loud. The crowds bustled around them, singing and laughing and generally making the most of their semiofficial holiday. The air was full of the smell of spiced food and wine and burning catherine wheels. A band came marching down the street towards them, waving brightly colored banners and signing loudly the praises of Conservatism. Hawk and Fisher stood back to let them go by. A burly man wearing chain mail approached them, carrying a bludgeon in one hand and a collecting tin in the other. He took one look at their faces, thought better of it, and hurried after the parade. The crowd, meantime, showed its traditional appreciation of free speech by pelting the singers with rotten fruit and horse droppings. Hawk watched the banner holders disappear down the street with fixed smiles and gritted teeth, and wondered where the Conservatives had found enough idiots and would-be suicides to enter the Northside in the first place.

Nice banners, though.

''I'll be glad when this election nonsense is over,'' said Fisher as they started on their way again. ''I haven't worked this hard in years. I don't think I've ever seen so many drunks and fights and street-corner rabble-rousers in my life. Or so many rigged games of chance, for that matter.''

''Anyone in this city stupid enough to play Find the Lady

with a perfect stranger deserves everything that happens to him," said Hawk unfeelingly. "And when you get right down to it, things aren't that bad, actually. You're bound to get some fights during an election, but there's hardly anyone here wearing a sword or a knife. You know, Isobel, I'm almost enjoying myself. It's all so *fascinating*. I'd heard all the stories about past elections, but I never really believed them till now. This is democracy in action. The people deciding their own future."

Fisher sniffed disdainfully. "It'll all end in tears. The people can vote till they're blue in the face, but at the end of the day the same old faces will still be in power, and things will go on just as they always have done. Nothing ever really changes, Hawk. You should know that."

"It's different here," said Hawk stubbornly. "The Reform Cause has never been stronger. There's a real chance they could end up dominating the Haven Council this time, if they can just swing a few marginal Seats."

Fisher looked at him. "You've been studying up on this, haven't you?"

"Of course; it's important."

"No, it isn't. Not to us. Come tomorrow, the same thieves and pimps and loan sharks will still be doing business as usual in the Northside, no matter who wins your precious election. There'll still be sweatshops and protection rackets and back-alley murders. This is Haven's dumping ground, where the lowest of the low end up because they can't sink any further. Let the Council have its election. They'll still need us to clean up the mess afterwards."

Hawk looked at her. "You sound tired, lass."

Fisher shrugged quickly. "It's just been a bad day, that's all."

"Isobel . . ."

"Forget it, Hawk." Fisher shot him a sudden smile. "At least we'll never want for work, while the Northside still stands."

Hawk and Fisher turned down Martyrs' Alley, and made their way out onto the Harbourside Promenade. The market stalls quickly disappeared, replaced by elegant shop-fronts with porticoed doors and fancy scrollwork round the windows, and an altogether better class of customers. The Promenade had been "discovered" by the Quality, and its fortunes had prospered accordingly. Of late it had become quite the done thing for the minor aristocracy to take the air on the Promenade, and enjoy a little fashionable slumming. There were goods for sale on the edge of the Northside to tempt even the most jaded palates, and it did no harm to a gentleman's reputation to be able to drop the odd roguish hint of secret dealings and watch the ladies blush prettily at the breath of scandal. Not that a gentleman ever went into the Northside alone, of course. Each member of the Quality had his own retinue of bodyguards, and they were always careful to be safely out of the Northside before dark.

But during the daylight hours the Promenade was an acknowledged meeting place for the more adventurous members of the Quality, and as such it attracted all kinds of well-dressed parasites and hangers-on. Scandalmongers did a busy trade in all the latest gossip, and confidence tricksters strolled elegantly down the Promenade, eyeing the Quality in much the same way as a cruising shark might observe a passing shoal of minnows. Hawk and Fisher knew most of them by sight, but made no move to interfere. If people were foolish enough to throw away good money on wild-sounding schemes, that was their business, and nothing to do with the Guards. Hawk and Fisher were just there to keep an eye on things, and see that no one stepped out of line.

For their part, the Quality ignored Hawk and Fisher. Guards were supposed to know their place, and Hawk and Fisher were notorious throughout Haven for not having the faintest idea of what their place was. In the past, members of the Quality who'd tried to put them in their place had been openly laughed at and, on occasion, severely manhandled. Which was perhaps yet another reason why Hawk and Fisher had spent the past five years patrolling the worst section of Haven.

The sun shone brightly over the Promenade, and the Quality blossomed under its warmth like so many eccentrically colored flowers. Youngsters wearing party colors hawked the latest editions of the Haven newspapers, carrying yet more details of candidates' backgrounds, foul-ups, and rumoured sexual preferences. A boys' brigade of pipes and drums made its way along the Promenade, following a gorgeously colored Conservative banner. The Conservatives believed in starting them young. Hawk stopped for a while to enjoy the music, but Fisher soon grew bored, so they moved off again. They left the bustling Promenade behind them, and made their way through the elegant houses and well-guarded establishments of Cheape Side, where the lower merchant classes held sway. They'd been attracted to the edge of the Northside by cheap property prices, and were slowly making their mark on the area.

The streets were reasonably clean, and the passersby were soberly dressed. The houses stood back from the street itself, protected by high stone walls and iron railings. And a fair sprinkling of armed guards, of course. The real Northside wasn't that far away. This was usually a quiet, even reserved area, but not even the merchant classes were immune to election fever. Everywhere you looked there were posters and broadsheet singers, and street-corner orators explaining how to cure all Haven's ills without raising property taxes.

Hawk and Fisher stopped suddenly as the sound of a gong resonated loudly in their heads. The sound died quickly away, to be replaced by the dry, acid voice of the Guard communications sorcerer:

Captains Hawk and Fisher, you are to report immediately to Reform candidate James Adamant, at his campaign headquarters in Market Faire. You have been assigned to protect him and his staff for the duration of the election.

A map showing the headquarters' location burned briefly in their minds, and then it and the disembodied voice were gone. Hawk shook his head gingerly. "I wish he wouldn't use that bloody gong; it goes right through me."

"They could do without the sorcerer entirely, as far as I'm concerned," said Fisher feelingly. "I don't like the idea of magic-users having access to my mind."

"It's just part of the job, lass."

"What was wrong with the old system of runners with messages?"

Hawk grinned. "We got too good at avoiding them."

Fisher had to smile. They made their way unhurriedly through Cheape Side and on into the maze of interconnecting alleyways popularly referred to as The Shambles. It was one of the oldest parts of the city, constantly due for renovation but somehow always overlooked when the budget came round. It had a certain faded charm, if you could ignore the cripples and beggars who lined the filthy streets. The Shambles was no poorer than anywhere else in the Northside, but it was perhaps more open about it. Shadowy figures disappeared silently into inconspicuous doorways as Hawk and Fisher approached.

"Adamant," said Fisher thoughtfully. "I know that name."

"You ought to," said Hawk. "A rising young star of the Reform Cause, by all accounts. He's contesting the High Steppes district, against a hardline Conservative Councillor. He might just take it. Councillor Hardcastle isn't what you'd call popular."

Fisher sniffed, unimpressed. "If Adamant's so important, how did he end up with us as his bodyguards?"

Hawk grunted unhappily. The last time he and Fisher had worked as bodyguards, everything had gone wrong. Councillor Blackstone had been murdered, despite their protection, and so had six other people. Important people. Hawk and Fisher had caught the killer eventually, but that hadn't been enough to save their reputation. They'd been in the doghouse with their superiors ever since. Not that Hawk or Fisher gave a damn. They blamed themselves more than their superiors ever could. They'd liked Blackstone.

"Well," said Fisher finally, "you've always said you wanted a chance to study an election close-up, to see how it worked. It looks like you've got your chance after all."

"Yeah," said Hawk. "Wait till you see Adamant in action, Isobel; he'll make a believer out of you."

"It'll all end in tears," said Fisher.

They were halfway down Lower Bridge Street, not far from the High Steppes boundary, when Hawk suddenly noticed how quiet it had become. It took him a while to realise, being lost in his thoughts of actually working with a Reform candidate, so the quiet hit him all the harder when it finally caught his attention. At first everything looked normal. The usual stalls lined the street, and the crowds bustled back and forth, like any other day. But the sound of the crowd barely rose above a murmur. The stall-holders stood quietly in their places, waiting patiently for customers to come to them, instead of following their usual practice of shouting and haranguing until the air itself echoed from the noise. The crowd made its way from stall to stall with bowed heads and downcast eyes. No one exclaimed at the prices, or browbeat the stall-holders, or tried to bargain for a lower price. And strangest and most unsettling of all, no one stopped to speak to anyone else. They just went from stall to stall, speaking only when they had to, in the lowest of voices, as though they were just going through the motions. Hawk slowed to a halt, and Fisher stopped beside him.

"Yeah," said Fisher. "I noticed it too. What the hell's going on here? I've been to livelier funerals."

Hawk grunted, his hand resting uneasily on the axe at his side. The more he studied the scene before him, the more unnerving it became. There were no street-corner orators, no broadsheet singers, and the few banners and posters in evidence flapped folornly in the drifting breeze, ignored by the crowd. There should have been street-conjurers and knife grinders and itinerant tinkers, and all the other human flotsam and jetsam that street markets attract. But there was only the crowd, quiet and passive, moving unhurriedly between the stalls. Hawk looked up and down the narrow street, and all around him the empty windows stared back like so many blank idiot eyes.

"Something's happened here," said Fisher. "Something bad."

"It can't be that bad," said Hawk. "We'd have heard something. News travels fast in Haven; bad news fastest of all."

Fisher shrugged. "Something still feels wrong. Very wrong."

Hawk nodded slowly in agreement. They started down the

street again, cloaks thrown back over their shoulders to leave their sword-arms free. The crowd made way before them, their heads averted so as not to meet the Guards' eyes. Their movements were slow and listless, and strangely synchronised, as though everyone on the street was moving in step with each other. The hackles began to stir on Hawk's neck. He glared about him, and then felt a sudden rush of relief as he spotted a familiar face.

Long Tom was a permanent fixture of Lower Bridge Street. Other stalls might come and go, but his was always there, selling the finest knives any man could wish for. He'd sell you anything from a kitchen knife to matched duelling daggers, but he specialised in military knives, in all their variations. Long Tom had lost both his legs in the army, and stomped around on a pair of sturdy wooden legs that added a good ten inches to his previous height. Hawk had gone to great pains to cultivate him. Long Tom always knew what was happening.

Hawk approached the stall with a friendly greeting on his lips, but the words died away unspoken as Long Tom raised his head to meet Hawk's gaze. For a moment Hawk thought a stranger had taken over the stall. The moment passed, and he quickly recognised the size and shape of the face before him, but still something was horribly wrong. Long Tom's eyes had always been a calm and peaceful blue; now they were dark and piercing. His mouth was turned down in a bitter, unfamiliar smile. He even held himself differently, as though his weight and figure had changed drastically overnight. They were small differences, and a stranger might not have noticed them, but Hawk wasn't fooled. He nodded casually to Long Tom, and moved off without saying anything.

"What was that all about?" said Fisher.

"Didn't you notice anything different about him?" said Hawk, looking unobtrusively about.

Fisher frowned. "He looked a bit off, but so what? Maybe he's had a lousy day too."

"It's more than that," said Hawk. "Look around you. Look at their faces."

The two Guards moved slowly through the quiet crowd,

and Fisher felt a strange sense of unreality steal over her as she saw what Hawk meant. Everywhere she looked she saw strange eyes in familiar faces. Everyone had the same dark, piercing eyes, the same bitter smile. They even moved to the same rhythm, as though listening to the same silent song. It was like a childhood nightmare, where everyday friends and faces become suddenly cold, menacing strangers. Hawk reached surreptitiously inside his shirt and grasped the bone amulet that hung on a silver cord round his neck. It was a simple charm; standard issue for Guards during an election. It detected the presence of magic, and could lead you to whoever was responsible. Its range was limited, but it was never wrong. Hawk closed his hand around the carved bone, and it vibrated fiercely like a struck gong. He swore silently and took his hand away. He knew now why all the crowd shared the same dark eyes.

"They're possessed," he said softly. "All of them."

"Oh, great," said Fisher. "You any good at exorcisms?"

"I was never any good at Latin."

"Terrific."

They'd kept their voices low, little more than murmurs, but already the crowd seemed to sense that something was wrong. Heads began to turn in the Guards' direction, and people began to drift towards them. Long Tom moved out from behind his stall, a knife in each hand. Hawk and Fisher began to back away, only to discover there were as many people behind them as in front. Fisher drew her sword, but Hawk put a hand on her arm.

"We can't use our weapons, Isobel. These people are innocent; just victims of the spell."

"All right; so what do we do?"

"I don't know! I'm thinking!"

"Then think quickly. They're getting closer."

"Look, it can't be a demon, or something escaped from the Street of Gods. Our amulets would have alerted us long before this if something that powerful was loose. No, this has to be some out-of-town sorcerer, brought in to stack the vote in this district."

"I think we're in trouble, Hawk. They've blocked off both ends of this street."

"We can't fight them, Isobel."

"The hell we can't."

The crowd closed in around them. The same dark eyes blazed in every face, and every hand held a weapon of some kind. Hawk reluctantly drew his axe, his mind working furiously. The sorcerer had to be somewhere close at hand, to be controlling so many people. He grabbed at his amulet with his free hand. The carved piece of bone burned with an uncomfortable heat. He spun round in a circle, and the amulet burned more fiercely for a moment. Hawk grinned. The amulet had been designed to track down sorcerers, as well as react to their spells. All he had to do was follow where it led him. He spun quickly back and forth to get a fix on the right direction, and then he charged into the crowd, knocking men and women out of the way with the flat of his axe. Fisher hurried after him.

The crowd fought back, lashing out with knives and cudgels and broken glass. Hawk parried most of the blows, but couldn't stop them all. He hissed with pain as a knife grated raggedly across his ribs, but fought down the impulse to strike back. Everywhere he looked he saw the same twisted smile, the same dark and angry eyes. The possessed washed against Hawk and Fisher like waves breaking on a stubborn rock, a never-ending tide of hollow men and women, fuelled by an alien anger. Knives and cudgels rose and fell, and blood flew on the quiet morning air.

Hawk careered down the street, the amulet burning painfully hot in his hand, and then ducked suddenly into a side alley. Fisher followed him in, and pulled over a stack of barrels so that they fell and blocked the alley mouth. The Guards leaned together against a cold brick wall, gasping for breath. Hawk wiped sweat and blood from his face with a shaking hand. He glanced across at Fisher, and winced at the cuts and bruises she'd acquired in their short run down the street.

"I hope you're still thinking," said Fisher, her voice calm and steady. "Those barrels won't hold them back for long."

''The sorcerer's here somewhere,'' said Hawk. ''Has to be. The amulet's practically burning a hole in my hand.''

There was a rasping clatter at the end of the alley as the hollow men pulled aside the fallen barrels. Light gleamed on knives and broken glass. Hawk glared quickly about him. There was a door to his right, set flush with the brickwork so that he almost missed it. He tried the handle, but it wouldn't budge. He shot a glance at Fisher.

''I'm going in. Hold them here as long as you can.''

''Sure, Hawk; I may have to kill some of them.''

''Do what you have to,'' said Hawk. ''Just hold the door. Whatever it takes.''

Fisher moved forward to block the alleyway, and Hawk swung his axe at the door. The blade bit deeply into the rotten wood, and Hawk had to use all his strength to pull the blade free. He could hear the scuff of moving feet behind him, and the muffled thud of steel cutting into flesh, but he didn't look round. He swung his axe again and again, taking out his anger and frustration on the stubborn door. Finally it collapsed inward, and he forced his way past the splintered edges into the dark hallway beyond. A little light spilled in through the broken door, but it quickly faded away into an impenetrable gloom.

Hawk moved quickly away from the door. The light made him an easy target. He crouched down on his haunches in the dark, and waited impatiently for his eyes to adjust to the gloom. He could still hear sounds of a struggle in the alleyway outside, and his hands closed tightly around the shaft of his axe. He tried to concentrate on the hall itself, and strained his ears for any sound in his vicinity, but there was only the dark and the quiet. Hawk had never liked the dark. His hands were sweaty, and he wiped them one at a time on his trousers. The hall and a long flight of stairs slowly formed themselves out of the shadows before him. Hawk moved forward, one foot at a time, alert for any sign of a trap. Nothing moved in the shadows, and the stairway grew gradually closer.

He'd just reached the foot of the stairs when he heard footsteps on the landing above. Hawk froze in his tracks as four armed men started down the stairs towards him. He lifted his axe threateningly, but there was no reaction from any of them. He couldn't make out their faces in the dim light, but he had no doubt they all shared the same dark eyes and smile. Hawk hesitated a moment, torn by indecision. They were innocent men, all of them. Victims of the sorcerer's will. But he couldn't let them stop him. He licked his dry lips once, and went forward to meet them.

The first man cut viciously at Hawk's throat with his sword. Hawk ducked under the blow, and slammed his axe into the man's gut. The force of the blow threw the man back against the banisters. Hawk jerked his axe free, and blood and entrails fell out of the hideous wound it left. The possessed man ignored the wound and swung his sword again. Hawk parried the blow and brought his axe across in a quick vicious arc that sank deep into the man's throat, nearly tearing his head from his shoulders. He fell backwards, still trying to swing his sword, and Hawk pushed quickly past him to face the other three men, who were already advancing down the stairs towards him.

There was a flurry of steel on steel, and blood flew on the air. For all their unnatural stubbornness, the hollow men weren't very good fighters. Hawk parried most of the blows, and his axe cut and tore at them without mercy. But still they pressed forward, blood streaming from hideous wounds, unfeeling and unstoppable. Even the broken figure on the stairs behind him tried to grab at his ankles to pull him down. Hawk swung his axe with both hands, already bleeding from a dozen minor wounds. The sheer force of his attack opened up a space for a moment, and he threw himself forward. He burst through the hollow men, and ran up the stairs onto the landing. He paused for a moment to get his bearings. Above the sound of his own harsh breathing he could hear the hollow men coming after him. Light showed round the edges of a closed door at the end of the hallway. Hawk ran towards it, the hollow men close behind.

He hit the door without slowing, and it burst open. Strange lights blazed and flared within the room, and Hawk flinched as the sudden glare hurt his eye. A crudely drawn pentagram covered the bare wooden floor, the blue chalk lines flaring with a fierce, brilliant light. Inside the pentagram sat a tall spindly man wrapped in a shabby grey cloak. He looked round, startled at Hawk's sudden entrance, and in his face Hawk saw the familiar dark eyes and a mouth turned down in a bitter smile. Hawk moved purposefully forward. The amulet round his neck burned fiercely hot.

The sorcerer gestured with one hand, and the lines of the pentagram blazed suddenly brighter. Hawk slammed into a wall he couldn't see, and staggered backwards, off balance. An arm curled round his throat from behind and cut off his air. Hawk bent sharply forward at the waist, and threw the hollow man over his shoulder. He crashed into the invisible barrier and slid to the ground, momentarily stunned. Hawk heard more footsteps outside on the landing. He swore briefly, and beat at the barrier with his fist, to no avail. He cut at it with his axe, and the great steel blade passed through, unaffected. Hawk grinned savagely. Cold iron. The oldest defence against magic, and still the best. He lifted his axe, and threw it at the sorcerer.

The axe cut through the barrier as though it wasn't there. The sorcerer threw himself frantically to one side, and the axe just missed him, but one of his hands inadvertently crossed one of the lines of his pentagram. The brilliant blue light snapped out in a moment. There was the sound of falling bodies in the doorway behind Hawk, and the hollow man at his feet stopped struggling to rise. He lay still, in a widening pool of his own blood. The sorcerer scrambled to his feet. Hawk drew a knife from his boot and started forward. The sorcerer turned and ran towards a full-length mirror propped against the far wall.

Hawk felt a sudden prickling of unease, and ran after him. The sorcerer threw himself at the mirror and vanished into it. Hawk skidded to a halt, and stood before the mirror, staring at his own scowling reflection. He reached out a hand and hesitantly touched the mirror with his fingertips. The glass was cold and unyielding to his touch. He turned away and recovered his axe, and then smashed the mirror to pieces. Just to be sure.

• • •

Out in the alley, Fisher was sitting on one of the barrels, polishing her sword. There was blood on her face and on her clothes, some of it hers. She looked up tiredly as Hawk emerged from the house, but still managed a small smile for him. There were bodies scattered the length of the alley. Hawk sighed, and looked away.

"Seventeen," said Fisher. "I counted them."

"What happened to the others?"

"They snapped out of it when you killed the sorcerer, and made a break for it." She saw the look on his face, and frowned. "Not dead?"

"Unfortunately, no. He got away."

Fisher looked down the alley. "Then, this was all for nothing."

"Come on, lass; it's not that bad." He sat down on the barrel beside her, and she leaned wearily against him. He put an arm round her shoulders. "All right, he got away. But once we've spread the word, he won't be able to try this scam again for years."

"What was the point of it, anyway?"

"Simple enough. He possesses a whole bunch of people, as many as he can control. A first-class sorcerer could easily manage a thousand or more, as long as they didn't have to do much. When polling starts, they all troop off and vote for whoever was paying the sorcerer. Afterwards, the sorcerer would kill them all, so they couldn't talk out of turn. The mastermind is elected, becomes a Councillor, and there's no one left to say it was anything but fair and aboveboard. Don't take this so badly, Isobel. We may have killed a few people here today, but we've saved a hell of a sight more."

"Yeah," said Fisher. "Sure."

"Come on," said Hawk. "We've just got time for a quick healing spell before we have to meet Adamant."

They got to their feet and started down the alley. The flies were already settling on the bodies.

2

A Gathering of Forces

High Steppes wasn't the worst area in Haven. That dubious honour went to the Devil's Hook; a square mile of festering slums and alleyways bordering on the docks. The Hook was held together by abject poverty on the one hand, and greed and exploitation on the other. Some said it was the place plague rats went to die, because they felt at home there. Those who lived in the High Steppes thought about the Hook a lot. It comforted them to know there was at least one place in Haven where the people were worse off than themselves.

There was a time when the High Steppes had been a fairly respectable area, but that was a long time ago. The only reminders of that time were a few weathered statues, a public baths closed down for health reasons, and some of the fancier street names. The old family mansions had long since been converted into separate rooms and apartments, and the long, terraced streets were falling apart from a general lack of care and repair. Predators walked the streets day and night, in all their many guises. A few minor merchant houses had moved into the fringes, attracted by the relatively cheap property prices, but so far their efforts to improve the area had met with little success. As with so many other things in Haven, there were too many vested interests who liked things they way they were. Politically, the Steppes had always been neutral. Not to mention disinterested. The Conservatives won the elections because they paid out the most in bribes, and because it was dangerous to vote against them.

James Adamant might just be the one to change all that.

He'd been born into a minor aristocratic line, and seen it collapse as a child when the money ran out. The Adamants eventually made it all back through trade, only to find themselves snubbed by the Quality, because they'd lowered themselves to become merchants. Adamant's father died young. Some said as the result of a weak heart; some said through shame. All of this, plus first-hand experience of what it was really like to be poor, had given James Adamant a series of insights not common to those of his standing. On coming of age he discovered politics and, more particularly, Reform. They'd done well by each other.

Now he was standing for the High Steppes Seat: his first election as a candidate. He had no intention of losing.

James Adamant was a tall, powerful man in his late twenties. He dressed well, but not flamboyantly, and favoured sober colors. His dark hair was long enough to be fashionable but short enough that it didn't get in his eyes. Most of the time it looked as though it could use a good combing, even after it had just had one. He had strong patrician features, and a wide easy smile that made him a lot of friends. You had to know him some time before you could see past the smile to recognise the cool, steady gaze and the stubborn chin. He was a romantic and an idealist, despite being a politician, but deep within him he kept a carefully cultivated streak of ruthlessness. It had stood him well in the past, and no doubt would do so again in the future. Adamant valued his dreams too much to risk losing them through weakness or compromise.

His political Advisor, Stefan Medley, was his opposite in practically every way there was. Medley was average height and weight, with bland, forgettable features saved by bright red hair and piercing green eyes that missed nothing. He burned with nervous energy from morning till night, and even standing still he looked as though he were about to leap on an enemy and rip his throat out. He was several years older than Adamant, and had seen a great deal more of political life. Perhaps too much. He'd spent all his adult life in politics, for one master or another. He'd never stood as a candidate, and never wanted to. He was strictly a backstage man. He worked in politics because he was good at it; no other reason. He had no Cause, no dreams, and no illusions. He'd fought elections on both sides of the political fence, and as a result was respected by both sides and trusted by neither.

And then he met Adamant, and discovered he believed in the man, even if he didn't believe in his Cause. They became friends, and eventually allies, each finding in the other what they lacked in themselves. Working together, they'd proved unstoppable. Which was why Reform had given them the toughest Seat to fight. Adamant trusted Medley, in spite of of his past. Medley trusted Adamant because of it. Everyone needs something to believe in. Particularly if they don't believe in themselves.

Adamant sat at his desk in his study, and Medley sat opposite him, perched on the edge of a straight-back chair. The study was a large, comfortable room with well-polished furniture and well-padded chairs. Superbly crafted portraits and tapestries added a touch of color to the dark-panelled walls. Thick rugs covered the floor, from a variety of beasts, few of them from the Low Kingdoms. There were wine and brandy decanters on the sideboard, and a selection of cold food on silver platters. Adamant liked his comforts. Probably because he'd had to do without so many as a child. He looked at the bank draft before him—the latest of a long line—sighed quietly, and signed it. He didn't like paying out money for bribes.

He shuffled the money orders together and handed them to Medley, who tucked them into his wallet without looking at them.

"Anything else you need, Stefan?" said Adamant, stretching slowly. "If not, I'm going to take a break. I've done nothing but deal with paperwork all morning."

"I think we've covered everything," said Medley. "You really should develop a more positive attitude to paperwork, James. It's attention to details that wins elections."

"Perhaps. But I'll still feel better when we're out on the

streets campaigning. You do your best work with paper; I do my best with people. And besides, all the time I'm sitting here I can't escape the feeling that Hardcastle is hard at work setting up traps and pitfalls for us to fall into.''

''I've told you before, James; let me worry about things like that. You're fully protected; Mortice and I have seen to that.''

Adamant nodded thoughtfully, not really listening. ''How long have we got before my people start arriving?''

''About an hour.''

''Perhaps I should polish my speech some more.''

''You leave that speech alone. It doesn't need polishing. We've already rewritten it within an inch of its life, and re-hearsed the damn thing till it's coming out of our ears. Just say the words, wave your arms around in the right places, and flash the big smile every second line. The speech will do the rest for you. It's a good speech, James; one of our best. It'll do the job.''

Adamant laced his fingers together, and stared at them pensively for a long moment before turning his gaze to Medley. ''I'm still concerned about the amount of money we're spending on bribes and . . . gratuities, Stefan. I can't believe it's really necessary. Hardcastle is an animal and a thug, and everyone knows it. No one in their right mind would vote for him.''

''It's not that simple, James. Hardcastle's always been very good at maintaining the status quo, and that's what Conservatism is all about. They're very pleased with him. And most Conservatives will vote the way their superiors tell them to, no matter whose name is on the ticket. Hardcastle's also very strong on law and order, and violently opposed to the Trade Guilds, both of which have made him a lot of friends in the merchant classes. And there are always those who prefer the devil they know to the devil they don't. That still leaves a hell of a lot of people unaccounted for, but if we're going to persuade them to vote for us, we've got to be able to operate freely. Which means greasing the right palms.''

''But seven and a half thousand ducats! I could raise a small army for not much more.''

"You might have to, if I didn't approach the right people. There are sorcerers to be paid off, so they won't interfere. There are Guard officers to sweeten, to ensure we get the protection we're entitled to. Then there's donations to the Street of Gods, to the Trade Guilds; do I really need to go on? I know what I'm doing, James. You worry about the ideals, and leave the politics to me."

Adamant fixed him with a steady gaze. "If something's being done in my name, I want to know about it. All about it. For example, hiring mercenaries for protection. Apparently we have thirty-seven men working for us. Is that really the best we can do? At the last election, Hardcastle had over four hundred mercenaries working for him."

"Yeah, well; mercenaries are rather scarce on the ground this year. It seems there's a major war shaping up in the Northern countries. And wars pay better than politicians. Most of those who stayed behind had long-term contracts with the Conservatives. We were lucky to get thirty-seven men."

Adamant gave Medley a hard look. "I have a strong feeling I already know the answer to this—but why weren't these thirty-seven men already signed up?"

Medley shrugged unhappily. "Nobody else would take them . . . ."

Adamant sighed, and pushed his chair back from the desk. "That's wonderful. Just wonderful. What else can go wrong?"

Medley tugged at his collar. "Is it me, or is it getting warm in here?"

Adamant started to reply, and then stopped as his Advisor suddenly stared right past him. Adamant spun round, and found that the great study window was completely steamed over, the glass panes running with condensation. As he watched, the lines of condensation traced a ragged face in the steam, with staring eyes and a crooked smile. A thick, choking voice eased through their minds like a worm through wet mud.

I know your names, and they have been written in blood

on cooling flesh. I will break your bones and drink your blood, and I will see the life run out of you.

The voice fell silent. The eye patches slowly widened, destroying the face, and the air was suddenly cool again.

Adamant turned his back on it. "Nasty," he said curtly. "I thought Mortice's wards were supposed to protect us from things like that?"

"It was just an illusion," said Medley quickly. "Very low power. Probably sneaked in round the edges. Believe me, nothing dangerous can get to us here. They're just trying to shake us up."

"And doing a bloody good job of it, from the looks on your faces," said Dannielle Adamant, sweeping into the study. Adamant got to his feet and greeted his wife warmly. Medley nodded politely, and looked away. Adamant took his wife's hands in his.

"Hello, Danny; I didn't expect you back for ages."

"I had to give up on the shops, dear. The streets are simply impossible, even with those nice men you provided to make a way for me. Oh, by the way; one of them is sulking, just because he dropped a few parcels and I was rude to him. I didn't know bodyguards were so sensitive. Anyway, the crowds got too much to bear, so I came home early. The Steppes must be bursting at the seams. I've never seen so many people out in daylight before."

"I know you don't like the area," said Adamant. "But it's politically necessary for us to live in the area I intend to represent."

"Oh, I quite understand, dear. Really."

She sank into the most comfortable chair, and nodded pleasantly to Medley. Away from Adamant, they didn't really get on. It was hardly surprising, considering the only thing they had in common was James Adamant.

Dannielle came from a long-established Society family, and until she met Adamant, she'd never even thought about politics. She voted Conservative because Daddy always had. Adamant had opened her eyes to a great many injustices, but like Medley she was more interested in the man than his politics. Still, her strong competitive streak made her just as

enthusiastic a campaigner as her husband. Even though most
of her family were no longer talking to her.

Dannielle was just twenty-one years old, with a neat figure,
a straight back, and a long neck that made her look taller.
She was dressed in the very latest fashion and wore it
with style, though she had strong reservations about the
bustle. She looked very lovely in ankle-length midnight-
blue, and she knew it. She particularly liked the way it set
off her powdered white shoulders and short curly black
hair.

Her face was well-known throughout Haven, having been
immortalized by several major portrait painters. She had a
delicate, heart-shaped face, with high cheekbones and dark
eyes you could drown in. When she smiled, you knew it was
for you, and you alone. James Adamant thought she was the
most beautiful woman he'd ever seen, and he wasn't alone in
that. The younger aristocracy had marked Dannielle as their
own from the moment she entered High Society. After she
married Adamant several young blades from among the Quality declared a vendetta against him for stealing her away from
them. They tended to be rather quiet about it after Adamant
killed three of them in duels.

"So," said Dannielle, smiling brightly, "How are things
going, darling? Are you and Stefan finished talking business?"

"For the moment," said Adamant, sinking back into his
chair. "I haven't had much time for you lately, have I, my
dear? I'm sorry, Danny, but it's been a madhouse round here
these last few weeks. Still, there's a good hour or so before
the big speech. Better get some rest while you can, love.
After the speech we have to go out into the streets to shake
hands and kiss babies. Or possibly vice versa."

"That can wait," said Dannielle. "Right now, your friend
Mortice wants a word with you."

Adamant looked at Medley. "Have you ever noticed that
whenever Mortice does something aggravating, he's always
my friend?"

Medley nodded solemnly.

• • •

Market Faire had a bad reputation, even for the Northside, which took some doing. You could buy anything at the Faire, if you had the price; anything from a curse to a killing. You could place a bet or buy a rare drug, choose a partner for the evening or arrange an unfortunate fire for a bothersome competitor. Judges lived in the Faire, and high-ranking members of the Guard, along with criminals and necromancers and anarchists. The Faire was a meeting ground; a place to make deals. Hawk couldn't help wondering if that was why Adamant had chosen to place his campaign headquarters in Market Faire.

He and Fisher made their way unhurriedly down the main street, and the crowds made way before them. The two Guards nodded politely to familiar faces, but their hands never moved far from their weapons. Market Faire was an old, rather shabby area, for all its brightly painted façade. The stone walls were weathered and discolored, there were cracks in the pavements, and from the smell of it the drains had backed up again. Still, all things were relative. At least the Faire had drains. Bravos swaggered through the bustling crowds, thumbs tucked into their sword belts, eyes alert for anything they could take as an insult. None of them were stupid enough to lock stares with Hawk and Fisher.

Adamant's house was planted square in the middle of the main street, tucked away behind high stone walls and tall iron gates. There were jagged spikes on the gates and broken glass on top of the walls. Two armed men in full chain mail stood guard before the gates. The younger of the two stepped forward to block Hawk and Fisher's way as they approached the gates. Hawk smiled at him easily.

"Captains Hawk and Fisher, city Guard, to see James Adamant. We're expected."

The young guard didn't smile back. "Anyone can claim to be a Guard Captain. You got any identification?"

"You're new in town, aren't you?" said Fisher.

Hawk lifted his left hand, to show the Captain's silver torc at his wrist. "The man's just doing his job, Isobel."

"Things have been a little unsettled around here recently,"

said the older of the two guards. "I know you, Captain Hawk, Captain Fisher. I'm glad you're here. Adamant's going to need some real protection before this election's over."

The younger guard sniffed loudly. Hawk looked at him. "Anything the matter?"

The young guard looked insolently at him. "You're a lot older than I thought you'd be. Are you really as good as they say?"

Fisher's sword leapt into her hand, and a split second later the point of her sword was hovering directly before the young guard's left eyeball. "No," she said calmly. "We're better."

She stepped back and sheathed her sword in a single fluid movement. The young guard swallowed loudly. The older guard smiled, unlocked the heavy gates, and pushed them open. Hawk nodded politely, and he and Fisher entered the grounds of Adamant's house.

"Show-off," said Hawk quietly. Fisher grinned.

The gates swung shut behind them with a dull, emphatic thud. The house at the end of the gravel pathway was a traditional two-storey mansion, with gable windows and a front porch large enough to shelter a small army. Anywhere else in the Steppes, a place like this would have had a whole family living in each room. Ivy sprawled across most of the front wall, its thickness suggesting that it alone was holding the aged brickwork together. There were four squat chimney pots at one end of the roof, all of them smoking. Hawk looked unhappily around him as he and Fisher made their way through the grounds towards the house. The wide grass lawns were faded and withered, and there were no flowers. The air smelled rank and oppressive. The single tree was dark and twisted, its branches bare. It looked as though it had been poisoned and then struck by lightning.

"This," said Fisher positively, "is a dump. Are you sure this is the right place?"

"Unfortunately, yes." Hawk sniffed the air cautiously. "Nothing's grown here for years. Still, not everyone likes gardening."

They walked the rest of the way in silence. Hawk strained his ears for some sound apart from their own boots on the gravel drive, but the grounds were unnaturally quiet. By the time they got to the massive front door, Hawk had managed to thoroughly unsettle himself. At the very least there should have been the bustling sounds of the heavy crowds outside, the everyday clamour of a city at work and at play. Instead, Adamant's house and grounds stood stark and still in their own little pool of silence.

There was a large and blocky brass knocker on the door, shaped like a lion's head with a brass ring in its jaws. Hawk knocked twice, raising loud echoes, and then quickly let go of the brass ring. He had an uneasy feeling the lion's head was looking at him.

"Yeah," said Fisher quietly. "I feel it too. This place gives me the creeps, Hawk."

"We've seen worse. Anyway, you can't judge a man by where he happens to be living. Even if he has got a graveyard for a garden."

They fell silent as the massive door swung silently open on its counterweights. The man standing in the doorway was tall, broad-shouldered, and dressed immaculately in the slightly out-of-date formal wear that identified him immediately as a butler. He looked to be in his early fifties, with a supercilious expression, a bald head, and ridiculous tufts of white hair above his ears. He held himself very correctly, and his gaze said that he had seen it all before, and hadn't been impressed then, either. He bowed very politely to Hawk, and, after a moment's hesitation, to Fisher.

"Good morning, sir and madam. I am Villiers, Master Adamant's butler. If you'll follow me, Master Adamant is expecting you."

He stepped back a careful two paces, and then stood at attention while Hawk and Fisher entered. He closed the door quietly, and Hawk and Fisher seized the opportunity for a quick look around the hall. It was comfortably spacious without seeming overbearing, and the wood-panelled walls glowed warmly in the lamplight. Hawk approved of the lamps. Too many halls were oversized and underlit, as though there was something fashionable about eyestrain. He realised Villiers was standing politely at his side, and turned unhurriedly to face him.

"Villiers, you're standing on my shadow. I don't normally like people that close to me."

"I'm sorry, sir. I was just wondering if you and your . . . partner would care to remove your cloaks. It is customary."

"I don't think so," said Hawk. "Maybe later."

Villiers bowed slightly, his impassive face somehow managing to convey that of course they knew best, even when they were wrong. He led the way down the hall, without looking to see if they were following, and ushered them into a large, comfortably appointed library. All four walls were lined with bookshelves, and leather-bound book spines gleamed dully from every direction. There was one comfortable chair by the fireplace, which Fisher immediately appropriated, stretching her legs out before her. Villiers cleared his throat politely.

"If you would be so kind as to wait here, I will inform Master Adamant of your arrival."

He bowed again, to just the right degree, and left the library, closing the door quietly but firmly behind him.

"I never did like butlers," said Fisher. "They're always such terrible snobs. Worse than their employers, usually." She looked at the empty fireplace, and shivered. "Is it just me, or is it freezing cold in here?"

"Probably just feels that way, coming in from the warmth outside. These big places hold the cold."

Fisher nodded, looking absently around her. "Do you suppose he's really read all these books?"

"Shouldn't think so," said Hawk. "Probably bought them by the yard. Having your own library is quite fashionable, at the moment."

"Why?"

"Don't ask me. I've never understood fashion."

Fisher looked at him sharply. There had been something in his voice. . . . "This isn't what you'd expected, is it?"

"No," said Hawk. "It isn't. James Adamant is supposed to be a man of the people, representing the poor and the downtrodden. This kind of lifestyle is the very thing he's always campaigned against. A big house, a butler, books he's never read. Dammit, he can't even be bothered to look after the place properly.''

"Don't blame me," said Adamant. "I didn't choose this monstrosity.''

Hawk turned round quickly, and Fisher rose elegantly to her feet as James Adamant entered the library, followed by Dannielle and Medley.

''I'm sorry to have kept you waiting,'' said Adamant. "Captains Hawk and Fisher, may I present my wife, Dannielle, and my Advisor, Stefan Medley."

There was a quick flurry of bows and handshakes. Dannielle extended a hand for Hawk to kiss. He shot a quick glance at Fisher, and shook the hand instead.

"I think we'd all be much more comfortable in my study," said Adamant easily. "This way."

He led them back down the hall and ushered them into the study, chatting amiably all the way. "My superiors insisted we take on this draught-ridden folly as Reform Headquarters, and in a moment of weakness, I agreed. It's quite unsuitable, of course, but the current thinking is that we have to put on as good a show as the Conservatives or the voters won't take us seriously. Personally, I think it's that kind of half-baked nonsense that's undermined Reform's credibility with the electorate these past few years. But since I'm only a very junior candidate, I don't get much say in these matters."

Medley brought in some more chairs, and Dannielle bustled around making sure that everyone was comfortably seated and had a brimming glass of wine in their hand.

"How do you feel about this place?" Hawk asked her politely.

"Ghastly old heap. Smells of damp, and half the time the toilets don't work properly."

"Your garden's not up to much, either," said Fisher. Hawk winced.

Dannielle and Adamant shared a look, their faces suddenly grim.

"We have enemies, Captain Fisher," said Adamant evenly. "Enemies not averse to using sorcery, when they can get away with it. Three days ago we had a splendid garden. Fine lawns, well-tended flower beds, and a magnificent old apple tree. And now it's all gone. Nothing will grow there. It's not safe even to walk far from the path. There are things moving in the dead earth. I think they come out at night, sometimes. No one's ever seen them, but come the morning there are scratches on the door and shutters that weren't there the night before.''

There was a cold silence for a moment.

''It's illegal for political candidates to use sorcery in any form,'' said Hawk finally. ''Directly or indirectly. If you can prove Hardcastle was responsible . . .''

''There's no proof,'' said Dannielle. ''He's too clever for that.''

There was another silence.

''You made good time in getting here,'' said Medley brightly. ''I only put in my request for you this morning.''

Hawk looked at him. ''You asked for us specifically?''

''Well, yes. James has many enemies. I wanted the best people I could get as his bodyguards. You and your partner have an excellent reputation, Captain Hawk.''

''That isn't always enough,'' said Fisher. ''The last time we got involved with guarding a politician, the man died.''

''We know about Councillor Blackstone,'' said Medley. ''It wasn't your fault he died; you'd done everything you reasonably could to protect him. And you found his murderer, long after any other Guards would have given up.''

Hawk looked at Adamant. ''Are you happy with this arrangement, sir Adamant? It's not too late for you to find somebody else.''

''I trust my Advisor,'' said Adamant. ''When it comes to picking the right people for a job, his judgement is impeccable. Stefan knows about such things. Now then, if you and your partner are going to be spending some time with us, I'd better bring you up to date on what's happening in the election. What kind of things do you need to know, Captain Hawk?''

''Everything,'' said Hawk flatly. ''Who your enemies are,

what kind of opposition you'll be facing. Anything that might give us an edge."

Dannielle got to her feet. "If you're going to get all technical, I think I'll go and see how dinner's coming along."

"Now, Danny, you promised you wouldn't bother the cook anymore," said Adamant. "You know she hates people looking over her shoulder."

"For what we're paying her, she can put up with a little criticism," said Dannielle calmly. She smiled graciously at Hawk and Fisher, and left the room, closing the door quietly behind her.

"Now then," said Adamant, leaning comfortably back in his chair. "When you get right down to it, there are only two main parties: Conservative and Reform. But there's also a handful of fringe parties, and a few well-supported independents, just to complicate things. There's Free Trade, the Brotherhood of Steel, No Tax on Liquor, (also known as the Who's for a Party Party,) and various pressure groups, such as the Trade Guilds and some of the better organised militant religions."

"The Conservatives are the main threat," said Medley. "They've got the most money. Free Trade is mainly a merchants' party. They make a lot of speeches, but they're short on popular support. Mostly they end up throwing their weight behind the Conservatives. No Tax on Liquor is the Lord Sinclair's personal party. He funds it and runs it, practically single-handed. There are always people willing to go along with him, if only for the free booze he dishes out. He's harmless, apart from this one bee in his bonnet. The Trade Guilds mean well, but they're too disorganised to mount any real threat to the Conservatives, and they know it. Usually they end up working hand-in-hand with Reform. That's where a lot of our funding comes from."

"What about the Brotherhood of Steel?" said Fisher. "I always thought they were more mystical than political."

"The two are pretty much the same in Haven," said Adamant. "Power and religion have always gone hand-in-hand here. Luckily most of the Beings on the Street of Gods are more interested in feuding with each other than getting in-

volved in the day-to-day politics of running Haven. The Beings have always been great ones for feuds. But, over the past
few years the Brotherhood of Steel has changed its ways.
They're nowhere near as insular as they used to be; they're
much better organised, and just lately a militant branch has
started flexing its political muscle. They've even got a candidate standing in this election. He won't win; they're not
that strong yet. But they could be a deciding factor in who
does win.''

Hawk frowned. ''Who would they be most likely to side
with?''

''Good question,'' said Medley. ''I can think of any number of political fixers who'd pay good money for the answer.
I don't know, Captain Hawk. Ordinarily I'd have said the
Conservatives, but the Brotherhood's mystical bent confuses
the hell out of me. I don't trust fanatics. There's no telling
which way they'll jump when the pressure's on.''

''All right,'' said Hawk. 'Now that we're clear on that . . . ''

''Speak for yourself,'' muttered Fisher.

''. . . perhaps you could explain exactly what's at stake in this
election. A lot of people have been saying Reform could end up
dominating the Council, even if the Conservatives still hold most
of the Seats. I don't get that.''

''It's really very simple,'' said Adamant, and Hawk's heart
sank. Whenever people said that, it always meant things were
about to become very, very complicated. Adamant steepled his
fingers, and studied them thoughtfully. ''There are twenty-one
Seats on the Council, representing the various districts of Haven. After the last election, Reform held four Seats, the Conservatives held eleven, and there were six unaffiliated Seats.
Which meant in practice that the Conservatives ran the Council
to suit themselves. But this time there are at least three Seats
that could go either way. All Reform has to do is win one extra
Seat, and together with the six independents we could take control of the Council away from the Conservatives. Which is why
this particular election is all set for some of the dirtiest and most
vicious political infighting Haven has ever seen.''

''Great,'' said Fisher. ''Just what the people need. Another excuse to go crazy, riot in the streets, and set fire to things. How long is this madness going to go on for?''

''Not long,'' said Medley, smiling. ''After the result has been announced this evening, there will be general fighting and dancing in the streets, followed by the traditional fireworks display and the paying off of old scores by the victorious party. After that, Haven will go deathly quiet, as everyone disappears to bind their wounds, get some sleep, and nurse their hangovers. Not necessarily in that order. Everything clear now?''

''Almost,'' said Hawk. ''What are we doing here?''

Adamant looked at Medley, and then back at Hawk. ''I understood you'd been told. You and your partner are here to act as my bodyguards until the election is over.''

''You don't need us for that,'' said Hawk flatly. ''You've got armed men at your gates, and probably quite a few more scattered around the house. And if you'd still felt the need for a professional bodyguard, there are any number of agencies in Haven that could have provided you with one. But you asked for us, specifically, despite our record. Why us, Adamant? What can we do for you that your own men can't?''

Adamant leaned back in his chair, and some of his strength seemed to go out of him for a moment, only to return again as he lifted his eyes and met Hawk's gaze squarely. ''Two main reasons, Captain Hawk. Firstly, there have been death threats made against me and my wife. Quite nasty threats. Normally I wouldn't worry too much. Elections always bring out the cranks. But I have reason to believe that these threats may be genuine. There have been three separate attempts on my life already, all of them quite professional. Stefan tells me there are whispers that the attacks were sanctioned by Councillor Hardcastle himself.

''Secondly, it seems I have a traitor among my people. Someone has been leaking information, important information, about my comings and goings, and my security arrangements. That person has also been embezzling money from my campaign funds. According to Stefan's investigations, it's been going on for some months; small amounts at first, but growing larger all the time. What evidence we have been able to piece together suggests the traitor has to be someone fairly close to me; my friends, my servants, my fellow campaign workers. Someone I trusted has betrayed me. I want you two to act as my bodyguard, and identify the traitor.''

Out in the hall, a woman screamed. Hawk and Fisher surged to their feet, reaching for their weapons. The scream came again, and was suddenly cut short.

''Danny!'' Adamant jumped up from his chair and ran for the door. Hawk got there first, and yanked the door open. Out in the hall it was raining blood. Thick crimson gobbets materialised near the ceiling and poured down with unrelenting ferocity. The walls ran with blood, and the rugs were already soaked. The stench was sickening.

Dannielle had been caught halfway up the stairs. She was drenched in blood. Her dress was ruined, and thick rivulets of gore ran out of her matted hair and down her face. She ran down the stairs to Adamant, and he held her in his arms, glaring about him through the pouring blood. Hawk and Fisher stood back to back in the middle of the hall, weapons at the ready, but there was only the blood, streaming down around them, thick and heavy. Medley flailed about him with his arms, as though trying to swat the falling drops of blood like flies.

''Get your wife out of here!'' Hawk yelled to Adamant. ''This is sorcerer's work!''

Adamant started to hurry Dannielle towards the front door, and then stopped short as a dark shape began to materialise between them and the door. The falling blood ran together, drop joining with drop, to form the beginnings of a body. In the space of a few moments it grew arms and legs and a hunched misshapen body. It stood something like a man, but the proportions were all wrong. It had huge teeth and claws, and swirling dark clots of blood where its eyes should have been. It moved slowly towards its prey, its body heaving and swelling with every movement.

Hawk stepped forward and cut at it with his axe. The heavy steel blade sliced through the creature's neck and out again without slowing, sending a wave of blood splashing against the wall. The creature stood its ground, unaffected. It was only blood, nothing more. Its substance ran away onto the floor, but more blood continued falling from the ceiling to replenish it.

Hawk and Fisher both cut at the figure, and it laughed silently at them. It lashed out at Hawk with a dripping arm. Hawk braced himself and met the blow with his axe, but even so, the impact sent him staggering backwards. The creature had weight and substance, when it chose to. It started towards Hawk, ignoring Fisher's attempts to draw its attention to her. It struck at Hawk again, and he ducked under the blow at the last moment. Its claws dug ragged furrows in the wall panelling. Hawk scuttled away from the creature, snarling curses at the thing as it turned to follow him.

"Right," he said breathlessly, "That's it. We're no match for this kind of magic. Adamant, get your people together and then herd them out the back door. We'll try and buy you some time. Most sendings can't travel far from where they materialise. Maybe we can outrun the bloody thing."

Adamant nodded quickly, and urged his wife down the hall away from the creature. The rain of blood suddenly increased, pouring down even more thickly than before. Through the crimson haze, Hawk could just make out a second shape beginning to form between them and the other exit. Hawk wiped blood from his face, and took a firmer grip on his axe.

He heard Fisher's warning scream behind him, and had just started to turn when the first blood-creature swept over him like a wave and all the world went red. As the creature enveloped him, he staggered back a pace, scrabbling frantically at the blood that covered his face, cutting off his air. Fisher was quickly at his side, trying to wipe the blood away from his nose and mouth, but it resisted her efforts and clung to his face like taffy. Hawk fell forward onto his hands and knees, shaking his head frantically as his lungs screamed for air. He caught a glimpse of Adamant hovering before him, and gestured weakly for him to make a run for the front door while he had the chance. Adamant hesitated; then lifting his head, he raised his voice in a carrying shout:

"Mortice! Help us!"

A blast of freezing air suddenly swept through the hall, a

bitter icy wind that froze the falling blood into shimmering
scarlet crystals. The creature enveloping Hawk cracked apart
around him and fell away in hundreds of crimson slivers. He
stayed hunched on his knees for a moment, gratefully drawing the icy air into his lungs, then rose slowly to his feet and
looked around him. The bloody rain had stopped, and the
hall was covered in a sheen of crimson ice. Fisher was standing nearby, beating scarlet ice from her cloak. Adamant,
Medley, and Dannielle looked shocked but otherwise unhurt.
Beyond them stood the second blood-creature, caught half-
formed by the icy wind. It stood, crouching and incomplete,
like an insane sculpture carved from blood-stained ice. Hawk
walked over to it and hit it once with his axe. It fell apart
and littered the hall floor with jagged shards of crimson ice.
Hawk kicked a few of them around, just to be sure, and then
turned to face Adamant.

"All right, sir Adamant; I think there are a few questions
that need answering. Like, what was all that about, and who
or what is Mortice?"

Adamant sighed quietly. "Yes. I was hoping you wouldn't
have to know about him, but . . . I think you had better meet
him."

"May I suggest we get out of these clothes first?" said
Dannielle. "I'm soaked and half-frozen, and this dress is
ruined."

"She has a point," said Fisher. "I look like I've been
skinny-dipping in an abattoir."

"I'm sure we can find you and your partner some fresh
clothes," said Dannielle. "Come with me, Captain Fisher,
and I'll see what I can dig out for you. James, you look after
Captain Hawk."

Fisher and Dannielle disappeared up the stairs together.
Hawk looked at Adamant. "All right, first a change of
clothes, but then I want to meet Mortice. No more delays; is
that clear?"

"Of course, Captain," said Adamant. "But . . . do try and
make allowances for Mortice's temper. He's been dead for
some five months now, and it hasn't done a thing for his
disposition."

• • •

Hawk walked up to the full-length mirror, and studied himself for some time. It didn't help. He still looked like a poor relation down on his luck. He and Adamant were roughly the same height, but Adamant had a much larger frame. As a result, the clothes Adamant had lent Hawk hung around him like he'd shrunk in the wash overnight. It wasn't even a particularly fetching outfit. Grey tights, salmon-pink knickerbockers, and a frilly white shirt; whatever the current fashion was, Hawk was pretty damn sure this wasn't it. The frilly shirt in particular worried him. The last time he'd seen a shirt this frilly a barmaid had been wearing it. And no matter what Adamant said, he was damned if he was going to wear that bloody silly three-cornered hat.

He looked at himself in the mirror one last time, and sighed deeply. He'd worn worse, in his time. At least he still had his Guardsman's cloak. He picked it up off the bed and put it on, pulling the heavy cloak around him so that it hid the clothes beneath. Luckily all Guards' cloaks came with a built-in spell that kept them clean and immaculate no matter what indignities they were subjected to. It was part of the Guard's image, and along with the occasional healing spell, was one of the few good perks of the job.

He ought really to be rejoining the others, but it wouldn't do them any harm to wait a while. He had several things he wanted to think through, while he had the chance. He looked around Adamant's spare bedchamber. It was clean, tidy, and very comfortably appointed. The bed itself was a huge four-poster, with hanging curtains. Very elegant, and even more expensive. What was a champion of Reform doing, living like a king? All right; no one expected him to live like a pauper just to make a point, but this ostentatious display of wealth worried Hawk. According to Adamant, the house had been provided by Reform higher-ups. So where were they getting the money from? Who funded the Reform Cause? The Trade Guilds, obviously, and donations from the faithful. Wealthy patrons like Adamant. But that wouldn't be enough to pay for houses like this. Hawk frowned. This wasn't really any of his business. He was just here to protect Adamant from harm.

Not that he was doing such a great job so far. The blood-creatures had caught him off guard. If Mortice hadn't saved their hides with his sorcery, the election would have been over before it had even begun. More mysteries. Mortice had to be a sorcerer of some kind. And Adamant had to know that associating with a sorcerer was grounds for disqualification. So why was he willing to let Hawk and Fisher meet him? And what was that crack about him being dead for five months? What was he? A ghost? Hawk sighed. He'd only been on the case an hour and already he had more questions than he could shake a stick at. This was going to be just like the Blackstone case all over again, he could tell. He settled his axe comfortably on his right hip, and made his way out onto the landing and down the stairs.

The hall was sparkling clean, with no trace of blood or ice. Mortice again, presumably. Fisher was waiting for him at the foot of the stairs, wrapped in her Guard's cloak. One look at the thunderclouds in her face was enough to tell Hawk that she'd been no luckier in her choice of new clothes than he. He went down to join her, looked ostentatiously round to make sure they were alone, and then whispered "I'll show you mine if you'll show me yours."

Fisher snorted a quick laugh, and smiled in spite of herself. "You first."

Hawk opened his cloak with a flourish and stood posed in the traditional flasher's stance. Fisher shook her head. "Hawk, you look like a Charcoal Street ponce. And it's still not as bad as mine."

She opened her cloak, and Hawk had to bite his lip to keep from laughing. Apparently they hadn't been able to find any of Dannielle's clothing that would fit Fisher, and had compromised by lending her men's clothing. Very old and very battered men's clothing. The shirt and trousers had probably started out white, but had degenerated over the years into an uneven grey. The cuffs were frayed, there were patches of different colors on the elbows and knees, and there were several important buttons missing.

"Apparently they originally belonged to the gardener,"

said Fisher through gritted teeth. "We can't go out looking like this, Hawk; people will laugh themselves to death."

"Then we'll just have to keep our cloaks shut and save what's underneath as a weapon of last resort," said Hawk solemnly.

"Ah, Captain Hawk," said Medley, poking his head out of the study door. "I thought I heard voices. Everything all right?"

"Fine," said Hawk. "Just fine."

Medley stepped out into the corridor, followed by Adamant and Dannielle. They were all in fresh clothes and looked very smart.

"If you're quite ready, could we please get a move on?" said Medley. "Mortice knows we're coming, and he hates to be kept waiting. The last time he got impatient, he called down a plague of frogs. It took us hours to get those nasty little creatures out of the house."

"If he's your friend," said Fisher dryly, "your enemies must really be something."

"They are," said Adamant. "If you'd care to follow me . . ."

He led them down the hall and through a series of corridors that opened eventually onto a simple stone-walled laundry room. There were tables and towels and a freshly scrubbed stone floor. Hawk looked expectantly around him, and wondered if he was supposed to make a comment of some sort. As he hesitated, Medley moved over to the middle of the floor and bent down. He took hold of a large steel ring set into the floor, and for the first time Hawk spotted the outlines of a trapdoor. Fisher looked at Adamant.

"You keep your sorcerer in the cellar?"

"He chose it," said Medley. "He finds the dark a comfort."

Hawk looked at Adamant. "You said Mortice was dead. Perhaps you'd care to explain that."

Adamant gestured for Medley to move away from the trapdoor, and he did. Adamant frowned unhappily. When he spoke, his voice was low and even, and he chose his words with care. "Mortice is my oldest friend. We've faced many troubles together. I trust him implicitly. He's a first-class sorcerer; one of the most powerful in the city. He died just over five months ago. I even went to his funeral.''

"But if he's dead," said Fisher, "what have you got in your cellar?''

"A lich," said Medley. "A dead body, animated by a sorcerer's will. We don't know exactly what happened, but Mortice was defending us from a sorcerous attack when something went wrong. Terribly wrong. The spell killed him, but somehow Mortice managed to trap his spirit within his dead body. In a sense he's both living and dead now. Unfortunately his body is still slowly decaying, despite everything he can do to prevent it. The pain and rot of corruption are always with him. It makes him rather . . . short-tempered.''

"He's haunting his own body," said Adamant. "Trapped in a prison of decaying flesh, because he wouldn't leave me unprotected.''

"His name was Masque, but he calls himself Mortice, these days," said Dannielle, a faint *moue* of distaste pulling at her mouth. "Igor Mortice. It's a joke. Sort of.''

Hawk and Fisher looked at each other. "All right," said Hawk. "Let's go meet the corpse.''

"I can see you and he are going to get on like a house on fire,'' said Medley.

He reached down and took a firm hold of the steel ring set into the trapdoor. He braced himself and pulled steadily. The trapdoor swung open on whispering hinges, and a rush of freezing air billowed out into the laundry room. Hawk shivered suddenly, gooseflesh rising on his arms. Adamant lit a lamp, and then started down the narrow wooden stairway that led into the darkness of the cellar. Dannielle lifted her dress up around her knees and followed him down. Hawk and Fisher looked at each other. Hawk shrugged uneasily, and followed Dannielle, his hand resting on the axe at his side. Fisher followed him, and Medley brought up the rear, slamming the trapdoor shut behind him.

It was very dark and bitterly cold in the cellar. Hawk wrapped his cloak tightly around him, his breathing steaming on the still air. The stairs seemed to go a long way down before they finally came to an end. Adamant's lamp revealed a large square box of a room, packed from wall to bare wall with great slabs of ice. A layer of glistening frost covered everything, and a faint pearly haze softened the lamplight. In the middle of the room, in a small space surrounded by ice, sat a small mummified form wrapped in a white cloak, slumped and motionless on a bare wooden chair. There was no way of approaching it, so Hawk studied the still figure as best he could from a distance. The flesh had sunk clean down to the bone, so that the face was little more than a leathery mask, and the bare hands little more than bony claws. The eyes were sunken pits, with tightly closed eyelids. The rest of the body was hidden behind the cloak, for which Hawk was grateful.

"I take it the ice is here to preserve the body," he said finally, his voice hushed.

"It slows the process," said Adamant. "But that's all."

Fisher's mouth twisted in a grimace. "Seems to me it'd be kinder to just let the poor bastard go."

"You don't understand," said Medley. "He *can't* die. Because of what he did, his spirit is tied to his body for as long as it exists. No matter what condition the body is in, or how little remains of it."

"He did it for me," said Adamant. "Because I needed him." His voice broke off roughly. Dannielle put a comforting hand on his arm.

Hawk shivered, not entirely from the cold. "Are you sure he's still . . . in there? Can he hear us?"

The mummified body stirred on its chair. The sunken eyelids crawled open, revealing eyes yellow as urine. "I may be dead, Captain Hawk, but I'm not deaf." His voice was low and harsh, but surprisingly firm. His eyes fixed on Hawk and Fisher, and his sunken mouth moved in something that might have been meant as a smile. "Hawk and Fisher. The only honest Guards in Haven. I've heard a lot about you."

"Nothing good, I hope," said Fisher.

The dead man chuckled dryly, a faint whisper of sound on the quiet. "James, I think you'll find you're in excellent hands with these two. They have a formidable reputation."

"Apart from the Blackstone affair," said Dannielle.

"Everyone has their off days," said Hawk evenly. "You can trust us to keep you from harm, sir Adamant. Anyone who wants to get to you has to get past us first."

"And there's damn few who've ever done that," said Fisher.

"You weren't doing so well against the blood-creatures," said Dannielle. "If Mortice hadn't intervened, we'd have all been killed."

"Hush, Danny," said Adamant. "Any man can be brought down by sorcery. That's why we have Mortice, to take care of things like that. Is there anything you need while we're here, Mortice? You know we can't stand this cold for long."

"I don't need anything anymore, James. But you need to take more care. It would appear Councillor Hardcastle is more worried about your chances in the election than he's willing to admit in public. He's hired a first-class sorcerer, and turned him loose on you. The blood-creature was just one of a dozen sendings he's called up out of the darkness. I managed to keep out the others, but there's a limit to what my wards can do. I don't recognise my adversary's style, but he's good. Very good. If I were alive, I might even be worried about him."

Adamant frowned. "Hardcastle must know he's forbidden to use sorcery during an election."

"So are we, for that matter," said Medley.

"That's different," said Dannielle quickly, darting a quick glance at Hawk and Fisher. "Mortice just uses his magic to protect us."

"The Council isn't interested in that kind of distinction," said Mortice. "Technically, my very presence in your house is illegal. Not that I ever let technicalities get in my way. But the Council's always had ants in its pants about magic-users. Right, Captain Hawk?"

"Right," said Hawk. "That's what comes of living so near the Street of Gods."

"Tough," said Mortice. "All the candidates have some kind of sorcery backing them up. If they didn't, they wouldn't stand a chance. Magic is like bribery and corruption; everyone knows about it and everyone turns a blind eye. I don't know why I should sound so disgusted about it. This is Haven, after all.''

''Being dead doesn't seem to have dulled your faculties at all,'' said Hawk.

Mortice's mouth twitched. ''I find being dead unclutters the mind wonderfully.''

''Where do you stand when it comes to sorcery, Captain Hawk?'' said Dannielle sharply. ''Are you going to turn us in, and get James disqualified from the election?''

Hawk shrugged. ''My orders are to keep James Adamant alive. As far as I'm concerned, that has overall priority. I'll put up with anything that'll make my job easier.''

''Well, if that's settled, we really should be going,'' said Adamant. ''We've a lot to do and not much time to do it in.''

''Do you really have to go, James?'' said Mortice. ''Can't you just stay and talk for a while?''

''I'm sorry,'' said Adamant. ''Everything's piling up right now. I'll come down and see you again, as soon as I can. And I'll keep searching for someone who can help with your condition, no matter how long it takes. There must be someone, somewhere.''

''Yes,'' said Mortice. ''I'm sure there is. Don't worry about Hardcastle's sorcerer, James. He may have caught me by surprise once, but I'm ready for him now. Nothing can harm you as long as I am here. I promise you that, my friend.''

His eyes slowly closed, and once again to all appearances he became nothing more than a mummified corpse, without any trace of life. Dannielle shivered quickly, and tugged at Adamant's arm.

''Let's get out of here, James. I'm not dressed for this kind of weather.''

''Of course, my dear.''

He nodded to Medley, who led the way out of the cellar and back into the laundry room. After the bitter cold of the cellar, the pleasant autumn day seemed uncomfortably warm. There was frost in their hair and eyebrows, and they all mopped at their faces as it began to melt. Adamant let the trapdoor fall shut, and blew out his lamp. Hawk looked at him.

"Is that it? Aren't you going to bolt it, or something? If Hardcastle is as ruthless and determined as you've made him out to be, what's to stop him sending assassins here to destroy Mortice's body?"

Medley laughed shortly. "Anyone stupid enough to go down there wouldn't be coming back out again. Mortice's temper wasn't very good when he was alive, and since he died he's developed a very nasty sense of humour."

Adamant's study seemed reassuringly normal after the freezing cold and darkness of Mortice's cellar. Hawk picked out the most comfortable-looking chair, turned it so he wouldn't have to sit with his back to the door, and sank down into it. Adamant started to say something and then thought better of it. He gestured for the others to take a seat, and busied himself with the wine decanters. Dannielle made as though to sit next to Hawk, and then quickly chose another chair when Fisher glared at her. Medley sat down beside Dannielle, who ignored him. Hawk leaned back in his chair and stretched out his legs. First rule of the Guard: If you get a chance to sit down, take it. Guards spend a lot of time on their feet, and it tends to color their thinking.

The last of the cellar chill began to seep out of Hawk's bones, and he sighed quietly. Adamant poured him a drink from one of the more expensive-looking decanters. Hawk sipped it, and made appreciative noises. It seemed a good vintage, though Fisher always insisted he had no palate for such things. Just as well, on a Guard's wages. He put down his glass, and waited patiently for Adamant to finish pouring wine for the others. There were things that needed to be said.

"Sir Adamant, just how reliable is Mortice?"

Adamant finished putting the decanter away before answering. "Before he died—very. Now—I don't know. After everything he's been through it's a wonder he's still coherent, never mind sane. The experience would have broken a lesser man. It still might. As it is, his life now consists mainly of pain and despair. He has no hope and no future, and he knows it. His friendship with me is his last link with normality."

"What about his magic?" said Fisher. "Is he still as powerful as he used to be?"

"He seems to be." Adamant emptied his glass and poured himself another drink. His hand was perfectly steady. "In his day, Mortice was a very powerful sorcerer. He says he's as strong now as he ever was, but there's no denying his mind does tend to wander on occasion. No doubt that's how those blood-creatures got in. If he ever cracks and gives in to all that pain and madness, I think we could all be in very great trouble."

"You must realise this changes things," said Hawk. "I can't overlook something like this. Mortice could end up as a threat to the whole city."

"Yes," said Adamant. "He could. That's why I'm telling you all this. I didn't have to. Originally, I'd hoped you wouldn't have to know about him at all. That's why he took so long to deal with those blood-creatures. I'd instructed him not to give away his presence unless he absolutely had to. It wasn't until I met him just now, and saw him through your eyes, that I realised how much he's changed since his death. He used to be such a powerful man."

"But as things stand we're in no danger," said Medley quickly. "You saw for yourself how calm and rational he is. Look; you'll be right here with us all through the election. You can keep a close watch on him. If he shows any sign that his control's slipping, then you can report him. It's not as if he was that dangerous. There's no doubt he's a very powerful individual, but he couldn't hope to stand against the combined might of all the Guard's sorcerers. I mean those people take on rogue Beings from the Street of Gods. And Mortice isn't exactly the High Warlock, now is he? In the meantime, we need him. Adamant won't survive the election without Mortice's support."

Hawk looked at Fisher, who nodded slightly. "All right," he said finally. "We'll see how it goes. But once the election is over . . ."

"Then we can talk about it again," said Adamant.

"And if he turns dangerous?" said Fisher.

"Then you do what you have to," said Adamant. "I know my responsibilities, Captain."

An uncomfortable silence fell across the room. Dannielle cleared her throat, and everyone looked at her. "This isn't the first time you've worked with a magic-user, is it, Captain Hawk? I seem to remember the sorcerer Gaunt was involved in the Blackstone case, wasn't he?"

"Only marginally," said Hawk. "I never knew him very well. He left Haven shortly afterwards."

"Damn shame, that," said Medley. "His loss was a great blow to the Reform Cause. Gaunt and Mortice were the only sorcerers of any note ever to ally themselves openly with the Reformers."

"You're better off without them," said Hawk flatly. "You can't trust magic, or the people who use it."

Dannielle raised a painted eyebrow. "You sound as though you've had some bad experiences with sorcery, Captain Hawk."

"Hawk has a long memory," said Fisher. "And he bears grudges."

"How about you, Captain Fisher?" said Adamant.

Fisher grinned. "I don't get mad. I get even."

"Right," said Hawk.

"We haven't discussed your politics yet," said Adamant slowly. "What beliefs do you follow, if any? In my experience, Guards tend to be uninterested in politics, apart from the usual favours and payoffs. Most of the time they just support the status quo."

"That's our job," said Hawk. "We don't make the laws, we just enforce them. Even the ones we don't agree with. Not all the Guards in Haven are crooked. You've got to expect some bribery and corruption, that's how Haven works, but on the whole the Guard takes its job seriously. We have to; if we didn't, the Council would replace us with someone who did. Too much corruption is bad for business, and the Quality doesn't like its peace disturbed."

"But what do you believe in?" said Medley. "You, and Captain Fisher?"

Hawk shrugged. "My wife is basically disinterested in politics. Right, Isobel?"

"Right," said Fisher, holding out her empty glass to Adamant for a refill. "Only thing more corrupt than a politician is a week-old corpse after the blowflies have been at it. No offence, sir Adamant."

"None taken," said Adamant.

"As for me . . . ." Hawk pursed his lips thoughtfully. "Isobel and I come from the far North. We were both raised under absolute monarchies. Things were different there. It's taken us both some time to adjust to the changes democracy has made in Haven and the Low Kingdoms. I don't think we'll ever get used to the idea of a constitutional monarch.

"On the whole, it seems to me that the same kind of people end up on top no matter what system you have, but at least in a democracy there's room for change. Which is why I tend to favour Reform. The Conservatives don't want any change because for the most part they're rich and privileged, and they want to stay that way. The poor and the commoners should know their place." Hawk grinned. "I've never known my place."

"But as far as this election is concerned, we're strictly neutral," said Fisher. "It's our job to protect you, and we'll do that to the best of our ability. No one will bother you while we're around. Not openly, anyway. But don't waste time preaching to us. That's not what we're here for."

"Of course," said Medley. "We quite understand. Still, you're being put to a great deal of trouble on our account. You'll become targets, just by being associated with us. Under the circumstances, perhaps you would allow James and myself to show our appreciation by providing you with a little extra money, for expenses and the like. Shall we say five hundred ducats? Each?"

He reached inside his coat for his wallet, and then froze as he took in Hawk's face. Silence fell across the room. Medley looked from Hawk to Fisher and back again, and a sudden chill went through him. A subtle change had come over the two Guards. There was a cold anger and violence in their faces; a violence barely held in check. For the first time,

Medley realised how the two Guards had earned their grim reputation, and he believed every word of it. He wanted to look to Adamant for support, but he couldn't tear his gaze away from the Guards.

"Are you offering us a bribe?" said Fisher softly.

"Not necessarily," said Medley, trying to smile. The joke fell flat. Medley could feel sweat beading on his forehead.

"Get your hand away from that wallet," said Hawk, "or we'll do something unpleasant with it. You don't want to know what."

"We don't take bribes," said Fisher. "Ever. People trust us because they know we can't be bought. By anyone."

"My Advisor meant no offence," said Adamant quickly. "He's just not used to dealing with honest people."

"Politics does that to you," said Dannielle.

"And you have to admit, you are rather . . . unusual, as Haven goes," said Adamant.

"As Haven goes, we're bloody unique," said Fisher.

Hawk grinned. "You got that right."

Medley pulled at his coat to straighten it, though it didn't need straightening, and looked at the ornate brass-bound clock on the mantelpiece. "We're running late, James. The faithful will be arriving soon for your big speech."

"Of course, Stefan." Adamant got to his feet, and smiled at Hawk and Fisher. "Come along, bodyguards. You should find this interesting."

"You got that right," said Dannielle.

Hawk leaned morosely against the landing wall and wished halfheartedly for a riot. Adamant's followers filled the ballroom below, all of them cheerful and excited and buoyantly good-natured. They listened politely to Adamant's stewards, and went where they were told without a murmur. Hawk couldn't believe it. Usually in Haven you tracked down a political meeting by following the trail of broken bottles and mutilated corpses. Adamant's followers were enthusiastic as all hell, particularly about him, but seemed uninterested in the traditional passtimes of cursing the enemy and planning his destruction. They actually seemed more interested in discussing the issues. Hawk shook his head slowly. As if elections in Haven had anything to do with issues. He'd bet good money that Hardcastle's people weren't wasting time discussing the issues. More likely they were busy planning death and bloodshed and general mayhem, and where best to make a start. Hawk glanced across at Fisher. She looked just as bored as he did. Hawk looked back at the crowd. Maybe someone would faint in the crush. Anything for a little excitement. Hawk had reached the stage where he would have welcomed an outbreak of plague, to relieve the tedium.

He looked hopefully at Adamant, but he seemed in no hurry to make his entrance. He sat quietly in his chair halfway down the landing, well out of sight of his followers. Thick velvet drapes had been hung the length of the landing, blocking off the view, just so that Adamant could make a dramatic entrance at the top of the stairs. He seemed cool and perfectly relaxed, hands laced together in his lap, his eyes vague and far away. Medley, on the other hand, was stalking back and forth like a cat with piles, unable to settle anywhere for a moment. He was clutching a thick sheaf of papers, and shuffling them back and forth like the cards in a losing hand. He kept up a muttered running monologue of comment and advice concerning Adamant's speech, even though it was obvious no one was listening to him. Dannielle glared at him irritably from time to time, but seemed mostly interested in studying her appearance in the full-length mirror on the wall.

Down below, the crowd was getting noisy. They'd been patient a long time, and some of them looked a little tired of being good-natured about it. Hawk moved a little to one side so that he could see the mirror opposite him more clearly. It was the last in a series of mirrors, all cleverly arranged so that he could see down into the ballroom without being seen himself. One of Medley's better ideas.

It wasn't a very big ballroom, as mansion ballrooms went, but the packed crowd made it seem larger. Massed lamps and candles supplied a blaze of light, though the air was starting to get a little thick. Portraits of stern-faced ancestors from the original owner's family lined the walls, all of them looking highly respectable. Hawk's mouth twitched. If they'd still been alive, they'd have probably had coronaries at what their house was being used for. Adamant's supporters filled the ballroom from one end to the other, latecomers pushed tight against the closed doors, while the front of the crowd spilled over onto the first few steps of the stairs to the second storey. They seemed to blend together into a mass of shiny faces and eager eyes. A handful of stewards stopped them from getting any further up the stairs. A few more moved slowly through the crowd, keeping an eye out for unfamiliar faces and paid saboteurs. They looked very alone and very vulnerable in the crowd. Everyone there was supposed to be Adamant's friend, but Hawk didn't trust any crowd that large. They'd been well-behaved so far, but Hawk had seen enough crowds in his time to know that they could turn ugly in a moment. Should things get out of hand, there was precious little Adamant's men would be able to do to restrain such a mob. They weren't even wearing swords. Hawk sniffed. It took more to handle a crowd than good intentions.

Hawk looked round as Adamant stirred in his chair, but the candidate was just shifting his weight more comfortably. He still looked cool and calm and utterly at ease. He could have been waiting for his second cup of tea at breakfast, instead of his first real test of popularity and support. At first, Hawk had thought it was all just a pose, a mask to hide his nervousness behind, but there was none of the over-stillness that betrayed inner tension. He shot a glance at Fisher, who nodded slightly to show she'd noticed it too. Adamant might be new to politics, but it seemed he already knew the first rule: Politicians inspire fervour, but they don't fall prey to it themselves. Or, to put it another way, Adamant was professional enough to be a coldhearted son of a bitch when he had to be. A point worth remembering.

Medley, on the other hand, looked as though he might explode at any moment. His face was covered with a sheen of sweat and his hands were shaking. His hair was a mess, and he ran his fingers through it like a comb when he thought no one was looking. He kept glancing at the crowd's image in the mirror as they grew increasingly noisy, and his running monologue became even more urgent as he ran through a list of things Adamant absolutely had to remember once he got out there in front of the crowd.

Medley began to repeat himself, and Dannielle shot him another dark look before going back to fussing over her appearance. Her dress was stylish, her makeup immaculate, but she couldn't seem to assure herself of that without constant checking. Hawk smiled. Everyone had their own way of dealing with nerves. For the most part, Hawk dealt with them by keeping busy. He studied the scene in the mirror again, and stirred uneasily. The crowd was definitely getting restive. Some of them had started chanting Adamant's name. The thin line of stewards at the foot of the stairs looked thinner than ever.

Hawk smiled briefly. It was one thing to wish for a little action to relieve the boredom, but quite another when it came to actually having to deal with it.

Medley made one comment too many, and Dannielle snapped at him. They locked gazes for a moment, and then Dannielle turned to Adamant for support. He smiled at both of them, and got up out of his chair. He traded a few quiet, reassuring words with each, taking just long enough for some of his calm to rub off on them. Down in the ballroom, the crowd was chanting *We want Adamant!* more or less in unison. He smiled at Hawk and Fisher.

"There's an art to this, you know. The longer we make them wait, the greater their response will be when I finally appear. Of course, let it go on too long, and they'll riot. It's all in the timing." He strode purposefully out onto the top of the stairs, and the crowd went mad.

They cheered and stamped and waved their banners, releasing their pent-up emotions in a single great roar of love and acclaim. The sound rose and rose, beating against the walls and echoing back from the ceiling. Adamant smiled and waved, and Dannielle and Medley moved out onto the top of the stairs to join him. The cheers grew even wilder, if that was possible. Dannielle smiled graciously at the crowd. Medley nodded briskly, his face grave and impassive.

Back in the hidden part of the landing, Hawk's gaze darted across the viewing mirror, checking the crowd for trouble spots. Letting this much raw emotion loose in a confined space was a calculated risk; all it needed was one unfortunate incident and the whole thing could turn very nasty. The trick, according to Medley, was to concentrate all the emotion on Adamant, through a combination of speeches and theatrics, and then turn the people loose on the city while they were still boiling over with enthusiasm. A good trick, if you can pull it off. Adamant probably could. He was good with words. The right words at the right time can topple thrones and build empires. Or bring on rebellions and civil wars, and dead men lying in burning fields.

Fisher stirred uneasily at Hawk's side, picking up some of his tension, and he made himself relax a little. Nothing was going to happen. Adamant and Medley had everything planned, right down to the last detail. Hardcastle's people wouldn't interfere here. They might not know about Mortice himself, but they had to know some magic-user was looking out for Adamant. Hawk gnawed at his lower lip, and looked across at Adamant. He was still smiling and waving, milking the moment for all it was worth. Dannielle stood serenely at his side, doing her best to be openly supportive without drawing any attention away from her husband. Medley looked uncomfortable in the spotlight, but no one expected him to be charismatic. It was enough that he was there, openly allied with Adamant.

Hawk looked back at the crowd in the mirror, which still showed no signs of cooling down. They all had flags or banners or placards, and they all wore the blue ribbon of the Reform Cause. They were a mixture of types and classes, with no obvious connections. There were a large number of poorly dressed, hard-worn characters whose reasons for supporting Reform seemed clear. But there were others whose clothes and bearing marked them clearly as tradesmen and merchants, and there were even some members of the Quality. Usually the only place you'd find such a combination gathered peacefully together was in the city morgue or the debtors' prison. And yet here they were, standing happily shoulder to shoulder, united in friendship and purpose by the man they trusted and cheered for. Politics made for strange bedfellows. Adamant lifted his hands suddenly, and the crowd's cheering died quickly away, replaced by an expectant hush.

Hawk watched closely from the shadows of the landing. There was something different about Adamant now. Something powerful. He seemed to have grown suddenly in stature and authority, as though the crowd's belief in him had made him the hero they needed him to be. The man Hawk had met earlier had been pleasant enough, even charming. But this new Adamant had a power and charisma that set him ablaze like a beacon in the night. His presence filled the ballroom. For the first time, Hawk understood why Hardcastle was afraid of this man.

The room was totally silent now. All eyes were fixed on Adamant. There was a hungry, determined feel to the silence that Hawk didn't like. It occurred to him that the relationship between Adamant and his followers wasn't just a one-way street. These people worshipped him, they might even die for him, but in a way they owned him too. They defined what he was and what he might be.

Adamant's speech lasted the better part of an hour, and the crowd lapped it up. He talked about the dark side of Haven, the sweatshops and the work gangs, the company shops that made sure their employees stayed poor, and the company bullies who dealt with anyone who dared speak out. He talked about rotten food and foul drinking water, about houses with holes in the roof and rats in the walls—and the crowd reacted with shock and outrage, as though they'd never known such things existed. Adamant made them see their world with fresh eyes, and see how bad it really was.

He told them about the powerful and privileged men who cared nothing for the poor because they were born into the wrong class and therefore were nothing more than animals, to be used and discarded as their betters saw fit. He told them of the titled men and women who gorged themselves on six-course meals in gorgeous banquet halls, while the children of the poor died in the streets from hunger and exposure—and the raw hatred from the crowd was a palpable presence in the ballroom.

And then he told them things didn't have to be that way anymore.

He told them of the Cause. Of Reform, and how the evils of Haven would finally be done away with, not by violence and revolution, but by slow, continued change. By people working together, instead of against each other, regardless of class or wealth or position. It wasn't going to be easy. There were those in Haven who would fight and die rather than see the system change. Reform would be a long fight and a hard fight, but in the end Reform would win, because working together the people were stronger by far than the privileged individuals who sought to keep them in their place, in the gutter. Adamant smiled proudly down at the men and women before him. *Let others call us trouble-makers and anarchists.* he said quietly; *We will show the people of Haven it isn't true. We are just men and women who have had enough, and will see justice done. Whatever it takes.*

They can't kill us all.

Adamant finally stopped speaking, and for a moment there was silence. And then the crowd roared its agreement in a single, determined voice. Adamant had taken a crowd of individuals and forged them into an army, and they knew it. All they needed now was an enemy to fight, and they'd find that soon enough out on the streets. Hawk watched the crowd in the mirror, impressed but deeply disturbed. Raising violent emotions like these was dangerous for everyone involved. If Hardcastle could raise similar feelings in his followers, there would be blood and death in the streets when the two sides met.

Adamant raised his hands again, and the crowd grew still. He paused a moment, as though searching for just the right words, and then talked to them slowly and calmly about how they should deal with the enemy. Violence was Hardcastle's way, not theirs. Let the voters see who needed to resort to violence first, and then they'd see who spoke the truth, and who dared not let it be heard. Adamant looked out over his people. It was inevitable that people were going to be hurt in the hours ahead, maybe even killed. But whatever happened, they were only ever to defend themselves, and then only as much as was needed. It was easy to fall into the trap of hatred and revenge, but that was the enemy's way, not theirs. Reform fought to change, not destroy.

He paused again, to let the thought sink in, and then suddenly raised his voice in happiness and good cheer. He filled the audience's hearts with hope and resolve, wished them all good fortune, bowed once, and then strode unhurriedly off into the shadows of the landing, followed by Dannielle and Medley. His audience cheered him till their hearts were raw, and then filed slowly out of the ballroom, laughing and chattering excitedly about the day ahead. Back in the concealing shadows of the landing, Adamant sank wearily into his chair and let his breath out in a long, slow sigh of relief.

"I think that went rather well," he said finally. He put out a hand to Dannielle, and she took it firmly in both of hers.

"It should have," said Medley. "We spent long enough rehearsing it."

"Oh, never mind him," said Dannielle, glaring at Medley. "You were wonderful, darling! Listen to them, James; they're still cheering you!"

"It's a hard life being a politician," said Adamant solemnly. "All this power and adulation . . . How will I ever stand the pressure?"

Medley snorted. "Wait till we get out on the streets, James. That's when the real work starts. They do things differently out there."

Half an hour later the faithful had all departed, but Adamant and company were back in the study again. Adamant had visitors. Garrett Walpole and Lucien Sykes were businessmen, so successful that even Hawk and Fisher had heard of them. Their families were as old as Haven, and if their money hadn't come from trade, they could both have been leading members of the Quality. As it was, the lowest member of High Society wouldn't have deigned to so much as sneer in their direction. Tradesmen used the back door, no matter how wealthy they were. Which was at least partly why Walpole and Sykes had come visiting. Not that they would ever have admitted it, of course. They shook hands formally with Ad-

amant, and nodded generally around them as Adamant made
the introductions.

"Your Advisor can stay," said Sykes briskly, "but the others will have to leave. Our business here is confidential, Adamant."

Hawk smiled, and shook his head. "We're bodyguards. We
stay with sir Adamant."

Walpole looked at Hawk and Fisher amusedly. "Call off
your dogs, will you, James? Perhaps your wife could take
them to the kitchens for a cup of tea, or something, until our
business is finished."

"Don't care much for tea," said Fisher. "We stay."

"You'll do as you're damned well told!" snapped Sykes.
"Now, get out, and don't come back till we call you. Adamant, tell them."

Hawk smiled slowly, and Sykes paled suddenly as his breath
caught in his throat. Without moving a muscle, a change had
come over Hawk. He suddenly looked . . . dangerous. The
scarred face was cold and impassive, and Sykes couldn't help
noticing how Hawk's hand rested on the axe at his side. The
room suddenly seemed very small, with nowhere to turn.

"We're bodyguards," said Hawk softly. "We stay."

"Gentlemen, please!" said Adamant quickly. "There's no
need for any unpleasantness. We're all friends here. Hawk,
Fisher, these gentlemen are my guests. I would be obliged if
you would show them every courtesy while they're in my
house."

"Of course," said Hawk. His tone was impeccably polite,
but the gaze from his single dark eye was still disturbingly
cold. Sykes looked at Fisher, but if anything her smile was
even more disturbing.

"There's no cause for alarm, my friends," said Adamant.
"My bodyguards fully understand our need for confidential-
ity. You have my word that nothing discussed here will go
beyond the walls of this room."

Walpole looked at Sykes, who nodded grudgingly. Hawk
smiled. Fisher leaned against the mantelpiece and folded her
arms.

"But your wife will still have to leave," said Sykes stubbornly. "This is not women's business."

Dannielle flushed angrily, and looked to Adamant for support, but he was already nodding slowly. "Very well, Lucien, if you insist. Danny, if you wouldn't mind . . ."

Dannielle shot him a quick look of betrayal, and then gathered her composure sufficiently to smile graciously round the room before leaving. She didn't slam the door behind her, but it felt as though she had. Adamant gestured for Walpole and Sykes to be seated, and waited patiently for them to settle themselves comfortably before pouring them wine from the most delicately fashioned decanter. Hawk and Fisher held out their glasses for a refill. Adamant handed them the decanter, and pulled up a chair opposite his visitors. The two Guards remained standing. Hawk studied the two businessmen surreptitiously over his wineglass. He didn't move in their circle, but he knew them both by reputation. Guards made it their business to know the movers and shakers of Haven's community by sight. You could avoid a lot of embarrassment that way.

Garrett Walpole was a bluff military type in his late fifties. He'd spent twenty years in the Low Kingdoms army before retiring to take over the family business, and it showed. He still wore his hair in a regulation military cut, and his back was straight as a sword blade. He wore sober clothes of a conservative cut, and sat back in his chair as though he owned the place.

Lucien Sykes was an overweight, ruddy-faced man in his late forties. He wore the latest fashion with more determination than style, and looked more than a little uneasy in present company. Sykes was big in the import-export business, which was why he'd come to Adamant. The Dock-workers Guild was in the second week of its strike, and nothing was moving in or out of the docks. The Conservative-backed DeWitt brothers were trying to break the strike with blackleg zombie workers, but so far that hadn't worked out too well. Zombies needed a lot of supervision, and weren't what you'd call efficient workers. As it was, the Dock-workers Guild had more reason than usual to be mad at the Conservatives, and had lined up firmly behind the Reformers. So if Sykes wanted to get his ships in or out of the docks any time soon, he was going to need help from the right people. Reform people.

Hawk grinned. He might be new to politics, but he knew a few things.

"Well," said Adamant finally, after everyone had sipped their drinks and the silence had dragged on uncomfortably long, "what exactly can I do for you, my friends? Normally I'd be only too happy to sit and chat for a while, but I have an election to fight, and very little time to do it in. If you'll just tell me what you want, I'll be happy to tell you what it will cost you."

Walpole raised a sardonic eyebrow. "Plain speaking may be a virtue, James, but if I were you I'd keep it to myself. There's no room for it in politics or business."

"You should know," said Medley, and Walpole laughed briefly.

"James, I can't say I'm hopeful of your chances, because I'm not. High Steppes has been a safe Conservative Seat for more than thirty years. All right, Hardcastle is a bit of a rotter, but people will vote for the devil they're familiar with rather than a Cause they don't know."

"Even though the devil has bled them dry for years, and the Cause will fight on their behalf?" Adamant smiled. "Or perhaps you don't believe in Reform?"

"My dear chap, it hasn't a hope." Walpole took a cigar out of his pocket, looked at it wistfully, and put it away again. "Only allowed one a day," he explained. "Doctor's orders. I'd get another doctor, but he's the wife's brother. James, Reform is a nice idea, but that's all. These fashions come and go, but they never last long. Too many vested interests concerned for it to get anywhere."

"Is that why you came here?" said Medley. "To tell us we can't win?"

Walpole laughed briefly. "Not at all. You asked me for money, James, and I'm here to give it to you. Who knows? you might win after all, and it wouldn't do me any harm to have you owe me a favour. Besides, I've been a friend of your family most of my life. Fought beside your father in the

Broken Ridges campaign. He was a good sort. I'm more than comfortably well-off these days, and I can afford to throw away a few thousand ducats.'' He took a banker's draft from his pocket and handed it to Medley. ''Put it to good use, James, and let me know if you need some more. And after this nonsense is over, do come and see me. I'm sure I can put some business your way. Now I really must be going. Things to do, you know. Good luck in the election.''

He didn't say *You're going to need it*. His tone said it for him.

He rose unhurriedly to his feet, and stretched unobtrusively as Adamant got up and rang for the butler. Medley tucked the banker's draft safely away in his wallet before rising to his feet. The butler came in, Walpole shook hands all around, and then the butler escorted him out. The room was suddenly very quiet. Adamant and Medley sat down again and turned their attention to Lucien Sykes. He glanced quickly at the two Guards, scowled unhappily, and then leant forward to face Adamant, his tone hushed and conspiratorial.

''You know my position. I have to get my ships in and out of the docks soon, or I stand to lose every penny I've got. You know I've donated money to the Cause in the past. I've been one of your main backers. Now I need your help. I need your word that the first thing you'll do as a Councillor is to put pressure on those bastards in the Dock-workers Guild to call off their strike. For a while, at least.''

''I'm afraid I can't do that,'' said Adamant. ''But I could put some pressure on the DeWitt brothers to be more reasonable. After all, they caused the strike, by refusing to spend the money needed to make the docks safe to work in.''

Sykes's scowl deepened. ''That won't do any good. I've already talked to Marcus and David DeWitt. They don't give a damn for anyone but themselves. It's become a matter of principle to them, not to give in to their workers. If they want to dig their own financial grave, that's up to them, but I'm damned if I'm going to let them drag me down with them.''

''You could always go to Hardcastle,'' said Medley.

''I tried,'' said Sykes. ''He wouldn't see me. Three thousand ducats, Adamant. That's my offer. I've got the bank draft right here.''

"I'll talk to the Guild and put what pressure I can on the DeWitts,'' said Adamant. "That's all I can promise you. If that's not good enough, then we'll have to do without your money.''

Sykes took a folded bank draft out of his coat pocket, hefted it in his hand, and then tossed it onto the desk. "I'll see you again, Adamant—if you win the election.''

He pulled his coat around him, glared briefly at Hawk and Fisher, and left the study. The door swung shut behind him. Hawk turned slightly to look at Adamant.

"Is it normally this blatant? I mean, when you get right down to it, those two were giving you bribes in return for future favours. Reform's always campaigned against that kind of corruption in the past.''

"Fighting an election costs money,'' said Medley. "Lots of it. James couldn't hope to pay all the bills on his own, and the Cause can't do much to help. What money they have has to be spread around among the poorer candidates. All they could give us was this house. So, we take funds where we can find them. You can bet Hardcastle isn't bothered by any such niceties. If his supporters don't make big enough donations, all he has to do is threaten to raise property taxes. And it's not as if we promised to do anything against our principles. In the end, all politics is based on people doing favours for each other. That's what keeps the system going. It may not be a very pretty system, but then, that's one of the things we're fighting to change.''

The door flew open, and Dannielle swept in. She glared at them all impartially, and then sank into her favourite chair. "I feel like I ought to open all the windows and set up incense sticks, just to get the smell of politics out of this room.''

"Sorry, Danny,'' said Adamant. "But they really wouldn't have talked freely with you there, and we needed the money they were offering.''

Dannielle sniffed. "Let's change the subject.''

"Let's,'' said Medley. "Is there anything more you need

to know before we start campaigning, Captain Hawk, Captain Fisher?''

"Yes," said Hawk. "I need more information on the other candidates. Hardcastle, for example. I gather he's unpopular, even among his own people.''

"The man's a brute," said Adamant. "He runs the High Steppes like his own private Barony. Even levies his own separate tax, though it's not called that, of course. It's an insurance policy. And people who don't or can't keep up their payments find their luck's suddenly changed for the worse. It starts with beatings, moves on to fires, and ends with murder. And no one says anything. Even the Guard looks the other way.''

Hawk smiled coldly. "We're the Guard here now. Tell me about Hardcastle himself.''

"He's a thug and a bully, and his word is worthless," said Medley unemotionally. "He takes bribes from everyone, and then welshes on the deal, as often as not. He's been very successful in business, and it's rumoured he knows where some very important bodies are buried. He has his own little army of men-at-arms and hired bullies. Anyone who tries to speak out against him gets their legs broken as a warning. I don't think he has any friends, but he has acquaintances in high places.''

"Anything else?" said Fisher.

"He's married," said Dannielle. "But I've never met her.''

"Not many have," said Medley. "She doesn't go out much. From what I hear, it was an arranged marriage, for business reasons. They've been married seven years now. No children.''

"An army of men-at-arms," said Hawk thoughtfully. "You mean mercenaries?''

"That's right," said Medley. "It's hard to get an accurate figure, but he's got at least three hundred armed men under his personal command. Probably more.''

"And this is the man you're standing against?" said Fisher. "You must be crazy. You're going to need your own private army just to walk the streets in safety.''

"What do I need an army for?" said Adamant. "I've got

you and Captain Hawk, haven't I? Relax, Captain Fisher. We have our own mercenaries. Not as many as Hardcastle, but enough. They'll keep the worst elements off our backs. We'll just have to play the rest by ear."

"Terrific," said Fisher.

"Tell me about the other candidates," said Hawk.

Adamant looked at Medley, who frowned thoughtfully before speaking. "Well, first, there's Lord Arthur Sinclair. Youngish chap, inherited the title a few years back under rather dubious circumstances, but that's nothing new in Haven. Plays politics for the fun of it as much as anything. Likes all the attention, and the chance to stand up in public and make a fool of himself. He's standing as an independent, because nobody else would have him, and he wants to see an end to all forms of tax on alcohol. He has some backing, mostly from the beer, wine, and spirits industry, and he's wealthy enough to buy himself a few votes, but the only way he'll get elected is if all the other candidates drop dead. And even then there'd have to be a recount."

"He means well," said Adamant, "but he's no danger to anyone except himself. He drinks like a fish, from what I've heard."

"Then there's Megan O'Brien," said Medley, having waited patiently for Adamant to finish. "He's a spice merchant, also independent, standing for Free Trade. Given that a great deal of Haven's income comes from the very taxes O'Brien wants stopped, I don't think much of his chances. He'll be lucky to get through the election without being assassinated."

"And, of course, there's General Longarm. Once a part of the Low Kingdoms army, now part of a militant movement within the Brotherhood of Steel. He's been officially disowned by the Brotherhood, though whether that means anything is open to question. The Brotherhood's always been devious. He's campaigning as an independent, on the Law and Order ticket. Believes every lawbreaker should be beheaded, on the spot, and wants compulsory military service introduced for every male over fourteen. He's crazier than a brewery-yard rat, and about as charismatic. His Brotherhood connections might get him a few votes, but otherwise he's harmless.''

"I wouldn't count him out completely," said Adamant. "Brotherhood militants took The Downs away from the Conservatives at the last election. I think it would be wise to keep a good weather eye on General Longarm."

"Any more candidates?" said Fisher, helping herself to more wine from the nearest decanter.

"Just one," said Medley. "A mystery candidate. A sorcerer, called the Grey Veil. No one's seen or heard anything about him, but his name's on the official list. Magician's aren't actually banned from standing in the election, but the rules against using magic are so strictly enforced, most magicusers don't bother. They say they're unfairly discriminated against, and they may well be right. Mortice says he's never even heard of the Grey Veil, so he can't be that powerful.''

Hawk frowned. "We had a run-in with a sorcerer, earlier today. It might have been him."

"Doesn't make any difference," said Fisher. "We ran him off. If he was the Grey Veil, I think we can safely assume he's no longer standing. Running, maybe, but not standing. The report we filed will see to that."

"Let me get this straight," said Hawk. "Apart from us, there's Hardcastle and his mercenaries, militant Brothers of Steel, and a handful of independents with whatever bullies and bravos they can afford. Adamant, this isn't just an election, it's an armed conflict. I've known battles that were safer than this sounds like it's going to be."

"Now you're getting the hang of it," said Dannielle.

"I think that's covered everything," said Adamant. "Now, would anyone like a quick snack before we leave? I doubt we'll have time to stop to eat once we've started."

Hawk looked hopefully at Fisher, but she shook her head firmly. "Apparently we're fine," said Hawk. "Thanks anyway."

"It's no trouble," said Dannielle. "It'll only take a minute to send word to the kitchen staff and the food taster."

Hawk looked at her. "Food taster?"

"People are always trying to poison me," said Adamant,

shrugging. "Reform has a lot of enemies in Haven, and particularly in the High Steppes. Mortice sees to it that none of the attempts get past the kitchens, so the food taster's really only there as a backup. Even so, you wouldn't believe what he's costing me in danger money."

"I don't think we'll bother with the snack," said Hawk. Fisher gave the wine at the bottom of her glass a hard look.

"You stick with us, Hawk," said Medley, grinning. "And we'll give you a solid grounding on politics in Haven. There's a lot more to it than meets the eye."

"So I'm finding out," said Hawk.

3

Wolves in the Fold

Brimstone Hall stood aloof and alone in the middle of its grounds, surrounded by a high stone wall emblazoned with protective runes. Armed men watched from behind the massive iron gates, and guard dogs patrolled the wide-open grounds. Rumour had it the dogs had been fed human meat just long enough to give them a taste for it. There used to be apple trees in the grounds. Hardcastle had them torn up by the roots; they offered shelter to potential assassins.

Cameron Hardcastle was a very careful man. He trusted nothing and no one, with good cause. He had destroyed many men in his time, one way or another, and helped to ruin many more. It was said he had more enemies than any other man in Haven. Hardcastle believed it, and took pride in the fact. In a city of harsh and ruthless men, he had made himself a legend. Constant death threats were a small price to pay.

The Hall itself was a crumbling stone monstrosity held together by ancient spells and never-ending repair work. It was stiflingly hot in the summer and impossible to heat in the winter, but it had been home to the Hardcastles for years past counting, and Cameron would not give it up. Hardcastles never gave up anything that was theirs. They were supposed to have been instrumental in the founding of Haven, which might have been why so many of them had been convinced they should be running it.

Cameron Hardcastle began his career in the Low Kingdoms army. It was expected of him, his class, and his family, and he hated every minute of it. He left the army after only seven years, retiring in haste before he could be court-martialled. It was said the charges would have been extreme cruelty, but no one took that seriously. Extreme cruelty was usually what got you ahead in the Low Kingdoms army. The men fought so well because they were more afraid of their officers than they were of the enemy.

More importantly, there were rumours of blood sacrifice behind locked doors in the officers' mess, but no one talked about that. It wasn't considered healthy.

Hardcastle himself was an average-height, stocky man, with a barrel chest and heavily muscled upper arms. He was good-looking in a rough, scowling way, with a shock of dark hair and an unevenly trimmed moustache. He was in his mid-forties, and looked it, but you only had to meet him for a few moments to feel the strength and power that radiated from him. Whatever else people said about him—and there was a lot of talk, most of it unpleasant—they all admitted the man had presence. When he entered a crowded room, the room fell silent.

He had a loud, booming laugh, though his sense of humour wasn't very pleasant. Most people went to the theatre for their entertainment; Hardcastle's idea of a good time was a visit to the public hangings. He enjoyed bear-baiting, prizefights, and kept a half-dozen dogs to go ratting with. On a good day he'd nail the rats' tails to the back door to show his tally.

He was Conservative because his family always had been, and because it suited his business interests to be so. The Hardcastles were of aristocratic stock, and no one was allowed to forget it. Of late, most of their money came from rents and banking, but no one was foolish enough to treat Hardcastle as a merchant or a businessman. Even as a joke. It wouldn't have been healthy. When he thought about politics at all, which wasn't often, Hardcastle believed in everyone knowing their place, and keeping to it. He thought universal suffrage was a ghastly mistake, and one he fully intended to rectify at the first opportunity. Reform was nothing more than a disease in the body politic, to be rooted out and destroyed. Starting with James bloody Adamant.

Hardcastle sat in his favorite wing chair, staring out the great bow window in his study and scowling furiously. Adamant was going to be a problem. The man had a great deal of popular support, more than any previous Reform candidate, and taking care of him was going to be difficult and expensive. Hardcastle hated spending money he didn't have to. Fortunately, there were other alternatives. He turned his gaze away from the window, and looked across at his sorcerer, Wulf.

The sorcerer was a tall, broad-shouldered man, with a fine noble head that was just a little too large for his body. Thick auburn hair fell to his shoulders in a mass of curls and knots. His face was long and narrow, and heavy-boned. His eyes were dark and thoughtful. He dressed always in sorcerer's black, complete with cape and cowl, and looked the part to perfection.

Wulf was a newcomer to Haven, and as yet hadn't shown much evidence of his power, but no one doubted he had it. A few weeks back he'd been attacked by four street thugs. It took the city Guard almost a week to find a horse and cart sturdy enough to carry the four stone statues away. They ended up on the Street of Gods. Tourists burn incense sticks before them, but the statues are still silently screaming.

Sitting quietly in a chair in the corner, with head bowed and hands clasped neatly in her lap, was Jillian Hardcastle, Cameron's wife. She was barely into her mid-twenties, but she looked twenty years older. She had been pretty once, in an unremarkable way, but life with Hardcastle had worn her away until there was no character left in her face; only a shape, and features that faded from memory the moment she was out of sight. She dressed in rich and fashionable clothes because her husband expected it of her, but she still looked like what she was: a poor little country mouse who'd been brought into the city and had every spark of individuality beaten out of her. Those who spent time in Hardcastle's company had learned not to comment on the occasional bruises and black eyes that marked Jillian's face, or the mornings she spent lying in bed, resting.

They'd been married seven years. It was an arranged marriage. Hardcastle arranged it.

He glared at Wulf for a long moment, and when he finally spoke his voice was deceptively calm and even. "You told me your magics could break through any barrier Adamant could buy. So why is he still alive?"

Wulf shrugged easily. "He must have found himself a new sorcerer. I'm surprised anyone would work with him after what I did to his last magic-user, but then, that's Haven for you. There's always someone, if the money's right. It won't make any difference in the long run. It may take a little time to find just the right opening, but I doubt this magic-user will be any more difficult to dispose of than the last one."

"More delays," said Hardcastle. "I don't like delays, sorcerer. I don't like excuses, either. I want James Adamant dead and out of the way before the people vote. I don't care what it costs, or what you have to do; I want him dead. Understand, sorcerer?"

"Of course, Cameron. I assure you, there's no need to worry. I'll take care of everything. I trust the rest of your campaign is running smoothly?"

"So far," said Hardcastle grudgingly. "The posterers have been out since dawn, and my mercenaries have been dealing with Adamant's men quite successfully, in spite of the interfering Guard. If Adamant is foolish enough to try and hold any street gatherings, my men will see they don't last long. Commoners don't have the guts to stand and fight. Spill some blood on the cobbles, and they'll scatter fast enough."

"Quite right, Cameron. There's nothing at all to worry about. We've thought of everything, planned for every eventuality. Nothing can go wrong."

"Don't take me for a fool, sorcerer. Something can always go wrong. Adamant's no fool, either; he wouldn't still be investing so much time and money in his campaign if he didn't think he had a bloody good chance of beating me. He knows something, Wulf. Something we don't. I can feel it in my bones."

"Whatever you say, Cameron. I'll make further enquiries. In the meantime, I have someone waiting to meet you."

"I hadn't forgotten," said Hardcastle. "Your chief of mercenaries. The one you've been so mysterious about. Very well; who is it?"

Wulf braced himself. "Roxanne."

Hardcastle sat up straight in his chair. "Roxanne? You brought that woman into my house? Get her out of here now!"

"It's perfectly all right, Cameron," said Wulf quickly. "I brought two of my best men to keep an eye on her. I think you'll find her reputation is a little exaggerated. She's the best sword-for-hire I've ever come across. Unbeatable with a blade in her hand, and a master strategist. She works well on her own, or in charge of troops. She's done an excellent job for us so far, with remarkably few fatalities. She's a genuine phenomenon."

"She's also crazy!"

"There is that, yes. But it doesn't get in the way of her work."

Hardcastle slowly settled back into his chair, but his scowl remained. "All right, I'll see her. Where is she?"

"In the library."

Hardcastle sniffed. "At least there's not much there she can damage. Jillian, go and get her."

His wife nodded silently, got to her feet and left the study, being careful to ease the door shut behind her so that it wouldn't slam.

Hardcastle turned away from the bow window, and stared at the portrait of his father, hanging on the wall opposite. A dark and gloomy picture of a dark and gloomy man. Gideon Hardcastle hadn't been much of a father, and Cameron had shed no tears at his funeral, but he had been a Councillor in Haven for thirty-four years. Cameron Hardcastle was determined to do better. Being a Councillor was just the beginning. He had plans. He was going to make the name Hardcastle respected and feared throughout the Low Kingdoms.

Whatever it took.

• • •

Roxanne prowled restlessly back and forth in Hardcastle's library, her boots sinking soundlessly into the thick pile carpet. The two mercenaries set to guard her watched nervously from the other side of the room. Roxanne smiled at them now and again, just to keep them on their toes. She was tall, six foot three even without her boots, with a lithe, muscular body. She wore a shirt and trousers of bright lime-yellow, topped with a battered leather jacket. She looked like a vicious canary. She wore a long sword on her left hip, in a well-worn scabbard.

At first sight she was not unattractive. She was young, in her early twenties, with a sharp-boned face, blazing dark eyes, and a mass of curly black hair held in place with a leather headband. But there was something about Roxanne, something in her unwavering gaze and disturbing smile that made even the most experienced mercenary uneasy. Besides, everyone knew her reputation.

Roxanne first made a name for herself when she was fifteen, fighting as a sword-for-hire in the Silk Trail vendettas. The rest of her company were wiped out in an ambush, and she had to fight her way back alone through the enemy lines. She killed seventeen men and women that night, and had the ears to prove it. The people who saw her stride back into camp that night, laughing and singing, covered in other people's blood and wearing a necklace of human ears, swore they'd never seen anything more frightening in their lives.

She went through a dozen mercenary companies in less than three years, and despite her swordsmanship they were always glad to see her go. She was brave and loyal, as long as she was paid regularly, and always the first to lead an attack, but there was no getting away from the fact that Roxanne was stark staring crazy. When there wasn't an enemy to fight she'd pick quarrels among her own people, just to get a little action. She was even worse when she got drunk. People who knew her learned to recognise the signs early, and head for the nearest exit. Roxanne had a nasty temper and a somewhat strange sense of humour. Her idea of a good night out tended to involve knife fights, terrorising the locals, and burning down inns that expected her to pay her bar bills.

Not that she limited her arson to inns. Quite often she'd set fire to a tent or two in her own camp, for reasons that made sense only to her. Roxanne liked a good fire. She also liked betting everything she had on one roll of the dice, and then refusing to pay up if she lost. She worshipped a god no one had ever heard of, had an entirely unhealthy regard for the truth, and picked fights with nuns. She said they offended her sense of the rightness of things. If Roxanne had a sense of the rightness of things, it was news to everyone who'd ever met her.

Everyone agreed that Roxanne would go far, and the sooner the better.

She ended up in Haven after a disagreement with a Captain of the Guard over the prices in a Jaspertown company store. When someone explained to her that she'd just killed the local Mayor's son, she decided it might be time to start looking for new employment. So she threw the Captain's head through the Mayor's front window, set fire to a post office as a distraction, and headed for Haven as fast as her stolen horse could carry her.

Roxanne roamed about Hardcastle's library, picking things up and putting them down again. She'd never seen so many resolutely ugly pieces of ornamental china in her life. And there wasn't a damn thing worth stealing. She broke a few ornaments on general principles, and because they made such a pleasant sound as they smashed against the wall. The two mercenaries stirred uneasily, but said nothing. Ostensibly they were there to keep her out of trouble and make sure she didn't set fire to anything, but Roxanne knew they wouldn't do anything unless they absolutely had to. They were scared of her. Most people were, particularly when she smiled. Roxanne smiled widely at the two mercenaries. They both paled visibly, and she turned away, satisfied. She started to pace up and down again, tapping her fingertips on her sword belt. She never could stay still for long. She had too much energy in her.

She looked round quickly as the library door swung open,

and then took her hand away from her sword as a pale, colorless woman came in. At first Roxanne thought she must be
a servant, but a quick glance at the quality of her clothes
suggested she had to be very upper-class, even if she didn't
act like it. She ignored the two mercenaries and addressed
herself to Roxanne, without raising her eyes from the floor.

"My husband will see you now," she said quietly, her
voice entirely free of inflection. "Please follow me and I'll
take you to him."

The two mercenaries looked at each other, and one of them
cleared his throat diffidently. "Pardon me, ma'am, but we're
supposed to stay with her."

Jillian Hardcastle glanced at him briefly, and then looked
back at the floor. "My husband wants to see Roxanne. He
didn't mention you."

The mercenary frowned uncertainly. "I don't really think
we should . . ."

"You stay put," said Roxanne flatly. "Don't touch the
booze and don't break anything. Got it?"

"Got it," said the mercenary. "We'll stay right here."
The other mercenary nodded quickly.

Roxanne followed Jillian Hardcastle out of the library and
into the hall. It was a large hall, wide and echoing, and Roxanne did her best to look unimpressed. She quickly realised
she needn't bother, as Jillian kept her gaze firmly on the
ground at all times. Roxanne stared at her thoughtfully. This
beaten-down little mouse was Hardcastle's wife? Perhaps the
rumours about him were true after all.

Jillian opened the study door, and gestured politely for
Roxanne to go in first. She did so, swaggering in with her
thumbs tucked into her sword belt. Hardcastle and Wulf got
to their feet. Hardcastle studied her narrowly. Roxanne smiled
at them both, and didn't miss the little *moue* of unease that
crossed their faces. She knew the effect her smile had on
people. That was why she used it. She glanced quickly round
the study. Not bad. Quite luxurious in its way. She did her
best to look as though she'd seen better, in her time.

"Welcome to my house, Roxanne," said Hardcastle heavily. "Wulf tells me you've done good work for me. As a

reward, I have a special assignment for you. You'll be working mostly alone, but there's an extra five hundred ducats in it for you."

"Sounds good," said Roxanne. "What's the catch?"

Hardcastle frowned. Out of the corner of her eye, Roxanne saw Jillian wince momentarily, and then her face was blank and empty again. Roxanne dropped insolently into the most comfortable-looking chair and draped one leg over the padded arm. Hardcastle looked at her for a moment, and then drew up a chair opposite her. Wulf and Jillian remained standing. Hardcastle met Roxanne's gaze for a moment, and then looked away, despite himself.

"James Adamant is standing against me in the election," he said finally. "I want him stopped. Hurt him, kill him, I don't care. Spend as much as you need, use whatever tactics you like. If there's any repercussions I'll get you out of Haven in plenty of time."

"The catch," said Roxanne.

"Adamant has two Captains of the city Guard as bodyguards," said Hardcastle steadily. "They're called Hawk and Fisher."

Roxanne smiled. "I've heard of them. They're supposed to be good. Very good." She laughed happily. It was an unpleasant, disturbing sound. "Hardcastle, I'd almost do this for free, just for the chance to go up against those two."

"They're not the target," said Hardcastle sharply. "If you have a grudge with them, you deal with it on your own time."

"Of course," said Roxanne.

"Even apart from them, Adamant's going to be hard to reach. He has his own mercenaries, and a new magic-user. I understand you have a special contact of your own among his people, so I'll leave the details to you. But it has to be done soon." He picked up his wineglass. "Jillian, get me some wine."

She moved quickly forward, took the glass from his hand, and went over to the row of decanters on the nearby table.

"Do I get any support on this?" said Roxanne, "Or am I working entirely on my own?"

"Use whatever people you need, but make sure there are

no direct links to me. Officially, you're just another of my mercenaries.''

Jillian brought him a glass of wine. Hardcastle looked at it without touching it. ''Jillian, what is this?''

''Your wine, Cameron.''

''What kind of wine?''

''Red wine.''

''And what kind of wine do I normally drink when I have guests?''

''White wine.''

''So why have you brought me red?''

Jillian's mouth began to tremble slightly, though her face remained blank. ''I don't know.''

''It's because you're stupid, isn't it?''

''Yes, Cameron.''

''Go and get me some white wine.''

Jillian went back to the decanters. Hardcastle looked at Roxanne, who was studying him thoughtfully. ''Have you got something to say, mercenary?''

''She's your wife.''

''Yes. She is.''

Jillian came back with a glass of white wine. Hardcastle took it, and put it down on the desk without tasting it. ''I'll talk with you about this later, Jillian.''

She nodded, and stood silently beside his chair. Her hands were clasped so tightly together that the knuckles showed white.

''It's time you spoke to your people, Cameron,'' said Wulf softly. ''We need them out on the streets as quickly as possible, and you need to speak to them before they go.''

Hardcastle nodded ungraciously and got to his feet. He looked at Roxanne. ''You'd better come too. You might learn something.''

''Wouldn't miss it for the world,'' said Roxanne.

The main hall at Brimstone Hall was uncomfortably large. Two chandeliers of massed candles spread a great pool of light down the middle of the hall, and oil lamps lined the walls. Even so, dark shadows pressed close around the borders of the light. Silence lay heavily across the hall, and the slightest sound seemed to echo on forever. Armed men stood at intervals along the walls, staring blankly straight ahead, somehow all the more menacing for their complete lack of movement. A wide set of stairs led up to a gallery overlooking the hall. Hardcastle stood at ease on the gallery, smiling faintly at some pleasant thought of things to come. Jillian stood at his side—quiet, pliant, head bowed, and eyes far away, as though trying to pretend she wasn't really there at all.

Roxanne stood back a way, hidden in the shadows of the gallery. Wulf sat on a chair beside her, legs casually crossed, hands folded neatly in his lap. He might have been waiting for a late dessert, or a promised glass of wine, but there was something unsettling in the air of anticipation that hung about him, something . . . unhealthy. Roxanne kept a careful watch on him from the corner of her eye. She didn't trust sorcerers. Not that she trusted anyone, when you got right down to it, but in her experience magic-users were a particularly treacherous breed.

Hardcastle finally nodded to the two armed mercenaries at the end of the hall, and they pulled back the bolts and swung open the heavy main doors. The crowd of Conservative supporters came surging in, herded by polite but firm stewards. There were flags and banners and a steady hum of anticipation, but it had to be said that the crowd didn't exactly look enthusiastic to be there. Roxanne couldn't help but wonder whether the armed guards were there to keep people out, or keep them in. The main doors slammed shut behind the last of the crowd. Hardcastle looked out over his supporters, and cleared his throat loudly. The hall fell silent.

Afterwards, Roxanne was never really clear what the speech had been about. It was an excellent speech, no doubt of that, but she couldn't seem to sort out what exactly had been so enthralling about it. She only knew that the moment Hardcastle began to speak he became magnetic. She couldn't tear her eyes away from him, and she strained to hear every word. The crowd below were besotted with him, cheering and applauding and waving their banners frantically every time he

paused. Even the stewards and mercenaries seemed fascinated by him. The speech finally came to an end, amid rap-
turous applause. Hardcastle looked out over the ecstatic
crowd, smiling slightly, and then gestured for silence. The
cheers gradually died away.

"My friends, there is one among you who has proved himself worthy of my special attention. Joshua Steele, step forward."

There was a pause, and then a young man dressed in the
gaudy finery of the minor Quality made his way through the
crowd to stand at the foot of the stairs. Even from the back
of the gallery Roxanne could tell he was scared. His hands
had clenched into fists at his sides, and his face was deathly
pale. Hardcastle's smile widened a little.

"Steele, I set you a task. Nothing too difficult. All you had
to do was use your contacts to find out whether James Adamant was still magically protected. You told me he wasn't.
That's not true, is it, Steele?"

The young man licked his lips quickly, and shifted his
weight from one foot to the other. "I did everything I could,
Councillor. Honestly! His old sorcerer, Masque, is dead, and
Adamant hasn't made any move to replace him. My inform-
ants were very precise."

Hardcastle shook his head sadly. "You lied to me, Steele.
You betrayed me."

Steele suddenly turned and ran, pushing his way through
the crowd. Hardcastle looked back at Wulf, and nodded
quickly. The sorcerer frowned, concentrating. Steele
screamed shrilly, and the crowd drew back from him in horror as he fell writhing to the floor. Blood spurted from his
nose and ears, and then from his eyes. He clawed at his face,
and then at his stomach as bloody spots appeared on his tu-
nic. Small fanged mouths burst out of his flesh all over his
body, as hundreds of bloodworms chewed their way out of
him. One of them ruptured the carotid artery in his neck and
blood flew out, soaking the nearest members of the crowd.
They moaned in revulsion, but couldn't tear their eyes away.
Steele kicked and struggled feebly for a few moments longer,
and then let out his breath in a long, ragged sigh. His body

continued to twitch and jerk as the bloodworms ate their way out. Some of the crowd stamped on the horrid things as they left the body, but it quickly became clear the worms were already dying. They couldn't survive for long once they'd left their host.

Roxanne looked thoughtfully at Hardcastle's back, and then at the sorcerer Wulf. There was a lesson here worth remembering. If she ever fell out with Hardcastle, she'd better make sure the sorcerer was dead first. She looked back at the crowd. They were silent and shocked, sullen now. Their holiday mood had been ruined. Hardcastle raised his voice to get their attention, and began to speak again.

And once more his marvelous oratory worked its magic. In a matter of moments, the crowd was won over again, and soon they were stamping and cheering and shouting his name, just as they had before. They seemed to have forgotten all about the dead man in their midst. Hardcastle filled their hearts and minds with good cheer, and sent them out into the streets to campaign on his behalf. The crowd filed out of the hall, laughing and chattering animatedly among themselves. Soon the hall was empty, apart from the stewards and the mercenaries. Hardcastle looked down at the body lying alone in the middle of the floor.

"Have someone clean up the mess," he said coldly, and then turned and left the gallery, followed by Wulf and Jillian. Roxanne looked at the torn and blood-soaked body down below.

Hardcastle strode into his study and poured himself a large drink. The speech had gone down well, and that little bastard Steele had got what was coming to him. Maybe there was some justice in the world after all. He was just lowering himself into his favourite chair when the commotion began. Someone was shouting in the corridor, and there was the sound of running feet and general panic. Hardcastle rose quickly from his chair, and his gaze went immediately to the family long-sword hanging on the wall over the fireplace. It had been a good few years since he'd last drawn that in anger, but he'd had a strong feeling he'd need the blade sooner or later during this campaign. And with Wulf's war on Adamant's house finally beginning to warm up, it was only to be expected that Adamant would resort in kind. Hardcastle snorted angrily as he put down his glass and pulled the longsword from its sheath. So much for Adamant's puerile insistence on playing by the rules. There was only one rule in politics, and that was to win.

It felt good to have a sword in his hands again. He'd spent too long in smoke-filled rooms, arguing with fools for money and support that should have been his by right. The commotion in the hall was growing louder. Hardcastle nodded grimly. Let them come. Let them all come. He'd show them he was a force to be reckoned with. He shot a quick glance at Jillian, who was standing uncertainly by the door, one hand raised to her mouth. Useless damned mouse of a wife. He'd tried to knock some backbone into her, and little good it had done him. He gestured curtly for her to get away from the door, and she fled to the nearest chair and stood behind it. The sorcerer Wulf stayed by the door, making hurried gestures with his hands and muttering under his breath.

"Well?" said Hardcastle impatiently, "What's out there? Are we under attack?"

"Not by magic, Cameron. My wards are still holding. The attack must be on the physical plane. Mercenaries, perhaps." He stopped suddenly, and sniffed at the air. "Can you smell smoke?"

They looked at each other as the same thought struck them both at the same time. They didn't need to say her name. Hardcastle hurried out into the hall, sword in hand, followed by Wulf. Roxanne had her back to the wall and her sword at the ready as she faced off against two of Hardcastle's mercenaries. She was grinning broadly. The mercenaries looked scared but determined. A little further down the hall, a huge wall tapestry was going up in flames. Several servants were trying to put it out with pans of water.

Hardcastle's face purpled dangerously. "Roxanne! What's the meaning of this?"

"Just having a little fun," said Roxanne easily. "I was

doing all right till these two spoilsports interfered. I'll be with you in a minute, as soon as I've dealt with them."

"Roxanne," said Wulf quickly, before Hardcastle could say something unwise, "please put away your sword. These men belong to your employer, Councillor Hardcastle. They are under his protection."

Roxanne sniffed ungraciously, and sheathed her sword. The mercenaries put away their swords, looking more than a little relieved. Wulf gestured for them to leave, and they did so quickly, before he could change his mind. Wulf looked at Roxanne reproachfully.

"When you signed the contract to work for Councillor Hardcastle, there was a specific clause stating that you wouldn't start any fires except those we asked you to."

Roxanne shrugged. "You know I can't read."

"I read it aloud to you."

"It was an ugly tapestry anyway."

"That's as may be. But as long as you work for the Councillor you will abide by your contract. Or are you saying your word is worthless?"

Roxanne glared at him. Wulf's stomach lurched, but he stood his ground. He knew any number of spells that would stop her in her tracks, but he had a sneaking suspicion she'd still survive long enough to kill him, no matter what he did to her. Confronting her this early was a definite risk, but it had to be done. Either her word was binding or it wasn't. And if it wasn't, then she was too dangerous a weapon to be used. He'd have to let her go, and hope he could kill her safely from a distance.

Roxanne scowled suddenly, and leaned against the wall with her arms folded. "All right, no more fires. You people have no sense of fun."

"Of course not," said Wulf. "We're in politics."

"If you've quite finished," said Hardcastle acidly, "perhaps you'd care to accompany me back to my study. I'm expecting some very important guests, and I want both of you present. If you can spare the time."

"Of course," said Roxanne cheerfully. "You're the boss."

Hardcastle gave her a hard look, and then led the way back

to his study. The DeWitt brothers were already there, waiting
for him. Hardcastle silently promised his butler a slow and
painful death for not warning him, and then smiled courteously at the DeWitts and walked forward to shake hands with
them. At the last moment he realised he was still holding his
sword, and handed it quickly to Wulf to replace on the wall.
At least Jillian had had the sense to get the DeWitts a glass
of wine. Perhaps the situation could still be saved.

Marcus and David DeWitt were both in their late forties,
and on first impression looked much the same: tall, slender,
elegant, and arrogant. Dark hair and eyes made their faces
appear pale and washed out, giving their impassive features
the look of a mummer's mask. There was a quiet, understated
menace in their unwavering self-possession, as though nothing in the world would dare disturb them. They'd left their
swords at the front door, along with their bodyguards, as a
sign of trust, but Hardcastle wasn't fool enough to believe
them unarmed. The DeWitts had many enemies and took no
chances. Even with a supposed ally.

Between them, Marcus and David DeWitt ran a third of
the docks in Haven, on the age-old principle of the minimum
investment for the maximum gain. Their docks were notorious for being the worst maintained and the most dangerous
work areas in Haven. If the DeWitts gave a damn, they hid
it remarkably well. Life was cheap in Haven, and labour even
cheaper. And the DeWitts' charges were attractively low, so
they never wanted for traffic. But now the dock strike was
crippling them, despite the zombie scab labour. The dead
men were cheap enough to run and never got tired, but they
weren't very bright and needed constant supervision. They
were also easy targets for dock-worker guerrilla units armed
with salt and fire.

A Conservative-backed Council would support the DeWitts
against the Dock-workers Guild, even if it came down to open
violence and intimidation. Reform would back the Guild. So
the DeWitts were making the rounds before the election, buy-
ing themselves Councillors. Unfortunately for them, they
needed Hardcastle more then he needed them. So if they

wanted his support, they were going to have to pay through the nose for it.

Wulf leaned back in his chair and quietly studied the DeWitt brothers. They were an unpleasant pair, by all accounts, but he'd worked with worse in his time. Like Hardcastle, for example. A brute and a bully and not nearly as clever as he thought he was. Wulf had done a great many unpleasant things himself, down the years; his style of magic demanded it. But he did them in a businesslike way, because they were necessary. Hardcastle did unpleasant things because he enjoyed it. He was one of those people who can only prove how important they are by showing how unimportant everyone else is. Wulf frowned slightly. Such men are dangerous—to themselves, and those around them.

But for the moment, he was a man with power, a rising star; a man on the way up. Wulf could go far, riding the coattails of such a man. And when Hardcastle's star began to wane, Wulf would move on. He had ambitions of his own. Hardcastle was just a means to an end.

"Twenty thousand ducats," said Marcus DeWitt in his cold, flat voice. He took a folded bank draft from his coat pocket and laid it carefully on the table before him. "I trust that will be sufficient?"

"For the moment," said Hardcastle. He gestured easily to Wulf, who leaned forward and picked up the bank draft.

"James Adamant has a hell of a lot of followers out on the streets," said David DeWitt, opening a small silver snuff box and taking out a pinch of white powder. He sniffed delicately, and then sighed slowly as the dust hit his system. He smiled, and looked steadily at Hardcastle. "Just how do you intend to deal with this very popular Reformer, sir Hardcastle?"

"The traditional way," said Hardcastle. "Money, and force of arms. The carrot and the stick. It never fails, providing it's applied properly. My people are already out on the streets."

"Adamant has money," said Marcus. "He also has Hawk and Fisher."

"They're not infallible," said Hardcastle. "They couldn't keep Blackstone from being killed."

"They caught his killer," said David DeWitt. "And made sure he didn't live to stand trial."

"There's no need to worry," said Wulf. "We have our own wild card. Gentlemen, may I present the legendary Roxanne."

She smiled at the DeWitt brothers, and they both flinched a little.

"Ah, yes," said Marcus. "I thought I smelt something burning as we came in."

"I always thought she'd be taller," said David. "Taller, and covered with fresh blood."

Wulf smiled. "She's everything the legends say she is, and more."

Marcus DeWitt frowned. "Does Adamant know she's working for you?"

"No," said Hardcastle. "Not yet. We're saving that for a surprise."

The sorcerer known as the Grey Veil huddled in a corner of the deserted church, shivering with the cold. He'd been there for several hours, gathering together what was left of his magic. He couldn't believe how fast everything had fallen apart. One moment he had been a force to be reckoned with, a sorcerer with hundreds of lesser minds under his command; and then suddenly his control was broken by an interfering Guard, and he'd had to run for his life like a thief in the night. His slaves were free again, and he was a wanted man with a price on his head.

It had all seemed so simple in the beginning. Enter the election as a candidate, and then possess enough people to raise an army of voters. Once on the Council, all kinds of powerful men would have been vulnerable to his possession. A simple plan; so simple it seemed foolproof. He should have known something would go wrong. Something always went wrong. Veil hugged his knees to his chest and rocked back and forth on his haunches. He had no idea how the Guards had found him out. It didn't really matter. He'd staked everything he had on one roll of the dice and had nothing left with which to start again. He'd be lucky to get out of Haven alive.

He pulled his thin cloak tightly about him. He should have known it would come to this. All his life everything he'd turned his hand to had failed him. He'd been born into a debt-ridden family, which, as time went on, only slid further and further into poverty. He was put to work as soon as he was able, at the age of seven. He spent his childhood in the sweat-shops of the Devil's Hook, and in his adolescence moved restlessly from one lousy job to another, searching always for the one lucky break that would change his life. Whatever money he made went on plans and schemes and desperate gambles, but none of them ever came to anything. Even the girl he loved went to another man.

And then he met the old man, who found in Veil a gift for magic. He worked himself to exhaustion to pay for the old man's lessons in sorcery, and when that wasn't enough he stole what he needed from his friends. When he was powerful enough he killed the old man, and took his grimoires and objects of power. He became the Grey Veil, and swore an oath on his own blood that whatever happened, whatever he had to do, he would never be poor again.

Veil smiled bitterly. He should have known better. A loser was still a loser, no matter what fancy new name he took. He breathed heavily on his hands, trying to coax some warmth into his numb fingers. It was very cold in the Temple of the Abomination.

There were many abandoned churches on the Street of Gods. A Being's power would wane, or its followers prove fickle, or perhaps simply the fashion would change, and over-night a church whose walls had once rung to the sound of hymns of adoration and the dropping of coins into offertory bowls would find itself suddenly deserted and abandoned. Eventually another congregation would take over the build-ing, worshipping another god, and business would go on as usual. But some abandoned churches were left strictly alone, for fear of what might linger in the silence.

The Temple of the Abomination had stood empty and alone for centuries; a simple, square stone building on the lower end of the Street of Gods. It wasn't very large, and from the outside it looked more like a downmarket mausoleum than a

church. It had no windows, and only the one door. It wasn't
locked or bolted. The Temple of the Abomination had a bad
reputation, even for the Street of Gods. People who went in
tended not to come out again. Veil didn't give a damn. He
needed a place to hide where no one else would think to look.
Nothing else mattered.

It slowly occurred to him that the church didn't seem as
dark as it had been. When he'd first crept inside the church,
he'd pulled the door shut behind him, closing out the light.
The pitch darkness had been a comfort to him then, an endless night that would hide him from prying eyes. But now he
could clearly make out the interior of the church, such as it
was. There wasn't much to see, just plain stone walls and a
broken stone altar set roughly in the centre of the room. Veil
frowned. Where the hell was the light coming from?

Curiosity finally stirred him from his hiding place in the
corner, and he rose slowly to his feet. He moved forward,
wincing as his stiff joints creaked protestingly. The small
sounds seemed very loud on the quiet. Outside on the Street
of Gods the clamour of a hundred priests filled the air from
dawn to dusk, augmented by the hymns and howls of the
faithful, but not a whisper of that turmoil passed through the
thick stone walls.

Veil peered about him, but there seemed no obvious source
to the dim blue light that filled the church. He glanced down
at his feet to see which way his shadow was pointing, and
his heart missed a beat. He didn't have a shadow. A cold
hand clutched at his heart, and for a moment his breath caught
in his throat. There had to be a shadow; there were other
shadows all around him. Some of them were moving. Veil
stumbled back a step and looked quickly about him, but there
was nothing and no one in the church with him, and the quiet
remained unbroken. He took a deep breath and made himself
hold it for a long moment before letting go. This was no time
to be letting his imagination get the better of him. The light
was nothing to worry about. There were bound to be stray
vestiges of magic in a place like this.

He made himself walk over to the stone altar. It didn't look
like much, up close. Just a great slab of stone, roughly the

shape and size of an average coffin. He winced mentally at the comparison, and walked slowly round the altar. It was cracked from end to end, and someone had cut runes of power into the stone with a chisel. Veil's lips moved slowly as he worked out the meaning. The runes were part of a restraining spell, meant to hold something in the stone.

Veil frowned. All he knew about the Temple of the Abomination was what everybody knew. Hundreds of years ago, when the city was still young, a cult of death and worse than death had flourished on the Street of Gods, until the other Beings had joined together to destroy the Abomination and all its worshippers. It all happened so long ago that no one even remembered what the Abomination was anymore. On an impulse, Veil placed his hands on the altar and called up his magic, trying to draw out whatever impressions still remained in the stone.

Power rushed through him like a tidal wave, awful and magnificent, blinding and deafening him with its intensity. He staggered drunkenly back and forth as strange thoughts and feelings swept through him, none of them his own. Memories of priests and carriers swept through him and were gone, blazing up and disappearing like so many candles snuffed by an unforgiving darkness. There were too many to count, but all of them had served the Abomination, and it had granted them power over the earth and everything that moved upon it.

Veil slowly lifted his head and looked about him. The church was lit as bright as day. He could feel the power surging within him, impatient to be released. He would use that power to gather followers, and bring them to what moved within him. And the thing that men had once called the Abomination would thrive and grow strong again.

That was not its true name, of course. Veil knew what the Abomination really was. He'd known it all his life. He laughed aloud, and the horrid sound echoed on and on in the silence.

4

Various Kinds of Truth

Hawk and Fisher lounged around Adamant's study, waiting impatiently for him to make an appearance. They were due to go out campaigning in the streets soon, but Adamant had promised them a chance to talk with everyone first. Hawk and Fisher still thought of themselves primarily as bodyguards, but there was still the problem of a possible traitor and embezzler somewhere in Adamant's inner circle. Hawk was determined to get to the bottom of that. He didn't like traitors.

Fisher helped herself to a large drink from one of the decanters, and looked enquiringly at Hawk. He shook his head. "You shouldn't either, Isobel. We're going to need clear heads to get through today."

Fisher shrugged, and poured half the drink back into the decanter. "Where the hell is Adamant, anyway? He promised us at least an hour for these interviews."

":We'll manage," said Hawk. "Maybe we should start with someone else. Adamant's got a lot on his mind right now."

"You like him, don't you?" said Fisher.

"Yes. He reminds me a lot of Blackstone. Bright, compassionate, and committed to his Cause. I'm not going to lose him as well, Isobel."

"Don't get carried away," said Fisher. "Remember, as Guards we're strictly neutral. We don't take sides. We're protecting the man, not his Cause. If you want to get enthusiastic about Reform, do it on your own time.''

"Oh, come on, Isobel. Doesn't Adamant stir your blood even a little? Think of the things he could do once he gets elected.''

"If he gets elected.''

The door opened, and they quickly fell silent. Adamant nodded briskly to the two Guards, and pretended not to notice the drink in Fisher's hand. "Sorry I'm late, but Medley keeps coming up with problems he insists only I can deal with. Now, what can I do for you?''

"We need more detail on the death threats, the information leaks, and the embezzlement,'' said Hawk. "Let's start with the death threats.''

Adamant sat on the edge of his desk, and frowned thoughtfully. "I didn't pay them much attention at first. There are always threats and crank letters. Reform has many enemies. But then the threats became specific. They said my garden would die, and it did. More magical attacks followed, including the one that killed Mortice. The last communication said I would die if I didn't resign. Blunt as that.

"There's not much I can tell you about the embezzling. My accountants stumbled across it quite by accident. Medley has the details. They've agreed to keep quiet about it until we can find the traitor, but they won't stay silent for long. They work for the Cause, not me personally.''

"The information leaks,'' prompted Fisher.

"After the embezzlement I started checking through my records, and I found that what I'd thought of as nothing more than a run of really bad luck was actually something more than that. Something more sinister. Someone had been tipping off the Conservatives about my plans and movements. Crowds were dispersed before I could address them, potential allies were intimidated, and meetings were disrupted by planted thugs. Not everyone has access to that kind of information in advance. It has to be someone close to me.''

"Assuming we identify the traitor,'' said Hawk slowly, "what if it turns out to be someone very close to you?''

"You let the law take its course,'' said Adamant flatly.

"Even if it's a friend?"

"Especially if it's a friend."

In the cellar, in the darkness, the sorcerer Mortice sat alone amid blocks of ice and felt his body decay. The pain howled within him, awful and never-ending, gnawing away at his courage and his sanity. At first the concentration needed to maintain Adamant's defences had helped to protect him from the pain and the horror of his situation, but it wasn't enough anymore. Through all the endless hours of the day and night there was nothing for him to do but sit and think and feel.

He had gone through anger and acceptance and horror, and now existed from minute to minute in quiet desperation. He had long ago given up on hope. He would have gladly gone mad, if he hadn't needed to keep control to protect Adamant. He still might. More and more his thoughts tended to wander and fray at the edges.

No one had been to see him for a long time. He could understand that. It was cold in the cellar, and they all had things to do, important things. But time passed slowly in the dark, and no one had been to see him in a very long time. And Adamant, his good friend James Adamant, came least of all.

Mortice sat alone in the cold, in the dark, in the pain, going slowly insane and knowing there was nothing he could do to stop it.

Medley came breezing into the study with a sheaf of papers in his hand, and then stopped dead as he saw Hawk and Fisher.

"Oh, damn! You wanted to see me, didn't you? Sorry, but James has been running me off my feet this morning. What can I do for you?"

"To start with, tell us about the embezzlement," said Hawk. "Exactly how much money has gone missing?"

"A fair amount," said Medley, sitting casually on the edge of Adamant's desk. "About three thousand ducats in all, spread over a period of three months. Small amounts at first, but growing steadily larger."

"Who has access to the money?" said Fisher.

Medley frowned. "That's the problem; quite a few people. James and myself, of course; Dannielle, the butler Villiers and half a dozen other servants, and of course several Reform people who worked on the campaign with us."

"We'll need a list of names," said Hawk.

"I'll see you get it."

"How was the money taken?" said Fisher.

"I'm not actually sure," said Medley. "The accountants were the first to notice something was wrong. Do you want to take a look at the books?"

Hawk and Fisher looked at each other. "Maybe later," said Hawk. "Tell me about Adamant. How has he responded to the death threats?"

"Fairly coolly. They're not the first he's had, and they won't be the last. It's a part of politics in Haven. The magic attacks worry him, of course; Mortice isn't as reliable as he once was."

"Then why doesn't he hire a new sorcerer?" said Fisher.

"Mortice is James's friend. And he lost his life defending James from attack. James can't just abandon him. And besides, when he's in form, Mortice is still one of the most powerful sorcerers in Haven."

They sat in silence for a while, each looking expectantly at the other.

"If there's nothing else . . . ." said Medley.

"You're in charge of Adamant's affairs," said Hawk. "Who do you think has been leaking information?"

"I don't know," said Medley. "It has to be someone with a grudge against James, but I'm damned if I know who. James is one of the fairest and most honourable men I know. The only enemies he has are political ones. Now if you'll excuse me . . . ."

He dropped his papers on the desk, nodded briskly to the Guards to indicate the interview was over, and left the study. Hawk let him go. He leafed through the papers on the desk, but they told him nothing.

"For a political Advisor, he's either extremely tactful or not very bright," said Fisher. "I can think of several possible enemies among Adamant's own people. Mortice, to start with. He saves Adamant's life, and ends up a rotting corpse for his trouble. And then there's his wife, Dannielle. She wouldn't be the first woman to be mad at her husband because he was more interested in his work than he was in her. And finally, what about Medley himself? He's in charge of the day-to-day running of the campaign; who has a better chance to embezzle money without it being missed?''

"Wait a minute," said Hawk. "Mortice and Dannielle I'll go along with, but Medley? What's his motive?''

"As I understand it, he worked both sides of the political fence before he came to work for Adamant. He could still be on the Conservative payroll as an undercover agent.''

Hawk scowled unhappily. "This is going to be another tricky one. If we point the finger at the wrong person, or even the right person but without enough proof, we could end up in a hell of a lot of trouble.''

"You got that right," said Fisher.

Up in the Adamants' bedroom, Dannielle sat elegantly on the edge of the bed and watched critically as James held a shirt up against himself for her approval. It didn't look any better than the first two, but she supposed she'd better agree to this one or he'd get annoyed with her. She wouldn't have minded if he just got red in the face and shouted at her, but James tended more to looking terribly hurt and put upon, and being icily polite. When he wasn't sulking. Dannielle sometimes found herself picking fights with the servants just to have someone she could yell at. At least some of them would yell back at her. She realised James was still waiting patiently, and she quickly smiled and nodded her approval of the shirt. He smiled, and put it on.

Dannielle bit her lip. Better to say it now, while he was in a good mood. "James, what do you think of Hawk and Fisher?''

"They seem competent enough. And surprisingly intelligent, for Guards.''

"But do you think they'll be good at their job? As bodyguards?''

"Oh, certainly."

"Then we don't need to rely on Mortice so much anymore, do we?" James looked at her sharply, and she hurried on before he could say anything. "You've got to do something about Mortice, James. We can't go on as we are. We need real magical protection. It was different when we had no one else we could trust, but now we've got Hawk and Fisher. . . ."

"Mortice is one of the most powerful sorcerers in Haven," said Adamant flatly.

"He used to be; now he's just a corpse with delusions of grandeur. His mind's going, James. Those blood-creatures weren't the first things to get past his wards, were they?"

"He's my friend," said Adamant quietly. "He gave his life for me. I can't just turn my back on him."

"When was the last time you went to see him, before today?"

Adamant came and sat down on the bed beside her. He suddenly looked very tired. "I can't bear to see him anymore, Danny. Just looking at him makes me feel sick and angry and guilty. If he'd just died, I could mourn for him and let him go. But he isn't dead or alive. . . . Just being in the cellar with him makes my skin crawl. The sorcerer Masque was my friend, not that thing rotting in the darkness! But he was my friend, and if it wasn't for him I would have died. Oh, Danny, I don't know what to feel anymore!"

Dannielle put her arms around him and rocked him back and forth. "I know, love. I know."

Dannielle came into the study only a few minutes after Hawk sent for her. She smiled brightly at the two Guards, and sank gracefully into her favourite chair.

"I do hope this won't take long. James is almost ready to go."

"We just need to get a few things clear," said Hawk easily. "Nothing too difficult. How involved are you with the day-to-day running of Adamant's campaign?"

"Not very. Stefan handles all that. I've no head for organising things, so I let the two men get on with it. My job is to stand conspicuously at James's side and smile at anyone who looks like they might vote for him. I'm rather good at that."

"What about the financial side?" said Fisher.

"I'm afraid I'm not very good with figures, either. It's all I can do to handle the household accounts. Once I went a few hundred ducats over budget and James was positively rude to me. Stefan handles all the money to do with the campaign. That's part of his job."

"Let's talk about the gossip," said Hawk.

Dannielle looked at him guilelessly. "What gossip?"

"Come on," said Fisher. "There's always gossip, and you're in the best position to know about it. Servants will talk to you where they wouldn't talk to Adamant or Medley. Or us."

Dannielle thought for a moment, and then shrugged. "Very well, but I can't vouch for how authentic any of this is. Stefan's been a bit . . . distracted recently. Apparently he's got a new girlfriend he's very fond of, but he's trying to keep it quiet because James wouldn't approve of her. It seems she's minor Quality, from a very Conservative family with strong connections to Hardcastle. You can imagine what the broadsheet singers would make of that, if it ever got out."

"How long has this been going on?" said Hawk.

"I'm not sure. About a month. I think."

"After the problems with the embezzlement began?"

"Oh, well after. Besides, Stefan would never betray James. He's far too *professional*."

Hawk caught the emphasis, and raised an eyebrow. "I thought that was why Adamant hired him?"

"There's such a thing as being too professional. Stefan lives, eats, and breathes his work. His word is never broken, and he defends his reputation the way some women defend their honour. What's more, he works all the hours God sends, and expects James to do the same. It's all I can do to get the pair of them to eat regularly. I'll be glad when this bloody campaign is over and we can all get back to normal."

"Is there anything else you can tell us?" said Hawk. "Has anything unusual happened recently?"

"You mean apart from my garden disappearing overnight and a rain of blood in my hall?"

Hawk nodded glumly. "I take your point."

Dannielle got to her feet. "Well, it was very nice talking to you both, but if you'll excuse me, James is waiting."

She swept out, without waiting for permission to leave. Hawk waited until the door had closed behind her, and then looked at Fisher. "So, Medley has a Conservative lover. That could be significant. Perhaps there's some kind of blackmail involved."

"Maybe; but the embezzlement started months before he met her."

"We can't be sure of that. He could have been seeing her for months before the servants got to hear of it."

Fisher scowled. "This is going to be another complicated case, isn't it?"

Stefan Medley sat alone in the library, staring at a wall of books and not seeing them. He should have told Hawk and Fisher about his lady love, but he hadn't. He couldn't. They wouldn't have understood.

Love was a new experience for Medley. The only passion he'd ever known before was for his work. Medley had long ago come to the conclusion that whatever women wanted in a man, he didn't have it. He wasn't much to look at, he had few social graces and even less money, and his chosen career wasn't exactly glamorous. He didn't want much out of life; he just wanted someone to care for him who didn't have to, someone to give him a reason for living. He just wanted what everyone else had and took for granted, and he'd never known.

Now he'd found someone, or she'd found him, and he wouldn't give her up. He couldn't. She was all he had. Except for James's friendship. Medley beat softly on the arm of his chair with his fist. James had believed in him, made him his right-hand man and his friend, trusted him above all others. And now here he was, selfishly keeping a secret that could destroy James's campaign if word ever got out.

But he had to do it. James would never understand. Of all the women he could have fallen in love with, it had to be *her*

. . . except, of course, he'd had no choice in the matter. It
had just . . . happened. Medley had always thought that falling in love, when it finally happened, would be gentle and
romantic. In fact, it was more like being mugged. Overnight,
his whole life had changed.

Medley sat quietly while his mind worked frantically, turning desperately this way and that, searching for a way out of
the trap he'd built for himself. There was no way out. Sooner
or later he was going to have to choose between his friend
and his love, and he didn't know what would happen then.
He couldn't give up either of them. They were the two sides
of his nature. And they were tearing him apart.

"More and more, this reminds me of the Blackstone case,"
said Fisher. "Something nasty's going to happen. We can all
feel it in the air, and there's nothing we can do about it."

"At least then we had a handful of suspects to choose
among," said Hawk. "Now we're stuck with two: the man's
wife and his best friend. And the only skeleton in the cup-
board we've been able to find is that Medley *might* be seeing
a Conservative girlfriend on the quiet. Hardly a burning motive for murder and betrayal, is it?"

"Don't look at me," said Fisher. "You're the brains in
this partnership; I just take care of the rough stuff. Conspir-
acies make my head hurt."

"Right." Hawk scowled. "There's still the butler, Villiers.
Maybe he knows something. Servants always know things."

Fisher smiled sourly. "Whether he's prepared to talk to us
about it is a different matter. If you ask me, Villiers is one
of the old school—faithful unto death and beyond, if necessary. We'll be lucky to get the time of day out of him."

Hawk looked at her. "That's great. Think positively, why
don't you?"

They both fell silent as the door swung open and Villiers
came in. He bowed politely to the two Guards, shut the door
firmly behind him, and then stood to attention, waiting to
hear what was required of him. His poker-straight back and
patient, dour expression gave him a solid dignity that was
only partly undermined by the fluffy white tufts of hair that

blossomed above his ears, in contrast to his resolutely bald head. He had dressed with exquisite care, and wouldn't have looked out of place in a Lord's mansion.

So what was he doing, working for a champion of the common people?

"Take a seat," said Hawk.

Villiers shook his head slightly but definitely. "I'd rather not, sir."

"Why not?" said Fisher.

"It's not my place," said Villiers, "ma'am." He added the last word just a little too late.

"How long have you been James Adamant's butler?" said Hawk quickly.

"Nine years, sir. Before that I was butler to his father. The Villiers family has served the Adamant family for three generations."

"Even during the bad times, when they lost everything?"

"Every family knows disappointments from time to time."

"How do you feel about Adamant's politics?" said Fisher.

"It's not my place to say, ma'am. My duty is to Master Adamant, and the Villiers have always known their duty."

"How do you get on with Mrs. Adamant?" said Hawk.

"An excellent young lady, from a fine background. A strong support to Master Adamant. Her health has been a little delicate of late, but she had never allowed that to interfere with her duties to her husband and the household. Mrs. Adamant is a very determined young lady."

"What's wrong with her health?" said Fisher.

"I really couldn't say, ma'am."

"How do you feel about Stefan Medley?" said Hawk.

"Master Medley seems quite competent in his work, sir."

"How about his private life?"

Villiers drew himself up slightly. "None of my business, sir," he said firmly. "I do not hold with gossip, and I do not encourage it below stairs."

"Thank you, Villiers," said Hawk. "That will be all."

"Thank you, sir." Villiers bowed formally to Hawk, nodded politely to Fisher, and left, closing the door softly behind him.

"I never met a butler yet who wouldn't be improved by a swift kick up the behind," said Hawk.

"Right," said Fisher. "Snobs, the lot of them. Even if he did know anything, he wouldn't tell the likes of us. It wouldn't be proper."

"Maybe there's nothing to tell," said Hawk. "Maybe there is no traitor, and this is all part of an elaborate smear job by the Conservatives to rattle Adamant and undermine his confidence."

Fisher groaned. "My head hurts."

"Stick with it," said Hawk. "The answer's here somewhere, if we just dig deep enough. Those blood-creatures were real enough. I'm damned if I'll let Adamant die the way Blackstone did. I'll keep Adamant alive, even if I have to kill all his enemies personally."

"Now you're talking," said Fisher.

All the day's talk and planning hadn't prepared Hawk and Fisher for the reality of life on the campaign trail. Adamant set out while the day was still young, taking with him Medley and Dannielle, Hawk and Fisher, and a small army of followers, mercenaries, and speech-writers. Hawk felt a little insulted by the presence of the mercenaries; it seemed to imply that Adamant felt Hawk and Fisher weren't enough to ensure his safety. But once Adamant and his party ventured into the streets, the crowds quickly grew so thick and so vociferous that only the mercenaries kept him from being mobbed. Hawk and Fisher contented themselves with walking on either side of Adamant and glaring at anyone who got too close.

The morning passed in a blur of streets and crowds and speeches. Adamant went from hall to hall, from meeting place to open gatherings, delivering endless speeches, raising the crowds to fever pitch and leaving them with a burning intent to vote Reform, which would hopefully last until polling time later that evening. Adamant's followers spread coins around to anyone with enough wit to stick out an empty palm, and the free booze flowed like water. The speech-writers busied themselves with constant rewrites to suit specific areas, often thrusting hastily scrawled extra lines into Adamant's hands only moments before he was due to make his speech. Somehow he always managed to learn them in time and deliver the lines as though he'd only just thought of them. Hawk was impressed. And yet for all the carefully crafted speeches and crowd-handling, the one thing that stood out whenever Adamant spoke was his sincerity, and the crowds recognised it. He believed in his Cause, and he made the crowds believe.

Down on Eel Street they found a landlord dictating how his tenants should vote, on pain of eviction. Adamant did a half-hour speech on the evils of oppression and the virtues of the secret ballot, and Fisher punched the landlord in the mouth. Not far away, in Baker Street, Hardcastle had planted a sorcerously altered double of Adamant to make damaging claims and speeches. Unfortunately for him, he grew too enamoured of the sound of his own voice and didn't get out of the area fast enough. Adamant's mercenaries took care of the double's protectors, and Hawk and Fisher caught up with him before he managed a dozen yards. Adamant made a blockbuster speech on the need to outlaw dirty tricks in politics, and Hawk and Fisher took turns ducking the double in a horse-trough until he admitted who hired him.

A bunch of rather shabbily dressed men began following Adamant and his people from location to location. They shouted impertinent questions and generally made a nuisance of themselves, but Adamant let them get away with it. Hawk and Fisher began to grow a little annoyed with them. Medley spotted the danger signs.

"They're reporters," he said quickly. "Please don't break them."

"We don't hit everyone we don't like," said Fisher.

"Of course not," said Medley. "It just seems that way. Look, we need the press on our side. The two main papers may be written by and for the Quality and the upper middle classes, but they have votes too, and they have a lot of influence over how other people vote. Luckily for us, Hardcastle's always hated the press and never made any bones about it. So, anything that makes us look good is going to get reported, and that's another nail in Hardcastle's coffin. Besides, a lot of the reporters out there are freelancers, making notes for broadsheets. We definitely don't want to upset them.''

Adamant finished his speech, about the opening of a small free Hospital for the Poor and Needy, and the crowd applauded loudly. Adamant then formally declared the hospital open, cut a length of ribbon that served no purpose Hawk could make out, and got cheered again. Hawk decided he'd never understand politics. A large and muscular heckler pushed his way to the front of the crowd, accompanied by two mercenaries in full chain mail. He started insulting Adamant, loudly and obscenely. The crowd stirred unhappily but did nothing, intimidated by the two mercenaries. Adamant's mercenaries were hesitant about going into the crowd themselves, for fear of starting a panic. Hawk and Fisher looked at each other, and drew their weapons. The fight lasted less than a minute, and the heckler was left on his own, looking a lot less imposing, and staring unhappily at Fisher's sword-point hovering before his eyes.

''If I were you,'' said Hawk, ''I'd leave now. Otherwise, Fisher will show you her party trick. And we haven't really got the time to clean up the blood afterwards.''

The heckler looked at the two dead men at his feet, swallowed hard, and disappeared back into the crowd. They let him go, being more interested in putting questions to Adamant while they had the chance. Most of their questions concerned sewers, or the lack of them, but on the whole the crowd was good-natured. Seeing one of Hardcastle's men put to flight had put them almost into a party mood. Adamant answered their questions clearly and concisely, with just enough wit to keep the crowd amused without dampening the fire he was trying to build in them.

Hawk leaned against a nearby wall and surveyed the scene before him. Everything seemed quiet. The crowd was friendly, and there was no sign of any more of Hardcastle's men. Hawk nodded, satisfied, and seized the chance for a short rest. The campaign trail so far had been hard and tiring, and there was still a lot of territory to cover. He looked round to see how the others were taking the strain.

Fisher looked calm and collected, but then, it took a lot to get to Fisher. Adamant was in his element and had never looked better. Dannielle, on the other hand, had found an overturned crate to sit on. Her face was pale and drawn, her shoulders were slumped with tiredness, and her hands were shaking. Hawk frowned. Villiers had said she was ill. . . . He decided to keep an eye on her. If she didn't find her second wind soon, he'd have Fisher escort her home. The last thing Adamant needed was something else to worry about. Dannielle would be safe enough with Fisher, and maybe a couple of mercenaries, just to be on the safe side. He looked round for Medley, to tell him what he intended, and felt a sudden chill as he realised there was no sign of him. He turned quickly to Fisher, who smiled briefly.

"Don't panic; he's just popped into the inn across the road for a swift drink. He'll be back before we have to move on. You're getting old, Hawk, missing things like that."

"Right," said Hawk. "This election is putting years on me."

The inn wasn't much to look at, even by High Steppes standards. Inside, the lights were dim enough to keep everything vague and indistinct. Most of the patrons preferred it that way, but then, they weren't much to look at either. It was that kind of neighborhood. Medley didn't give a damn. This was where he'd first met his lady love, and it would always be a special place to him. He nodded to the indifferent bartender behind the stained wooden bar, and moved quickly on to the private booths at the back of the inn. She was there, waiting for him, just as she'd promised. As always, just the sight of her was enough to make his heart beat faster. He sat down beside her, and his hands reached out and found hers. They sat staring into each other's eyes for a long moment, and it seemed to Medley that he'd never been so happy.

"I can't stay long," he said finally. "Now, what's so important that I had to come here today? You know I'm always glad to see you, but with Adamant's people just outside . . . "

She smiled, and squeezed his hands. "I know, I'm sorry. But I had to see you. I didn't know when I'd be able to get away again. How's your campaign going?"

"Fine, fine. Look, I can't stay long, or they'll come looking for me. And we can't afford to be seen even talking together."

"I know. They wouldn't understand. They'd stop us from seeing each other."

"I wouldn't let them," said Medley. "There's nothing in the world I value more than you."

"You say the nicest things."

"I love you."

"I love you too, Stefan," said Roxanne.

Cameron Hardcastle strode steadily and purposefully through the High Steppes, and the people lined the streets to watch him pass. Armed mercenaries surrounded him at all times, making sure the crowds kept a respectful distance. There was scattered applause from the onlookers, but little cheering. The bunting he'd ordered put up hung limply on the still air, and although his people had handed out Conservative flags and banners by the dozen well in advance, he could only see a few being waved. If it hadn't been for his followers singing campaign songs as they marched, the streets would have been embarrassingly quiet. Hardcastle smiled tightly. That would change soon enough. It always did, once he started to speak.

Jillian hurried quietly along beside him, eyes downcast as always. Hardcastle would just as happily have left her behind, but that was politically unacceptable. A strong marriage and a stable family were central tenets of Conservative thinking, so he had to show off his own wife in public. It was expected of him. She wouldn't disgrace him. She wouldn't dare.

The sorcerer Wulf walked a few paces behind them, disguised as one of the mercenaries. He couldn't afford to be recognised in public as Hardcastle's sorcerer. Firstly, it would have upset the crowds. They tended to distrust magic, and everyone associated with it. Usually with good reason. Secondly, his support was illegal. And thirdly, he would have made too tempting a target. A great many people would have liked a chance at him. But he couldn't let Hardcastle walk the streets unprotected, for the same reason. Even more people would have liked to see Councillor Hardcastle dead. So the great sorcerer Wulf tramped the streets of Haven in Hardcastle's shadow, sweating profusely under a mercenary's chain mail. Besides, he had to be there. Hardcastle couldn't make his speeches without him.

Hardcastle himself was in a surprisingly good mood. His speeches had all gone down very well and, according to first reports, his mercenaries were winning practically every encounter with Adamant's. He reached the platform his people had prepared for him, and climbed the steps onto the stage. Jillian came and stood silently at his side, smiling blankly at the crowd. The campaign song came to an end, and the crowd cheered him, one eye warily watching the mercenaries. Hardcastle lifted his hands for quiet, and silence fell quickly across the packed street. He began to speak, and the crowd's attention became fixed and rapt. A wave of euphoria and commitment swept over them, and soon they were stamping and shouting, and cheering at the end of every sentence. By the end of the speech the crowd was his, to a man. He could have ordered them naked and unarmed into battle, and they would have gone. Hardcastle smiled out over the cheering crowd, relishing the power he had over them.

There was a slight disturbance to one side, as someone pushed their way through the crowd towards him. Hardcastle tensed, and then relaxed a little as he recognised Roxanne. He gestured quickly for her to join him on the platform.

"I was beginning to wonder where you were," he said quietly, still smiling at the crowd.

"Just taking care of business," said Roxanne.

"I suppose I might as well make use of you while you're here." Hardcastle nodded graciously to her, as though he'd been expecting her, and then held up his hands for quiet again. The crowd was silent in a moment. "My friends, may I present to you the latest addition to our ranks, the renowned warrior, Roxanne! I'm sure you all know her fine reputation!"

He paused for a cheer that didn't come. The crowd stirred uneasily. "Oh, great," said an anonymous voice. "Someone send for the fire brigade now, while there's still time."

One of the mercenaries moved in quickly to shut him up with a mailed fist to the kidneys, but the damage had been done. The mood of the crowd had been broken. Most of the people there had heard of Roxanne, and while they were undoubtedly impressed, they were also extremely worried. If not downright scared. Her reputation had preceded her. She looked out over the crowd with a raised eyebrow, but had enough sense not to smile. Wulf glared surreptitiously about him, testing the feel of the crowd, and didn't like what he found. The euphoria of a moment before had vanished, as though it had never been. Wulf shrugged. There would be other times. He moved in close beside the platform and looked up at Hardcastle.

"I think we should be leaving now, Cameron. And in the future it might be wise to keep Roxanne in the background."

Hardcastle nodded curtly. He turned to give the order to leave, and at that moment the crowd went mad. Suddenly everyone was screaming and shouting and kicking out in all directions, and then scattering as fast as their legs would carry them. Hardcastle stared blankly about him, angry and confused, and then he saw the rats moving among the crowd. Hundreds of rats, in all shapes and sizes, many still sleek and shining with slime from the sewers. They scurried this way and that, mad with rage, sinking fangs and claws into anything that came within range. Hardcastle's hands clenched into fists and his face reddened. There was only one way so many rats could have appeared in one place at one time, and that was by magic. A sorcerer must have teleported them into the crowd. Adamant's sorcerer . . .

Wulf fought his way back to the platform. "We have to get out of here, Cameron! There's too many of them! There's nothing I can do!"

Hardcastle nodded stiffly, and signalled for his mercenaries to open a path through the chaos. A blazing anger pulled at his self-control as he descended from the platform, followed by Jillian and Roxanne. One way or another, Adamant would pay for this insult . . . whatever it cost.

Hardcastle arrived at his next meeting place to find a crowd already gathered, listening to someone else address them. He brought his people to a halt and gestured to one of his mercenary officers.

"I thought you said you'd cleared the Reformers out of this area."

"I did, sir. I can't understand it; my people were most thorough. I left men here with strict instructions not to allow any other speakers. If you'll excuse me, sir, I'll go and see what's happening.''

He gestured quickly to half a dozen of his men. They drew their swords and followed him into the crowd. Wulf stirred suddenly at Hardcastle's side.

''There's trouble here, Cameron. Bad trouble.''

Hardcastle smiled grimly. ''My people will take care of it.''

''I don't think so,'' said Wulf. ''Not this time. There's a power here, and I don't like it. It's old magic; Wild Magic.''

Hardcastle frowned impatiently and turned to glare at him. ''What the hell are you talking about, Wulf?''

The sorcerer was staring at the man addressing the crowd, and Hardcastle reluctantly followed his gaze. The man was tall and slender, wrapped in a shabby grey cloak that had seen better days. He was too far away for Hardcastle to hear what he was saying, but there was no denying the impact his words had on the crowd. They couldn't take their eyes off him. And yet there was none of the shouting and clapping that Hardcastle's own speeches always elicited. The crowd was almost eerily silent, utterly engrossed with the speaker. Hardcastle suddenly realised the mercenaries he'd sent into the crowd hadn't come back. He looked quickly about him, but there was no sign of them anywhere. There was a faint whisper of steel on leather as Roxanne drew her sword from its scabbard.

''They've been gone too long,'' she said quietly. ''Want me to go look for them?''

''Not on your own,'' said Hardcastle. ''Jillian, you stay here with my people. Wulf, you and Roxanne follow me. We're going to take a closer look at this . . . phenomenon.''

He gestured to two of his mercenaries, and they opened up a path through the crowd for him. More mercenaries spread out through the crowd, flanking Hardcastle and his party as they moved. No one in the crowd paid them any attention, their gaze fixed on the slight grey figure on the platform. *My platform*, thought Hardcastle resentfully. There was still no sign of any of the missing mercenaries.

''I am the Lord of the Gulfs,'' said the Grey Veil, his eyes wide and unblinking, his face full of a cold and awful wonder.

"He has given me power, power beyond imagining, and he will do the same for you. Only come to him and serve him, and he will make you masters among men. He is ancient and magnificent, older than mankind itself, and his time has come round again."

Hardcastle frowned, and looked about him. The grey figure was saying nothing new, and on the Street of Gods no one would have given him a second glance. So why was everyone so rapt? Why weren't there any hecklers in the crowd? He muttered instructions to the nearest mercenary, who nodded and moved quickly through the crowd, passing the instructions on to the other mercenaries. Soon the silence was broken by jeers and insults and catcalls, and the crowd began to stir.

The Grey Veil turned slowly to face the jeers, and some of the mercenaries' voices faltered. The Veil stopped speaking, and raised his hands above his head. The day suddenly grew dark. Hardcastle looked up and saw the sky was full of angry, swollen clouds, cutting off the daylight and spreading a chill across the crowd. He frowned uncertainly. He would have sworn the sky had been clear only moments before. He looked back at the grey figure, just in time to flinch as lightning cracked down to strike the upraised hands. An eerie blue glow crackled around the Grey Veil's hands, and then the lightning leapt out into the crowd, striking down each and every one of Hardcastle's men who'd raised their voices in mockery. The crowd screamed and shrank back as the mercenaries burst into flames and fell dying to the ground. The smell of burnt flesh filled the air, but somehow the crowd still held their ground instead of scattering, bound together by the Grey Veil's will. He slowly lowered his hands, and the sky began to clear.

The Veil smiled at Hardcastle, and fixed him with his disturbingly direct gaze. "What else would you have me do? Shall I call down the rain or call up a hurricane? Shall I fill your lungs with water, or cause your blood to boil in your veins? Or shall I heal the sick and raise the dead? I can do all those things, and more. The Lord of the Gulfs has given me power beyond your petty dreams."

"Want me to kill him?" said Roxanne.

"You wouldn't get within ten feet of him," snapped Wulf. "Cameron, let me deal with him."

"Do it," said Hardcastle. "Destroy him. No one murders my men and gets away with it."

"I wouldn't stand any more of a chance than Roxanne," said Wulf. "I told you; he has the Wild Magic in him."

"So what do we do?" said Hardcastle.

"If we're lucky, we make a deal."

Wulf made his way through the silent crowd and approached the platform. He and the Grey Veil spoke together for some time, and then Wulf bowed to him and made his way back to Hardcastle and Roxanne. His face was carefully impassive, but there was no hiding its pallor, or the beads of sweat on his forehead.

"Well?" said Hardcastle.

"He's agreed to meet us privately," said Wulf. "I think we can do business."

"Who the hell is he? And what's this Lord of the Gulfs nonsense? I've never heard of him."

"You wouldn't," said Wulf. "It's a very old name. You probably know him better as the Abomination."

Hardcastle looked at him sharply. "The Abomination was destroyed. Every schoolchild knows that. Its Temple on the Street of Gods has been abandoned for centuries."

"Apparently he's back. Not as powerful as he once was, or he wouldn't need to make deals with us."

Hardcastle nodded, back on familiar ground. "All right; what does he want?"

"That's what we're going to discuss." Wulf looked sharply at Hardcastle. "Cameron, we've got to get him on our side. Whatever it takes. With his power, he could hand us the election on a plate."

"What if the price is too high?" said Roxanne.

"No price is too high," said Hardcastle.

5

Harlequin and Other Beings

Dressed in chequered black and white, with a white, clown's face and a domino mask, Harlequin dances on the Street of Gods. No one has ever seen his eyes, and he casts no shadow. He dances with a splendid ease, graceful and magnificent, pirouetting elegantly to a music only he can hear. And he never stops.

Morning, noon, and night, Harlequin dances on the Street of Gods.

Everyone needs something to believe in. Something to make them feel safe and secure and cared for. They need it so badly they'll give up anything and everything, just for the promise of it. They'll pay in gold and obedience and suffering, or anything else that has a market value. Which is why religion is such big business in Haven.

Right in the centre of the city, square in the middle of the high-rent district, lies the Street of Gods. Dozens of different churches and temples stand side by side and ostentatiously ignore each other. Then there are the smaller, more intimate meeting houses, for adherents of the lesser known or more controversial beliefs, who for the most part deal strictly in cash. And then there are the street preachers. No one knows where they come from or where they go, but every day they turn up by the hundreds to line the Street of Gods and spread the Word to anyone who'll listen.

There's never any trouble in the Street of Gods. Firstly, the Beings wouldn't like it, and secondly, it's bad for business. The people of Haven firmly believe in the right of everyone to make a profit.

Or prophet.

Hawk and Fisher looked curiously about them as they accompanied Adamant down the Street of Gods. It wasn't a part of Haven they knew much about, but they knew enough to be wary. Anything could happen on the Street of Gods. Not for the first time, Hawk wondered if they'd done the right thing in leaving the mercenaries behind, but Adamant had insisted. He'd left his followers behind as well. Apart from his bodyguards, only Medley and Dannielle remained with him now.

We're here to ask a favour, said Adamant. *That means we come as supplicants, not as heads of a private army.*

Besides, said Medley, *We're here to make deals. We don't need witnesses.*

The Street itself was a mess. The assorted temples and churches varied widely in size and shape and style of architecture. Fashions from one century stood side by side with modes and follies from another. Street preachers filled the air with the clamour of their cries, and everywhere there was the din of bells and cymbals and animal horns, and the sound of massed voices raised in praise or supplication. The Street itself stretched away into the distance for as far as Hawk could see, and his hackles stirred as he realised the Street of Gods was a hell of a lot larger than the official maps made it out to be. He pointed this out to Medley, who just shrugged.

"The Street is as long as it has to be to fit everything in. With so many magics and sorceries and Beings of Power jammed together, it's no wonder things get a little strange here from time to time."

"You got that right," said Fisher, watching interestedly as a street preacher thrust metal skewers through his flesh. He showed no sign of pain, and no blood ran from the wounds.

Another preacher poured oil over his body, and set himself on fire. He waited until he'd burned out, and then did it again.

"Ignore them," said Adamant. "They're just exhibitionists. It takes more than spectacle to impress anyone here." He looked expectantly at Medley. "What's the latest news, Stefan?"

Medley gathered together a handful of notes and papers, presented to him by messengers reporting on the day's progress. "So far, not too bad. Hardcastle's mercenaries are wiping the streets with ours whenever the two sides meet, but they can't be everywhere at once. All the main polls show us running neck and neck with Hardcastle, which is actually pretty good this early in the campaign. We could even improve as the day goes on. Wait until the drink wears off and they've spent all their bribe money; then we'll see how many Conservative voters stay bought. . . .

"Mortice has been keeping busy. Apparently he's broken up several Conservative meetings by teleporting rats into the crowd. His sense of humour's got very basic since he died.

"As for the other candidates: General Longarm has been making some very powerful speeches. He seems to be building quite a following among the city men-at-arms. Megan O'Brien isn't getting anywhere. Even his fellow traders don't believe he can win. And Lord Arthur Sinclair was last seen hosting one hell of a party at the Crippled Cougar Inn, and getting smashed out of his skull. No surprises there."

They walked on a while in silence. In the Street of Gods the time of day fluctuated from place to place, so that they walked sometimes in daylight and sometimes in moonlight. Once it snowed briefly and rained frogs, and the stars in the sky outshone the sun. Gargoyles wept blood, and statues stirred on their pedestals. Once, Hawk looked down a side alley and saw a skeleton, held together by copper wire, beating its skull against a stone wall over and over again, and for a time a flock of burning birds followed Adamant's party down the Street, singing shrilly in a language Hawk didn't recognise. Adamant looked always straight ahead, ignoring everything outside of his path, and after a while Hawk and Fisher learned to do the same.

"How many Gods are there here?" said Fisher finally.

"No one knows," said Medley. "The number's changing all the time. There's something here for everyone."

"Who do you believe in?" said Hawk to Adamant.

Adamant shrugged. "I was raised orthodox Brotherhood of Steel. I suppose I'm still a believer. It appeals to my pragmatic nature, and unlike most religions they're not always bothering me for donations."

"Right," said Medley. "You pay your tithes once a year, show up at meetings once a month, and they pretty much leave you alone. But it's a good church to belong to; you can make very useful contacts through the Brotherhood."

"Tell me about the Brotherhood," said Hawk. "Isobel and I haven't had much contact with them here, and they're not very well-known in the Northlands where we were raised."

"They're pretty straightforward," said Adamant. "Part militaristic, part mystical, based upon a belief in the fighting man. It started out as a warrior's religion, but it's broadened its appeal since then. They revere cold steel in all its forms as a weapon, and teach that all men can be equal once they've trained to be fighting men. It's a particularly practical-minded religion."

"Right," said Medley. "And if we can get their support, every man-at-arms in the High Steppes will vote for us."

"I would have thought they'd be more interested in Hardcastle," said Fisher.

"Normally, yes," said Adamant. "But luckily for us, Hardcastle has not only not paid his tithes in years, he also had the effrontery to levy a special tax on the Brotherhood in his territory. And on top of that, just recently the Brotherhood's been split down the middle by an argument over how involved they should get in local politics. The new militant sect already has one Seat on the Council: The Downs. Their candidate in the Steppes is General Longarm. We're going to see the High Commander of the orthodox sect, and see if we can stir up some support for us, as part of their struggle against the militants."

"Great," said Fisher. "Just what this campaign needed. More complications."

Adamant looked at Hawk. "How about you, Captain? What do you believe in?"

"Hard cash, cold beer, and an axe with a good edge." Hawk walked on in silence for a while, and then continued. "I was raised as a Christian, but that was a long time ago."

"A Christian?" Dannielle raised a painted eyebrow. "Takes all sorts to make a world, I suppose."

"Who exactly are we here to see?" said Fisher, changing the subject.

"There are only a few Beings who will talk to us," said Adamant. "Most of them won't interfere in Haven's civil affairs."

"Why not?" said Hawk.

"Because if one got involved, they all would, and it wouldn't be long before we had a God War on our hands. No one wants that, least of all the Beings. They've got a good racket here, and no one wants to rock the boat. But there are a few Beings who've developed a taste for a little discreet and indirect meddling. The trick is to get to them before Hardcastle does. I think we'll start with the Speaking Stone."

The Speaking Stone turned out to be a huge jagged boulder of granite, battered and weather-beaten beyond all shape or meaning. Plainly robed acolytes guarded it with drawn swords all the time Adamant and his party were there. After all the things he'd seen so far on the Street of Gods, Hawk was very disappointed in the Stone. He tried hard to feel some holy atmosphere or mystical aura, but the Stone looked like just another lump of rock to him. Adamant spoke with the Stone for some time, but if it had anything to say for itself, Hawk didn't hear it. Adamant seemed neither pleased nor displeased, but if he had got anything out of his visit, he kept it to himself.

The Madonna of the Martyrs had a bad reputation. Her church was tucked away in a quiet little backwater of the Street of Gods. There were no signs to proclaim what it was; the people who needed to would always find their way there. There was a constant stream of supplicants to the Madonna's doors; the lost and the lonely, the beaten and the betrayed.

They came to the Madonna with heavy hearts, and she gave them what they asked for: an end to all pain. After they died, they rose again in her service, for as long as she required them.

Some called her a God, some a Devil. There isn't always that much difference on the Street of Gods.

The Madonna herself turned out to be a plain, pleasant woman dressed in gaudily colored robes. She had a tray of sickly looking boiled sweets at her side and sucked one noisily all the time they were there. She didn't offer them round, and Hawk, for one, was grateful. Dead men and women shuffled through her chamber on unknown errands. Their faces were colorless and slack, but once or twice Hawk thought he caught a quick glimpse of something damned and suffering in their eyes. He kept his hand near his axe, and his eye on the nearest exit.

Adamant and the Madonna made a deal. In return for her withdrawing her support for the DeWitt brothers, Adamant would allow the Madonna access to the High Steppes hospitals. It wasn't quite as cold as it sounded. The Madonna was bound by her nature only to take the willing, and every hospital has some who would welcome death as a release from pain. Even so . . . Hawk studied Adamant thoughtfully. He'd always suspected the politician had a ruthless streak. He caught Medley's eye on the way out, but the Advisor just shrugged.

La Belle Dame du Rocher, the Beautiful Lady of the Rocks, refused to see them. So did the Soror Marium, the Sister of the Sea. They were both old patrons of Haven, and Adamant was clearly disappointed. He left an offering for each of them anyway, just in case.

The Hanged Man was polite but noncommittal, the Carrion In Tears asked too high a price, and the Crawling Violet's answer made no sense at all. And so it went down the Street of Gods. Even those few Beings who would allow Adamant to approach them were usually uninterested in his problems. They had their own affairs and vendettas to pursue. Adamant remained calm and polite throughout it all, and Hawk kept his hand near his axe. The various Beings were disturbing enough, but their followers gave him the creeps. They all had the same flat, unwavering stare of the fanatic.

And finally, when they had been everywhere else, Adamant brought his party to the Brotherhood of Steel. Their Headquarters looked less like a church, and more like an upmarket barracks. The carved wood and stonework was only a few hundred years out of date, which made the place look almost modern compared to most of the Street of Gods. Armed guards patrolled the front of the building, but fell back respectfully once they recognised Adamant. Hawk looked at him sharply.

"You're not just a casual visitor here, are you?"

"I've had dealings with the Brotherhood before," said Adamant. "Every politician has."

A scarred man-at-arms in brightly shining chain mail led them through a series of open corridors to an impressively large library, where he left them. Fisher grabbed the most comfortable chair and sank into it, stretching out her long legs with a satisfied sigh. Hawk was tempted to do the same. His feet were killing him. But every instinct he had was telling him to keep alert. Every man he'd seen in the Headquarters had been wearing a sword, and looked like he knew how to use it. If by some chance Hardcastle had already been here and struck a deal with the Brotherhood, getting out of the Headquarters might prove a lot more difficult than getting in. He sat on the arm of Fisher's chair and fixed Adamant with a steady gaze.

"All right, sir Adamant. Who are we waiting to see?"

"Jeremiah Rukker. He's the Commander here. Not a bad sort; we can talk with him."

"How does he feel about Reform?"

"Couldn't care less, one way or the other. Officially, the Brotherhood is above politics. Actually, they'll work with anyone, if it's kept under the table and the price is right. And the Brotherhood strikes a very hard bargain."

"Fill me in on the Brotherhood," said Fisher. "Just how much influence do they really have in Haven?"

"More than you'd think," said Medley. "Essentially, any man who can wield a sword or an axe can apply for membership in the Brotherhood. Once admitted, they can learn skills and tactics preserved over hundreds of years and become part of a mystical fellowship that owes loyalty to nothing save itself. A Brother of Steel will defy any law, ruler, or religion—if the Brotherhood requires it.''

"And there are Brothers everywhere," said Adamant. "In the Council, in the Guard, and in all the political parties."

Hawk frowned. "How can you be sure of that?"

"This is Haven, remember? Nothing stays secret here for long." Adamant looked at Hawk steadily. "According to my sources, the Brotherhood has spread throughout the Low Kingdoms; even among the King's Advisors. So far, they've managed to avoid a purge of declaring themselves totally impartial when it comes to politics, but the new militants may change all that."

"So why have we come here?" said Hawk. "Why should the orthodox Brotherhood want to make a deal with Reform?" And then he paused, and his face cleared suddenly. "Of course; the most important thing for them is to see that the militants lose this election. In the Steppes, that means backing either Hardcastle or you, and they know they can't trust Hardcastle. I think I'm getting the hang of politics."

"There's more to politics than just being cynical," said a deep, resonant voice behind him. Hawk spun round, one hand dropping to his axe. A tall, impressively muscled man in his mid-forties stood smiling in the library doorway. He paused a moment to make sure they'd all got a good look at him, and then he strode forward into the room. His polished chain mail gleamed brightly in the lamplight, and a long sword hilt peered over his left shoulder. The sword on his back reached almost to the floor. He had jet-black hair, sharp classical features that were a little too perfect to be handsome, and a broad smile that wasn't reflected in his eyes. All in all, he looked more like a politician than Adamant did. Hawk decided that if he had to shake hands, he'd better count his fingers afterwards. He nodded warily to the newcomer, who smiled briefly in his direction before bowing formally to Adamant.

"Jeremiah Rukker, at your service once again, sir Adamant. It's always good to see you here. Won't you introduce me to your companions?''

"Of course, Commander. This is my wife, Dannielle. You know my Advisor. The two Guards are Captain Hawk and Captain Fisher. Perhaps you've heard of them.''

"Yes," said Rukker. "I've heard of them.''

Hawk raised an eyebrow at the ice in Rukker's voice. "Do we have a problem, Commander?''

"We don't," said Rukker carefully. "Your reputation as a warrior precedes you. But your woman also claims the rights of a warrior, and that is unacceptable.''

Fisher rose lithely to her feet and stood next to Hawk, one hand resting idly on her sword hilt. Rukker drew himself up to his full height, and fixed her with a cold stare.

"Women do not use weapons," he said flatly. "They are not suited to it. They know nothing of the glory of steel.''

"Nice-looking sword you've got there," said Fisher easily. "Want to go a few rounds?''

"Isobel . . ." said Hawk quickly.

"Don't worry; I won't damage him too much. Just take some of the wind out of his sails. Come on, Rukker, what do you say? Best out of five, and I'll give you two points to start with. Just to make the match even.''

Adamant glared at her, and then at Hawk. "Captain, if you wouldn't mind . . .''

"Don't look at me," said Hawk. "She goes her own way. Always has. Besides, if Rukker's stupid enough to take her on, he deserves everything that happens to him. If I were you, I'd send for a doctor. And a mop.''

Rukker stared haughtily at Fisher. The effect was rather spoiled because he had to look up slightly to do it. "A Brother of Steel does not fight with women," he said coldly. "It is not seemly.''

"Yeah," said Fisher. "Sure.''

She turned away and sat down in the chair again. Rukker ignored her and inclined his head courteously to Hawk.

"I understand you worked with the legendary Adam Stalker on your last case, Captain Hawk. He was a great man. His death is a loss to us all.''

"There's no doubt he'll be missed," said Hawk. "Was he a Brother of Steel?"

"Of course. All the great heroes are. You might care to make application yourself, some day. Your skills and reputation would make you a valued member."

"Thanks," said Hawk. "But I'm not really the joining type."

"Don't dismiss us so casually, Captain. We have much to offer." Rukker fixed Hawk with a burning gaze, and his voice became earnest and compelling. "The Brotherhood is dedicated to the glory of Steel. It is the symbol that holds mankind together, that enables him to impose order on a savage and uncaring universe. Steel gives us mastery over the world and ourselves. In learning to control our bodies and our weapons, we learn to control our minds and our destinies.

"Think of what we could teach you, Captain. Every move, every trick and skill of fighting there has ever been is to be found here somewhere, in our libraries and instructors. Our fighters are unbeatable, our warriors suitable to advise Kings. We are the future; we decide the way the world will turn."

"Thanks," said Hawk. "But I have enough problems dealing with the present. Besides, Isobel and I are a team. We work together. Always."

"And that's why you'll never be anything more than a city Guard," said Rukker. "A pity. You could have gone far, Hawk; if it hadn't been for your woman."

Hawk smiled suddenly. "Commander, I'm giving you a lot of slack, because I'm here as Adamant's guest. But if you insult my wife one more time, I will hurt you severely. Even worse, I might let Isobel to it. Now, be a good fellow and get on with your business with Adamant."

Rukker flushed pinkly, and his hand rose to the sword hilt at his shoulder. Hawk and Fisher were both on their feet facing him, weapons drawn and at the ready, before Rukker's hand could close around the hilt. Adamant moved quickly forward to stand between them.

"That's enough! Hawk, Fisher, put your weapons away. That's an order. I do apologise, Commander. We've had a very trying day, and I fear all our nerves are somewhat on edge.''

Rukker nodded stiffly and took his hand away from his sword. Bright spots of color burned on his cheekbones, but when he spoke his voice was perfectly steady. ''Of course, James. I quite understand. Let's get down to business, shall we? What exactly can I do for you?''

''Hardcastle's mercenaries are grinding my campaign into the ground,'' said Adamant. ''My people are holding their own for the moment, but they can't last long without armed support. I need your support, Jeremiah; I need your men.''

Rukker pursed his lips thoughtfully. ''The Brotherhood doesn't take sides, James; you know that. We're above politics. We have to be.''

''The militants feel differently.''

''They're fools. We're only allowed free rein as long as we support all sides equally. We're not strong enough yet to stand as a political force in our own right. We survive because we're useful, but the powers that be would crush us in a moment if they thought we were dangerous. No, James. We've worked together in the past when we found ourselves walking the same path, but we can't afford to be openly allied with your Cause.''

''You can't afford not to,'' said Adamant. ''According to all the reports, General Longarm and his militants are doing very well at the moment. They haven't got enough support to win on their own, but if they were to ally themselves with Hardcastle, they'd make an unbeatable team. And Hardcastle's just rattled enough by their successes and mine to agree to such an alliance.''

''You make a good argument, James. But not good enough. Longarm's certainly ambitious, but he's not stupid enough to trust promises from Hardcastle.''

''Who said anything about trust? For the moment they need each other, but all kinds of things could happen once the election is safely over. After all, Hardcastle maintains his position through armed force. Forces that in the future would be exclusively controlled by General Longarm . . . But you're missing the point, Jeremiah. The point is, can you afford to bet that Longarm won't make an alliance with Hardcastle?''

''No,'' said Rukker. ''I can't. All right, James. I'll have to consult with the High Commander, but I'm pretty sure he'll say *yes*. We can't allow Longarm to win this election. You'll have your men in a few hours. And we should be able to call off most of Hardcastle's mercenaries. A large proportion of them belong to the Brotherhood. You've got your support, James. But you'd better make damned sure I don't have reason to regret it.''

Out on the Street of Gods, three different clocks were striking fifteen, although it was still barely midday. Given some of the Street's earlier excesses, Hawk felt only a mild relief that nothing worse was happening. He looked carefully about him, and then stopped as a commotion broke out further down the Street. Fisher noticed his reaction, and her hand dropped to her sword.

''Trouble, Hawk?''

''Could be. Take a look.''

Halfway down, on the other side of the Street, a very tall woman dressed in bright yellow and battered leathers was beating up half a dozen nuns from the Convent of the Bright Lady. The nuns were armed with wooden staves and lengths of steel chain, but the tall woman was wiping the floor with them, using only her bare hands.

''Who the hell is that?'' said Hawk.

''That is Roxanne,'' said Medley. ''I'm surprised you haven't heard of her.'' He winced as Roxanne lifted a nun bodily into the air and slammed her face-first into the nearest wall.

''So that's Roxanne,'' said Hawk. ''I always thought she'd be taller.''

''There's a good price on her head,'' said Fisher.

''With her reputation as a fighter, there'd have to be. I'm not tackling her without being paid extra.''

''She's probably overrated. No one's that good.''

''Bets?'' said Hawk, as Roxanne head-butted one nun and punched out another.

''All right,'' said Fisher. ''Who goes first?''

"Toss you for it."

Fisher fumbled for a coin.

"Wait a minute," said Dannielle. "Look."

Hawk and Fisher looked back just in time to see two new figures dragging Roxanne away from her latest victims, just as she was about to start putting the boot in. She shrugged them off easily, but made no move to attack them. Hawk whistled softly as he realised one of them was Councillor Hardcastle. The other man, dressed in ill-fitting chain mail, was the sorcerer Wulf. Hawk studied him thoughtfully. He'd heard about Wulf.

"Now, that is interesting," said Adamant. "I didn't know Roxanne was working for Hardcastle."

"She won't be much longer," said Hawk. "She's about to be arrested."

"I'd rather you didn't," said Medley quickly. "We don't want to draw attention to ourselves. Officially, we were never here. Our agreement with the Brotherhood will last only as long as we can keep it quiet. In fact, we'd better get out of here now, before Hardcastle spots us. Right, James?"

"I'm afraid so," said Adamant. "If it's a question of the bounty money, Captain Hawk . . ."

"It isn't," said Hawk shortly. "She's wanted on a dozen warrants, most of them for murder and arson. But she can wait. Protecting you has top priority until I receive fresh orders. Let's go."

Fisher nodded reluctantly, and the party moved quickly off down the Street of Gods, keeping to the shadows.

"It's probably just as well," said Medley. "Roxanne's supposed to be unbeatable with a sword."

Fisher sniffed. "I could take her."

"I'm sure you could," said Adamant. "After the election."

"Well, at least now we've got something to look forward to," said Hawk.

Roxanne liked the Street of Gods. Its constantly shifting realities appealed to her own mercurial nature. She almost felt at home. Of course, not everyone felt the same. The Street

had terrorised Jillian to the point that not even Hardcastle's
threats could make her accompany them. He'd had to send
her home, along with all his followers and mercenaries. The
Grey Veil had insisted on that. Apparently his God didn't like
large audiences when it came to hard bargaining. Roxanne
kept a close watch on Veil. She didn't trust him any further
than she could spit into the wind.

Veil led them past churches and temples decorated with
imps and gargoyles and demons. None of them looked particularly healthy places. Veil passed them all by, and Roxanne
pouted disappointedly. Finally they came to the Temple of
the Abomination, and Veil smiled sardonically as he took in
their reactions. It wasn't much to look at, just a plain stone
building with no windows, the stonework scarred and pitted
by long years of neglect, but something about it put Roxanne's teeth on edge.

Veil gestured for his guests to enter. Hardcastle and Wulf
looked at the rough wooden door hanging slightly ajar, and
then looked at Roxanne. She grinned broadly, drew her sword,
and moved forward to kick the door open. At the last moment, the door swung open before her. Roxanne stopped and
waited a moment, but there was no one there. The gloom
beyond the door was still and quiet. She looked back at Veil.
He was watching her mockingly with his disquieting eyes.
Roxanne turned her back on him and swaggered into the Temple of the Abomination.

A dim crimson glow filled the huge stone hall, radiating in
some obscure fashion from a broken stone altar. The hall
stretched away into the distance, and the ceiling towered im-
possibly high above her. She moved slowly forward, her
sword held out before her. There was a sluggish movement
of shadows, but nothing came out of the gloom to challenge
her. Roxanne curled her lip disappointedly. Faint scuffing
sounds behind her spun her round, but it was only Veil, leading Hardcastle and Wulf into the Temple. Roxanne went back
to join them.

Hardcastle looked briefly about him, and did his best to
look unimpressed. "All right," he growled finally. "We're

here. Now tell me why I've come all this way to a deserted Temple when I could be talking with Beings of real Power.''

"Gently, Cameron," murmured Wulf. "You don't know what you're dealing with here.''

"And you do?" said Veil.

"I think so, yes," said Wulf. "You're one of the Transient Beings, aren't you?''

Veil laughed delightedly. It wasn't a healthy sound. The echoes seemed to go on forever in the great hall.

"What the hell's a Transient Being?" said Roxanne.

"An abstraction given shape and form," said Wulf. "A concept clothed in flesh and blood and bone. They have Power beyond reason, for their birth lies in the Wild Magic, and once summoned into the world of men they cannot easily be dismissed.''

Roxanne frowned at the slender figure wrapped in grey before her. "You mean he's a God?''

Veil laughed, but when he spoke his voice was subtly different, as though something else spoke through him. "The Lord of the Gulfs has been asleep for centuries, and it will be some time before he can physically manifest himself in this world again. For now, he needs a host to walk in the world of men.''

Hardcastle scowled unhappily. "What kind of Being are you?''

The light around them grew subtly darker, like sunset fading into night. Here and there in the gloom, pale sparks of light appeared, growing quickly into transparent human shapes. Soon there were hundreds of ghosts glowing palely in the great hall, drifting endlessly back and forth as though in search of something they could no longer remember. All of them were hideously shrivelled and emaciated, reduced by some awful hunger to nothing more than flesh-covered skeletons with distended bellies and wide, agonised eyes. More and more appeared until they filled the hall from end to end, and then without warning they turned upon each other, tearing ravenously at their ghostly flesh with frenzied hands and teeth. They ate each other with desperate haste, screaming silently at the horror of what they did, but the broken bones and ripped flesh brought no end to their hunger.

"I have had many names but only one nature," said the Being through Veil's voice. "Call me Hunger. Call me Famine."

The ghosts were suddenly gone, and the gloom in the Temple of the Abomination was still and quiet once again.

"The Lord of the Gulfs has more power than you could ever dream of," said Veil. "They drive me out again and again, but I always come back. Serve me, and my power is yours."

"Serve you?" said Wulf. "How?"

"Bring me followers. The more who worship me, the greater my power will become. They will feed me with their devotion, and my influence will spread across the land, as it did before. My host must be protected. I cannot be destroyed by the living or the dead—that gift was given to me at my creation—but my host is always . . . vulnerable."

"Can you destroy my enemies?" said Hardcastle.

"Of course."

"Then you've got a deal; whatever you are."

"Excellent," said the Lord of the Gulfs. "But this host has done all it can. It had enough power to raise me, but not enough to sustain me. As a sign of good faith, you must provide me with a new host."

"Take me," said Wulf. "Let me share your power. I have enough sorcery to contain you until we can find you a new host."

Veil looked at him, and then smiled suddenly. "Very well, sorcerer. If that's what you want."

Hardcastle frowned at Wulf. "Are you sure you know what you're doing?"

"Of course I'm sure," muttered Wulf. "Don't rock the boat."

The Grey Veil grinned widely, the smile spreading and spreading until the mouth cracked and broke, splitting the cheeks and opening up the face to show the bones and muscle beneath. The face sloughed off like a mask, and the muscles turned to dust and fell away. The eyes sank back into the sockets and disappeared, leaving only a grinning skull. Dust fell out of the grey robe in streams, and then it crumpled and fell limply to the floor. The jaw fell away from the skull in one silent laugh, and then they too were gone and there was only dust and an empty grey robe. A wind rose up out of nowhere and blew the dust away.

Wulf put an unsteady hand to his mouth and shook his head slightly. His eyes were glazed, as though he was listening to a faint voice very far away. Hardcastle looked at Roxanne, and then back at Wulf.

"I'm all right, Cameron," said Wulf quietly. He lowered his hand slowly and smiled at Hardcastle. "He really wasn't very bright, for a God. He hasn't been awake long, and he wasn't nearly as strong as he thought he was. I've got him, held securely within my wards, and all his power is mine. Adamant doesn't know it yet, but the election is yours, Cameron. No other sorcerer can stand against me now. Let's go."

The wooden door swung open, and Hardcastle and Wulf went back out into the Street of Gods. Roxanne looked round the deserted hall one last time and then followed them out. She put away her sword, and wondered if there'd be time to stop for dinner any time soon.

6

Truth and Consequences

The afternoon dragged slowly on towards evening as Adamant led his party through the bustling streets of the High Steppes, making speeches, addressing gatherings, and generally beating the drum for Reform. The crowds were thicker than ever as even those who'd been working spilled out onto the streets to make the most of the unofficial holiday. Street traders sold out their wares, closed their stalls, and joined the celebrations. Conjurers and mummers provided traditional entertainments, innkeepers ran low on stock and began hauling dusty bottles from off the back shelves, and fireworks spattered the darkening sky.

Adamant finally took a break from the crowds, who were more interested in partying than politics, and led his people into the more upmarket sections of the Steppes. He was looking for personal endorsements and promises of funds. What he got were kind words, good wishes, and vague promises. When anybody could be bothered to speak to him. Adamant declined to be disheartened, and pressed on with unfailing enthusiasm.

And along the way two new members joined his party and walked along with him: Laurence Bearclaw and Joshua Kincaid.

Bearclaw was a big man in his late forties, with broad shoulders, and a barrel chest that was slipping slowly towards his belt. He first won fame by killing a bear with nothing but a knife, and he still wore the animal's claws on a chain around his neck to prove it. His shoulder-length hair was still jet-black because he dyed it regularly. He'd served in a hundred different campaigns as a freelance mercenary, and he'd come away with credit and scalps from all of them. He didn't really give much of a damn for Reform, but he liked Adamant, and the idea of supporting the underdog appealed to him.

Kincaid was an average-height man in his mid-forties, with a shock of butter-yellow hair and icy blue eyes. He was muscular in a lean kind of way, didn't smile much, and was even more dangerous than he looked. He'd made his reputation by fighting in the infamous Bloody Ridges campaign alongside the legendary Adam Stalker. He was famous throughout Haven, and moderately well-known outside it. There were several broadsheets and songs telling of his heroic deeds, all of them written by Kincaid under an assumed name. Like his friend and sometime fighting companion Bearclaw, Kincaid wasn't what you'd call political. But it had been too long since his last campaign, and he was bored sitting around waiting for a call to action that never came. He hated just sitting around; it made him feel old. If nothing else, working with Adamant was bound to supply enough material for a new broadsheet.

The afternoon wore on, and took its toll from all of them. Adamant seemed as full of bounce and vinegar as ever, but some of his party were beginning to wilt under the strain. Dannielle in particular seemed to be having an increasingly hard time keeping up with him. She'd disappear now and again for a quick sit-down and a rest, and return later revitalised and full of bounce. But it never lasted. Dark bruises began to appear under her eyes. Medley was becoming increasingly distracted as he tried to keep up with the growing number of reports on how the campaign was going. Hawk and Fisher stayed close by Adamant and kept their eyes open for trouble. As Guards, they were used to spending long hours on their feet, but the pace was getting to them too. Things nearly came to a head when Adamant visited the few members of the Quality who lived on the edges of the Steppes, in a last-ditch gamble for funding and support. Mostly they got the door slammed in their faces; the rest of the time they were invited in, only to be subtly sneered at or not-so-subtly threatened. This did not go down well with Fisher. She tended to take it personally when she got looked down on. In fact, she tended to get very annoyed and hit people. After one unfortunate incident, Adamant decided it would be better if she waited outside thereafter.

But finally even Adamant had to admit they'd done all they could. Evening was falling, and the voting would begin soon. He looked out over the milling crowds for a long moment, his eyes far away, and then he smiled and shook his head and took his people home.

Back in Adamant's study, Hawk and Fisher sank immediately into the nearest chairs, put their feet up on his desk, and watched interestedly as Adamant bustled around checking reports and planning future strategy. Medley did his best to listen and pay attention, but he was beginning to look decidedly wilted round the edges. Dannielle had already disappeared upstairs for a little lie-down. Hawk for one did not blame her. He could quite happily have spent the next few months just sitting in his chair doing nothing. He smiled slightly. He'd always suspected he was officer material.

Bearclaw and Kincaid had gone in search of the kitchens to do a little restorative foraging. The butler Villiers came and went bearing messages and reports for Adamant, with a haughty expression that suggested he considered himself above such things. Hawk and Fisher helped themselves to the wine. Medley finally shuffled the reports into some kind of order, and Adamant settled down behind his desk to listen. He glared at Hawk and Fisher until they took their boots off his desk, and then looked expectantly at Medley.

"First the good news," said Medley. "The Brotherhood of Steel is out on the streets in force. Together with our people, they're knocking the hell out of Hardcastle's mercenaries. Also, street crimes have dropped sixty per cent.

"Megan O'Brien, the spice trader, has pulled out of the

election. He's given his money and support to Hardcastle, in return for future favours. No surprises there.

"Lord Arthur Sinclair, standing on the No Tax On Liquor platform, was last seen passed out cold in the middle of a riotous party that covered an entire block. The Guard have roped off the area and set up barricades. Anyway, Sinclair is officially out of the running, or will be as soon as anyone can wake him up long enough to tell him.

"The mystery candidate known as the Grey Veil has disappeared. No one's seen hide nor hair of him since midday. He's probably retired quietly to save face.

"Now we come to the bad news. Hardcastle has been campaigning just as hard as we have, if not more so. His speeches have all gone down very well, and his people are handing out booze and money like they're going out of fashion. He's made the rounds of some very influential people, and gained a lot of support. The Quality may not like him much, but they're scared to death of James Adamant. It also appears that Hardcastle has picked up some very powerful support from something on the Street of Gods. Mortice isn't sure who or what is behind it, but just recently Hardcastle's sorcerer Wulf has been using all kinds of powerful magics he didn't have access to before. He's still not strong enough to break through Mortice's wards, but Mortice can't break through Wulf's either. So, as far as magic goes we have a stalemate. For the moment.

"The rest of the bad news concerns General Longarm." Medley paused for a moment to gulp thirstily at a glass of wine before continuing. "Longarm and his militants are doing surprisingly well. There's no doubt his armed supporters have been practicing subtle and not-so-subtle intimidation, but there does seem to be some real grass-roots support for Longarm. People are responding well to his theme of political strength through military strength. He's also sworn to accept any man with a sword into the militant branch of the Brotherhood, once he's elected. A lot of people want that. Being a Brother of Steel opens a lot of doors, and not just in Haven."

Medley checked his papers to make sure he'd covered

everything, and then dropped them on the desk before Adamant. Adamant frowned thoughtfully.

"What do we know about General Longarm, Stefan?"

"Solid, professional soldier; not very imaginative. Had a reasonably good record with the Low Kingdoms army, before he retired and moved here. Came to politics late in life, which is probably why he takes it so seriously. Speaks well in public, as long as he sticks to a prepared text. This offer of guaranteed entry into the militant Brotherhood sounds a lot like desperation tactics. Might be worth sounding out other militants to find out whether it's a genuine offer or just something Longarm came up with off his own bat."

Adamant looked at Hawk and Fisher. "The militants already have one Seat on the Council: The Downs. Have you heard anything about that district since the militants took over?"

"It's not really our district," said Hawk slowly. "But I have heard a few things. Ever since Councillor Weaver came to power in The Downs, street crime has dropped by more than half throughout the area. That's been very popular. On the other hand, it seems clear that militant Brothers have been working as unofficial Guards in The Downs, and that hasn't been at all popular. There's no doubt they've been cracking down on street violence, but they've also been pushing their beliefs very strongly, and anyone who dares speak out against that gets very short shrift. I'm not just talking about bloody noses either; apparently the militants can turn quite nasty if they're crossed. I haven't any hard figures on how the election's going there, but I wouldn't be at all surprised if Weaver lost his Seat."

"Thank you, Captain," said Adamant. "There may be something there I can use. Campaign rhetoric is always better for having some basis in truth."

The door flew open and Dannielle swept in, looking much refreshed. She smiled brightly at Hawk and Fisher, still slumped in their chairs.

"What's this; still tired? I don't know what the Guard's coming to these days. James, darling, will you please come with me and talk to the cook? I've been trying to get her to agree to the menu we decided on for tonight's banquet, but she keeps going all mulish on me.''

"Of course, Danny," said Adamant tolerantly. He nodded to Medley and the two Guards, and allowed his chattering wife to drag him out from behind his desk and out into the hall. Hawk looked at Fisher.

"I don't know where she gets her energy from, but I could sure use some of it."

Hardcastle and his people trudged determinedly round the High Steppes, making speeches, shaking hands, and generally waving the flag. The crowds had been drinking most of the day and were starting to get a little rowdy, but Roxanne and the mercenaries kept them in line. And the speeches were still going down very well. As long as Hardcastle kept talking the crowds would listen, rapt and enthusiastic. Hardcastle was glad something was still going right; the news from the rest of the Steppes was almost universally bad. Somehow Adamant had put together an army of fighting men and turned them loose, and they were wiping the streets with Hardcastle's mercenaries. He'd lost nearly every advantage he'd gained, and areas that should have been safely under his thumb were now singing Reform songs and throwing stones at his people.

Hardcastle fought to hold on to his temper. He couldn't afford to let himself be distracted. He still had to make the rounds and talk to the people who mattered; people of standing and influence. Adamant might crawl to the commoners for their grubby little votes, but it was the Quality and the merchant houses who really ran Haven. That was where the real power lay. When they spoke, people listened—if they knew what was good for them. And so Hardcastle went from house to house, knocking on doors and glaring at servants, only to find himself fobbed off with vague promises and excuses as often as not. Apparently they were disturbed by the rising violence in the streets. Hardcastle fumed quietly to himself. These were the same people who'd bleated the loudest to the Council at the advances Reform had been making.

The afternoon darkened towards evening, and Hardcastle

headed for the last address on the list. His last friend, and his last hope.

He stood before Tobias' door, and waited impatiently for an answer to the bell pull. It was taking a long time. Roxanne was idly trimming a fingernail with a nasty-looking dagger, and Wulf was staring off into the distance, lost in his dreams of power. Hardcastle looked at his followers and mercenaries, standing clumped together and muttering rebelliously under their breath, and he gestured irritably for them to disperse across the street. He wouldn't put it past Adamant to launch a sneak attack, if he thought he could get away with it. It was what Hardcastle would have done. Besides, he didn't need an army to visit a friend. Assuming the friend would talk to him.

Geoffrey Tobias had a reputation for being tight with money, and his house reflected it. Tobias was one of the six richest men in Haven, but his house was a cheap and nasty two up, two down, in one of the more subdued areas of the Steppes. The walls hadn't been painted in years, and wooden shutters covered the windows, locked tight even though it was still light. Tobias believed there were always thieves and cut-throats waiting for a chance at his money. Hardcastle shrugged. The man was probably right. A miser living on his own and apparently unprotected was an obvious target. Not that he was unprotected, of course. Hardcastle had no doubt the nasty little house was absolutely crawling with defensive spells.

Tobias had always been careful with money, but since he'd lost his Seat on the Council he'd given all his attention to his financial dealings. The man who had once been one of the real firebrands of the Conservative Cause had become a bitter and secretive recluse. He wouldn't see anyone he didn't absolutely have to, and even then strictly only by appointment. But he'd see Hardcastle. Hardcastle was a friend, and more importantly, he had something Tobias wanted. The offer of a Seat on the Council . . .

In return for a sizeable contribution to campaign funds, of course.

The door finally opened a crack, and Tobias glared out at

them. He recognised Hardcastle with a scowl and opened the
door a little wider. He was a grey, shabby man with pale skin
and stringy grey hair that hung listlessly around his shoulders. His clothes were filthy and years out of style, and you
had to look hard to see that under the dirt and wrinkles they
had once been of exquisite style and cut. His face was all
sharp planes and angles, with a down-turned mouth, and his
eyes were cold and knowing. Tobias looked at Hardcastle for
a long time and then sniffed loudly.

"Hello, Cameron. I should have known you'd come
scratching at my door, with the election so close. Are all
these people with you?"

"Yes, Geoffrey," said Hardcastle patiently. "I vouch for
them."

Tobias sniffed again. "They stay out here, all of them. I
won't have them in my house."

He stepped back to allow Hardcastle to enter, and then
slammed the door shut behind him. The narrow hall was
gloomy and oppressive and smelled of damp. There was
cracked plaster on the walls, and the floor was nothing but
bare boards. Tobias led Hardcastle down to the end of the
hall, pushed open a door and gestured for him to enter. He
did so, and found himself in a comfortable, brightly lit room.
The walls were covered with highly polished wood panels,
and there was a deep pile carpet on the floor. A huge padded
armchair stood by the fireplace, next to a delicate wooden
table covered with papers and set with an elegant silver tea
service. Tobias grunted with amusement at Hardcastle's surprise.

"I may be eccentric, Cameron, but I'm not crazy. I haven't
much use for show or vanity anymore, but I still like my
comforts."

He sank carefully into the armchair, and gestured for Hardcastle to pull up the only other chair opposite him. They sat
looking at each other for a moment.

"Been a while, Geoffrey."

"Two years, at least," said Tobias. "I've kept busy, with
one thing and another."

"So I hear. They tell me you've doubled your fortune since you left the Council."

"Leave? I didn't *leave* anything, and you damned well know it! I was forced out of my Seat, by that little snot Blackstone and his whining Reformers. He promised them the earth and the moon, and they believed it. Little good it did them. Their precious Blackstone is dead, and his successor couldn't make money if his life depended on it. Just wait till the Heights is hurting for money and can't balance its budget, and see how fast they scream for me to come back and save them!"

His voice had been rising steadily, and by the end he was practically shouting. He stopped as his breath caught in his throat, and he coughed hard for several moments.

"You should take better care of yourself," said Hardcastle. "You've let yourself go."

"That's one way of putting it, I suppose." There were flecks of blood around Tobias' mouth. He patted his lips with a folded handkerchief, looked indifferently at the crimson stains on the cloth, and put it away. "What do you want here, Cameron? I've no influence anymore."

"That could change," said Hardcastle. "With a little persuasion I think I can get you official Conservative backing in the next election for the Heights. Full support; right across the board. Of course, a large contribution to Conservative funds would help to sway things in the future. That's how the world works."

"Oh, I know all about how the world works, Cameron." Tobias chuckled briefly. "Sorry to disappoint you, but I don't really care about the Heights anymore. I still get mad about how they treated me, but I wouldn't go back if they got down on their knees and begged. Being a Councillor always meant more to my poor Maria than it ever did to me. I still miss her, you know. . . ." Hardcastle looked nonplussed for a moment, and Tobias chuckled again. "Not used to being caught out, are you, Cameron? You've been surrounded by Advisors for too long. You can't trust Advisors. They just tell you what they think you want to hear."

"I need them," said Hardcastle. "I can't do everything

myself. And my friends haven't always been there when I needed them.''

"You never needed me," said Tobias quietly. "You never really needed anyone. And I had my own problems.''

"Why didn't you tell me you were ill? I would have come to you long before this.''

"I go my own way, Cameron. Always have, always will. I don't lean on anyone. Don't worry; you can have your contribution. Tell my lawyers how much you need, and I'll see it gets to you. Buy some more mercenaries. Buy whatever it takes to crush those Reform scum into the dirt. Make them pay for what they did to me.''

"I'll do that, Geoffrey, I promise you. Is there anything else I can do for you?''

"Yes. Leave me in peace. Goodbye, Cameron. Don't slam the door on your way out.''

In Brimstone Hall Jillian Hardcastle sat on her bed, her back pressed against the headboard, hugging her knees to her. Her husband had finally returned. She could hear him moving about downstairs, talking to people. His people; none of them were hers. She had no friends, no one came to visit her, and she wasn't even allowed a servant of her own. All she had was her husband, the great Cameron Hardcastle.

She looked at her bare arms, and the bruises stood out plainly even under the extra layer of makeup. She'd have to put on some long gloves before she went downstairs. Her back still ached, but it was bearable now. At least there hadn't been any blood in her urine this time.

She often thought about leaving, but she had no one to go to. And wherever she went, Cameron would be sure to find her. He had people everywhere. She sometimes thought about killing herself, but she could never find the courage. Hardcastle had beaten all the courage out of her.

She heard footsteps outside on the landing, and fear rushed through her like icy water, freezing her in place. It was Cameron, come to look for her. She knew it. She stared fixedly at the closed bedroom door, barely breathing, her stomach churning with tension. The footsteps approached the door, and then went on past it, continuing on down the hall. It wasn't Cameron. Just one of the servants.

She ought to go down and welcome Cameron home. He expected it of her. If she didn't go downstairs, he would come looking for her, and then he would be angry. But she couldn't go down to meet him. Not yet. She'd go downstairs in a minute, and greet him in the polite monotone he'd taught her. She would go down. In a minute. Or two.

Hardcastle sank into his favourite chair, looked round his warm, comfortable study, and sighed gratefully. It had been a long hard day, and he wasn't as young as he used to be. He started to order Jillian to fetch him a drink, and then scowled as he realised she wasn't there. She ought to have been there. It was her place to be at his side, to carry out his wishes. He'd have to have another little talk with her, later on.

He got to his feet, ignoring his protesting back, and poured himself a large drink. He rather thought he'd earned it. There was a polite knock on the door. He grunted acknowledgement, and Wulf and Roxanne came in. He dropped back into his chair, noting sourly that neither of them looked particularly tired. Roxanne leaned against the fireplace with her arms folded, waiting patiently for new orders. Hardcastle made a mental note that she wasn't to be offered a guest room for the night. They'd probably wake up in the early hours to find the whole damned Hall going up in flames. Wulf was standing to attention before him, waiting to report on the day's activities. Let him wait. Do him good to be reminded of his place. Hardcastle sipped unhurriedly at his wine and then nodded to the sorcerer to begin.

Most of the reports were pretty straightforward. All the minor candidates had dropped out. That simplified things; he wouldn't have to have them crushed or killed, after all. General Longarm was still making a nuisance of himself, but he was nothing more than a retired soldier with delusions of grandeur. And with all the mercenaries currently battling on the streets, soldiers weren't particularly popular right now. Adamant was still a problem. The Brotherhood of Steel had declared in his favour, and were actually out on the streets sticking their noses into things that didn't concern them. Hardcastle scowled. He'd better send word to the right people, and have them called off.

Wulf droned on, showing off as usual on how professional he was, and Hardcastle waited impatiently. He had a question he wanted to ask, but he didn't interrupt. He didn't want the sorcerer to be able to hide behind the excuse of any other business. Wulf eventually ground to a halt, and Hardcastle looked at him steadily.

"You said you had power now, Wulf. Real power. Power enough to break through Adamant's wards and destroy him and his new sorcerer. So why are they still alive?"

Wulf met Hardcastle's gaze unflinchingly. "It will take time before I can use my power safely. For the moment I'm still concentrating on the wards that hold the Abomination safely within me. We were lucky to find him while he was still relatively weak after his awakening. If he was to escape now, he would be very angry with us. He'd destroy us, the whole of Haven, and probably most of the Low Kingdoms. We're talking about one of the Transient Beings, Cameron, not some low-level demon. We can't risk something like that getting loose."

"So what am I supposed to do about Adamant?"

"Nothing, for the moment. Let's wait and see how the polling goes. There's still plenty of time to intervene directly, if it should prove necessary."

Hardcastle glared at him. "That's not good enough, sorcerer." He looked across at Roxanne. "According to my sources, Longarm is planning an attack on Adamant tonight. I want you to use your inside contact to get into Adamant's house. Stay hidden and wait for the attack, and then take advantage of the confusion to make sure Adamant dies. You'd better kill your contact as well. Is that clear?"

"Of course," said Roxanne. "Sounds like fun." She smiled at Hardcastle, and he had to look away. Few people could meet Roxanne's smile without flinching. Even when she was on their side.

• • •

The banquet at Adamant's mansion was a noisy affair. There were so many guests that even the main dining hall was barely sufficient to hold them all. The single great table had all but disappeared under huge servings of food and wines, and there wasn't a spare place left for anyone. The huge candelabra and dozens of wall lamps filled the hall with a blaze of light, and the guests filled the air with a roar of chatter. It was a victory celebration, in every way that mattered. No one had any doubts as to the election's outcome. This night would be Reform's night. They could tell. They could feel it on the air and in the streets.

Adamant sat in the seat of honour, of course, with Dannielle on one side and Medley on the other. Dannielle was busy feeding Adamant by hand, with something covered in a sticky sauce, half of which seemed to be ending up on his face, to their mutual amusement. Medley was busy sampling several wines to see which was the tastiest. The two warriors, Bearclaw and Kincaid, sat side by side discussing old battles, and using the table cutlery to mark troop positions. The rest of the guests were Adamant's followers and party faithfuls, being rewarded for their services to Adamant's campaign. Servants came and went, bringing yet more courses and side dishes. Adamant's food taster sat quietly to one side, nibbling at a light salad, having given up trying to keep up with everyone else. A dozen or so dogs wandered round the hall, enjoying all the noise and attention, and feeding on bones and scraps thrown to them by indulgent guests.

Hawk and Fisher were there too, but they weren't part of the banquet. They were on duty. They'd get their dinner later, in the kitchens. If they were lucky. Reform only went so far, after all. Hawk was fatalistic about such things and, if anything, preferred to have his attention free to watch for threats, but Fisher was simmering with barely repressed bile. Hawk kept a watchful eye on her. She tended to take such things personally. At the moment she was scowling dubiously at a chicken leg she'd snatched from under the nose of a resentful hound. The animal was about to challenge her for it, but one glare from Fisher was enough to change his mind.

"You're not really going to eat that, are you?" said Hawk.

"Damn right I am," said Fisher. "I'm hungry." She gnawed industriously at the leg for a while, and then gestured with it at the banquet table. "Look at them all, stuffing their faces. There's not one of them who's worked half as hard as we have today. I hope they all get wind."

"Don't take it so hard," said Hawk. "I'm sure Adamant would have invited us to table if he could, but it would do his image no good at all, and he knows it. The Cause is great for political reform, but it's got a long way to go before it can start meddling with the social structure."

"I'd like to meddle with his structure," muttered Fisher. "Preferably with a large mallet."

"It's not as if we've been singled out," said Hawk reasonably. "Adamant's got a good twenty to thirty mercenaries and men-at-arms scattered round this house standing guard, and none of them were invited either."

"We're different," said Fisher.

"Maybe," said Hawk. "Hello! Where's Medley going?"

Hawk and Fisher watched interestedly as Medley made his excuses to Adamant, and left the table. He seemed to be in something of a hurry, and by the time he got to the main door he was practically running.

"The fish must be off," said Hawk.

Fisher looked at him fondly. "You have no romance in your soul, Hawk. Now he's no longer needed here, he's probably off to see his mysterious girlfriend. I wonder if we'll get to meet her?"

"I doubt it. Hello! Now Dannielle's leaving as well."

Hawk and Fisher watched again as Dannielle made her excuses to Adamant and left the table.

"Maybe the fish *is* off," said Fisher.

"I don't know," said Hawk thoughtfully. "She's been up and down all day. Maybe her illness is catching up with her."

"Or she's gone after Medley to try and sneak a look at his girlfriend."

"Either that, or someone's slipped poison in their food . . ."

They looked at each other.

"No," said Hawk finally. "They haven't eaten anything

the others haven't, and anyway, Mortice is keeping a close watch on the banquet.''

Fisher shrugged. ''No doubt we'll find out what's happening eventually. We usually do.''

''That was before we got involved in politics.''

''True.''

They watched everyone else eating for a while. Hawk's stomach rumbled.

''Something's wrong,'' said Fisher suddenly.

Hawk looked at her. ''How do you mean?''

''We're supposed to get regular security updates from Adamant's people, but no one's been by here in almost half an hour.''

''That's right,'' said Hawk. He frowned, and bit his lip thoughtfully. ''You wander over and take up a position by Adamant. I'll take a quick look out the door and see if anyone's about. It's always possible Adamant's people are just getting slack now the worst is over, but . . .''

''Yeah,'' said Fisher. ''But.''

She headed casually in Adamant's direction, while Hawk made unhurriedly for the main door. No point in upsetting the guests if they didn't have to. The banquet hall was set right in the centre of the mansion and had just the two doors. The far door led straight to the kitchens; a servants' route. Hawk had checked it out earlier. It was too narrow and twisting to move an attack force through. The main door led out onto a wide corridor that ran pretty much the length of the house, with only a couple of bends. Hawk scowled. He didn't like the direction his thoughts were taking. Any attack force would have to get past all of Adamant's men and Mortice's protective wards. He'd have been bound to hear something. Unless the attack force was very, very good. Hawk stopped before the main door and listened. He couldn't hear a thing over the racket the dinner guests were making. Why the hell had Medley and Dannielle chosen this particular time to disappear? He reached out a hand to the doorknob, and then stopped as the doorknob began to turn slowly on its own. Hawk backed away.

The door flew open and a dozen cloaked and masked men

burst in. Hawk yelled a warning to Fisher, and drew his axe. The guests at table screamed and yelled and struggled to get to their feet. Fisher moved to stand between Adamant and his attackers, sword at the ready. Bearclaw and Kincaid rose to their feet and looked around for weapons. Neither of them had worn swords to table. That would have been an insult to Adamant. Bearclaw seized a heavy silver candlestick and hefted it professionally. Kincaid broke a bottle against the wall with practiced ease.

The attackers came spilling round Hawk like rushing water past a rock. He stood his ground and cut down two men with his axe. Bearclaw came charging forward, deftly avoided a vicious sword stroke, and clubbed the man to the ground. He quickly stepped over the fallen body to tackle another intruder, and Kincaid came forward to guard his back with the broken bottle. Two swordsmen thought he'd be an easy target. Kincaid smiled easily, cut one man's throat, and blinded the other, his hand moving too quickly to be seen. He threw aside the bottle and snatched up a dead man's sword. Blood flew on the air as he moved swiftly among the scattering enemy, his sword darting back and forth in textbook cuts and parries.

Three men got past Hawk and the two warriors, and made straight for Adamant. Fisher met them with her sword. The first man went down almost immediately, clutching at the wide rip in his gut. The second forced Fisher back step by step with a whirlwind attack of cuts and thrusts. The third man closed in on Adamant. Fisher tried desperately to finish her man so that she could get back to protect Adamant, but her opponent was too good to be that easily dismissed. Fisher cut and parried and then faked a stumble. The masked man thought he saw his chance and moved in, and Fisher ran him through. She jerked her sword free and turned quickly round just in time to see Adamant throw a bowl of soup into the third man's face, blinding him. The intruder clawed at his eyes, and Adamant kicked him in the groin. As the man sank to his knees, Adamant took away his sword and looked around for another victim.

Hawk cut down two more men, the wide head of his axe punching through hidden chain mail as though it wasn't there.

Bearclaw and Kincaid fought back to back, and the last two intruders went down in a flurry of blood and steel. A sudden silence fell across the dining hall, broken only by the gradually slowing breathing of the fighting men and mutters of shock and amazement from the guests. Bearclaw bound up a nasty-looking gash in his shoulder with a dubious-looking handkerchief taken from his sleeve.

"I must be getting old, Joshua," he said easily. "Was a time they'd never have got near me."

Kincaid nodded solemnly. "Well, it must be said the candlestick never was your preferred weapon. Grab one of their swords and we'll go and see if there are any more of these bastards in the house."

The guests stirred uneasily at that, and Adamant moved quickly forward to address them. "It's all right, my friends, the worst is over. Please stay where you are while I have my people search the house and make it secure." He moved quickly over to Bearclaw and Kincaid and kept his voice low as he spoke to them. "Joshua, Laurence, find out what's happened to my men-at-arms, and report back here when the house is fully secure again. And remember, Danny and Stefan went off on their own just before the attack; make sure they're all right."

The two warriors nodded silently and left the hall sword in hand. Hawk wanted to go with them, but knew he couldn't. His priority had to be Adamant's safety. He went over to Fisher, and made sure she was all right. They looked around at the mayhem they'd helped to cause, and shared a grin. Adamant approached them and nodded his thanks.

"It may not look like it," he said quietly, "but this is still something of a disaster. A whole lot of nasty questions come to mind, starting with how the hell they got in. Mortice's wards are supposed to keep out anyone I haven't personally vouched for. And why the hell didn't Medley's intelligence people warn him there was a raid in the offing?"

"No problem," said Hawk. "We handled it. Any idea who they were?"

"Not really," said Adamant. "A last-chance assault by Hardcastle's people, presumably. Let's take a look."

They moved quickly among the bodies, pulling off masks and studying faces. Hawk and Fisher didn't recognise anyone, but Adamant remained kneeling beside the body of a grey-haired man with a harsh, scarred face that hadn't relaxed at all in death. Hawk and Fisher moved over to join him.

"General Longarm himself," said Adamant. "He always did take his politics too personally."

"Let's keep looking," said Fisher. "Maybe we'll get really lucky and find Hardcastle's here as well."

Adamant smiled in spite of himself, and then looked round quickly as the main door opened and Kincaid came in. He walked straight over to Adamant, who rose to his feet.

"We have something of a problem, James," he said quietly. "Not with the house; that's secure. It seems there were fifty of the intruders originally. Your people took care of the others before they got this far. No one heard anything because of the noise of the banquet. We've got quite a few casualties, and even more dead. These people were professionals."

"Militant Brothers of Steel," said Hawk.

Kincaid nodded, but didn't look all that impressed. "Well, they're dead militants now."

"So what's the problem?" said Fisher.

"I think you'd better come and see for yourself, James." Kincaid couldn't seem to meet Adamant's eyes. "It's Dannielle."

Adamant's face lost all its color, as though someone had just punched him in the gut. "How badly is she hurt?"

"I really think you'd better see for yourself James."

"You're not going anywhere without us" said Hawk quickly.

Adamant nodded impatiently. "Let's go."

Kincaid led the way out into the main corridor. There were bodies and blood everywhere. Preoccupied as he was, Adamant still had room in him to be sickened at the sight of so many men who had died in his behalf. He stepped carefully over the bodies, nodding here and there at a familiar face, and then he stopped and knelt by one man. It was the butler,

Villiers. He'd taken a dozen wounds before he died, and a broken sword was still clutched in his hand.

"He never believed in Reform," said Adamant. "But he stayed with me anyway, because I was family. He never left us, even during the bad days. He protected me as a child. And all it got him was a bad death, in a house where he should have been safe." He got to his feet, and nodded for Kincaid to carry on. They walked on down the corridor. When Adamant spoke again his voice was perfectly steady. "You haven't said anything about Stefan. Is he all right?"

"Oh, he's fine," said Kincaid. "Locked himself in your study with his girlfriend. I don't think he knows anything's happened. Just shouted at me to go away when I knocked on the door."

Adamant nodded, not really listening, and Kincaid led the way up the stairs to the next floor. His face was fixed and drawn. *She must be dead*, thought Hawk. *Anything else, he would have said*. The moved along the hallway to Adamant's bedroom. Bearclaw was waiting outside the door. There was pity in his face as he looked at Adamant. Pity, and something else Hawk couldn't read. Bearclaw opened the bedroom door, and everyone drew back a few steps to let Adamant go in first.

In the bedroom, Dannielle was sitting on the bed. Her face was flushed, and she wouldn't look Adamant in the eye. Kincaid picked up a small silver snuff box from the dressing table and handed it to Adamant. He looked at it blankly for a moment and then opened it. Inside was a small amount of grey-white powder.

"Cocaine," said Bearclaw. "We found her helping herself when we were searching this floor."

"Oh, great," said Fisher. "That's going to look really good when it gets out."

"It's not going to get out," said Adamant. "Not until after the election." He looked at Dannielle, and his mouth tightened. "How could you, Danny? How could you do this to me?"

"Oh, that's typical, James. Never mind why I'm taking drugs; all you care about is your precious reputation." Dannielle glared at him sullenly, her voice shrill and bitter. "I've been sniffing dust ever since you started campaigning for the Steppes. The best part of three months, and it's taken you till now to notice. It's all your fault, anyway. You never had time for me any more; all you talked and thought and dreamed about was your bloody campaign. I tried to go along, to be a part of it for your sake, but you never even noticed I was there.

"We aren't all as strong as you, James. You've been full of energy right from the beginning, inspired by your Cause, running full tilt from one thing to the next, with the rest of us straggling along behind you, trying to keep up. I just couldn't anymore. I was tired all the time, and lonely and depressed. So I started sniffing dust now and again, just to give me a boost, make me feel human, and keep me going. Only the campaign just ground on and on, and I got more and more tired, and there were always more and more things that needed doing for your bloody Cause. And I needed more and more dust just to feel normal and get me through the day. I even had to embezzle from you to pay for the dust."

"Why didn't you tell me?" said Adamant. He realised he was still holding the snuff box, and put it down on the dressing table. He wiped his fingers unconsciously on his sleeve, as though they were dirty.

"When did I ever get a chance to talk to you?" said Dannielle. "We haven't had a moment to ourselves in months."

Adamant started to say something heated in reply, and then stopped himself. When he spoke again his voice was low and cold and very controlled. "Perhaps you're right, Danny. I don't know. We'll talk about it later. In the meantime, I have to think about how best to keep this quiet. A lot of people are counting on me to win this election, and I won't let them down. If news of this gets out, I'll be ruined. I've made a lot of enemies in my stand against the drug trade, and they'd use a scandal like this to destroy me. Who else knows, apart from us? Who was your supplier?"

Dannielle smiled almost triumphantly. "Lucien Sykes."

"What?"

"Drugs come in through the docks, and he takes his share.

Where do you suppose all the money came from that he's been donating to your campaign?''

Adamant turned away and closed his eyes for a moment. Nobody said anything. Adamant turned to Hawk and Fisher. "How much of this do you need to report?"

"Not all of it," said Hawk. "Keeping quiet about your wife comes under the general heading of protecting you. But Sykes is a different matter. We can't ignore someone in his position. But he can wait until after the election tonight."

"Thank you," said Adamant. "That's all I can ask. Danny, pull yourself together, and then come down and help with my guests. People have been hurt."

"Do I get to keep my dust?"

"Do you need it?"

"Yes."

"Then keep it."

Adamant turned and left the room, and the others followed him out.

"I'm going to have to put out some kind of statement about the attack," said Adamant as they went back downstairs. "To reassure my followers that I'm all right. Rumours spread like wildfire in Haven, particularly when it's bad news. I'd better talk to Stefan. He's probably still in my study with his lady friend." He smiled briefly. "I did promise no one would barge in on them while they were there, but I'm sure he won't mind, under the circumstances."

He led the way back to his study, and knocked briskly on the door. "Stefan, it's James. I need to see you. Something's come up." He waited a moment, but there was no reply. Adamant smiled slightly, produced a key, and unlocked the door. He knocked again, and pushed the door open. Medley and Roxanne were sitting together. For a moment nobody moved as the two sides stared at each other, and then Roxanne grabbed her sword belt and drew her sword.

"Get out of here, Stefan! They'll kill us both!"

She started towards Adamant, sword at the ready, and then stopped as Hawk and Fisher moved quickly forward to protect him. Medley got to his feet, but stood where he was, staring at Adamant's horrified face. Roxanne grabbed a burning brand from the fire and set it to a hanging tapestry. Flames ran up the wall. She grabbed Medley's arm and urged him towards the other door. Hawk and Fisher went after them as Bearclaw and Kincaid tried to beat out the fire before it could spread. Adamant just stood where he was, watching.

Roxanne backed away from Hawk and Fisher one step at a time, her sword sweeping back and forth before her, keeping the Guards at bay. She was grinning broadly, and her eyes were full of death. She glanced back over her shoulder just long enough to be sure that Medley was safely through the door. Then after a moment's hesitation, she turned and ran after him. Hawk and Fisher plunged after her, but she slammed the door in their faces and turned the key on the other side. Hawk lifted his axe to break down the door, and then lowered it again. His job was to protect Adamant, not to chase after traitors. Medley and Roxanne would keep for another day. He put away his axe, and after a moment Fisher sheathed her sword. Kincaid and Bearclaw had torn down the burning tapestry, and were stamping out the flames. Adamant was still standing in the doorway, staring at nothing. Hawk glanced at Fisher, who shrugged uncertainly. He moved tentatively towards Adamant, and the politician's eyes came back into focus. He had to swallow two or three times before he could speak.

"My wife is taking drugs supplied by one of my main backers. My guests have been attacked in my own dining hall, and most of my men-at-arms are dead. And now it turns out my closest friend has been a traitor all along. I never knew politics could cost so much." For a moment he couldn't get his breath, and Hawk thought Adamant might cry, but the moment passed and some of his strength came back to him. His face hardened, and when he spoke again his voice was strained but steady.

"Not a word of this to anyone. We can't afford for my supporters to know how badly we've been betrayed. It will all come out after the election, but by then it won't matter, whatever the result. So, we'll go back to the dining hall, reassure my guests, and keep our mouths shut about all this.

"But win or lose, Stefan Medley is a dead man."

Medley followed Roxanne through the packed streets, dazed and unquestioning. It was all like some horrible nightmare he couldn't wake up from. One moment he'd been cherishing a snatched moment with Roxanne, and the next he was running for his life. He didn't know where he was running to; Roxanne had taken over as soon as they left the house. He couldn't seem to concentrate on anything; all he could see was Adamant's face, and the look of betrayal in his eyes. Roxanne led him through increasingly narrow and squalid streets until finally they came to the Sheep's Head Inn, a quiet backwater tavern they'd used before for their few assignations.

The bartender showed no interest in seeing them again, but then he never did. That was one of the reasons why they'd chosen the place. Roxanne collected the key and led the way up the back stairs to their usual room, and for the first time they were able to sit down and look at each other.

"All in all, it's been an interesting day," said Roxanne. "Pity I didn't have time to kill Hawk and Fisher, but there'll be other times."

"Is that all you've got to say?" said Medley. "My life is ruined, my reputation isn't worth spit any more, and all you can think about is fighting a couple of Guards? We've got to get out of Haven, Roxanne. James won't move against us while the election's still running, but once that's over he'll send every man he's got after us. His pride won't let him do anything else. And you can bet he won't have given them orders to bring us back alive."

"We can go to Hardcastle," said Roxanne. "He'll protect us. If only to spite Adamant."

"No," said Medley. "Not Hardcastle. I've hurt him too badly in the past. He has scores to settle with me. Look, Roxanne, this is our chance to get away from all this and start over."

"But I don't want to leave," said Roxanne. "I don't run from anyone. Besides, I like working for Hardcastle. The pay's good, and the work is interesting. I'm staying."

Medley looked at her for a long moment. "Why are you doing this to me, Roxanne?"

"Doing what?"

"I love you, Roxanne, but I can't go to Hardcastle. If you love me, you won't ask me to."

Roxanne looked down at the floor, and then back at him again. "Sorry, Stefan, but I told you; I work for Hardcastle. You were just another job. Hardcastle's sorcerer set me on you, as a way of getting to Adamant. You told me all kinds of useful things without realising it. You were fun, but now the masks are off and the game's over. You lost. I'm sorry to rush you, Stefan, but I have to be going now."

She got to her feet, and Medley stood up to face her. "So it was all nothing but lies; all the things you said to me. I betrayed my best friend and dragged my honour through the mud, all for you; and now you're telling me it was all for nothing? I can't believe that, Roxanne. I won't believe that."

She shrugged. "Don't take it so personally. It's just business. No hard feelings?"

Medley sat down again, as though all the strength had gone out of his legs. "No; no hard feelings, Roxanne."

She smiled at him briefly, and left, closing the door quietly behind her. Medley stared at the closed door, listening to the sound of her footsteps disappearing down the stairs.

7

Desperate Choices

All the clocks in Haven struck eight in the evening, and the polls finally opened. Brightly colored election booths appeared on the designated street corners, in the time it took for the bells to toll the hour. Magically created and maintained by the Council's circle of sorcerers, they were as near to being corruption-proof as anything in Haven could be. Once a vote had been registered and placed in the metal box, nothing but the most powerful sorceries could get at it again. There were fingerprint checks to make sure everyone was who they claimed to be, and to keep out simulacra and homunculi. Haven's voters were a devious lot when it came to corruption and cheating.

The inns and the brothels were still going strong, though the free booze had run out long ago. Some of the day-long revellers were busy sleeping it off on tavern floors and tables, uncaring that they were missing the very chance to vote that they'd been celebrating. Bets were still being made, at widely varying odds, and rumour and speculation ran rife. People thronged the streets, dressed in their best. An election was an Occasion, a chance to see and be seen. Pickpockets and cutpurses had never had it so good. Ballad singers stood at every street corner, singing the latest broadsheets about the two main candidates, interspersed now and then with requested old favourites. There were jugglers and conjurers and

151

stilt-walkers, and of course any number of street preachers making the most of the occasion, always on the lookout for a crowd and anyone who looked like they might stand still long enough to be preached at.

The voting began, as Haven made its choice.

Roxanne leaned back in her chair and stretched her legs languorously as Hardcastle poured her a glass of his best wine. He was smiling broadly, and positively radiating good cheer. It didn't suit him. Wulf and Jillian stood quietly in the background.

"You've done well, Roxanne," said Hardcastle, pouring himself a large drink. "Without Medley to help him, Adamant's organisation will fall apart at the seams, and he'll lose every advantage he's gained. All it needs now is a few more pushes in the right places, and everything he's built will collapse around him. It's a pity you didn't get a chance to kill him, but it's just as well. I've changed my mind. I don't want him dead just yet. I want him to suffer first.

"It's not enough to kill Adamant. Not anymore. I want to beat him first. I want to humiliate the man; rub his nose in the fact that all his whining Reformers are no match for a Conservative. I don't just want him dead; I want him broken."

Roxanne shrugged noncommittally and sipped at her wine. She'd taken advantage of the speech to study Jillian Hardcastle and the sorcerer Wulf. Both of them looked rather the worse for wear. Jillian had a bruised and swollen mouth, and was holding herself awkwardly, as though favouring a hidden pain. Wulf looked tired and drawn. There were dark bruises of fatigue under his eyes, and his gaze was more than a little wild. He seemed preoccupied, as though listening to a voice only he could hear. Roxanne realised Hardcastle had stopped talking, and quickly turned her attention back to him.

"All right," she said equably. "What do we do now?"

"We need to isolate Adamant even further," said Hardcastle. "We've taken away his Advisor. Who does that leave him to lean on? The two Guards, Hawk and Fisher. They've been acting all along like Adamant's paid men, for all their vaunted impartiality. With them out of the way, Adamant should crumble and fall apart nicely.''

Roxanne nodded. "I can take either of them on their own, but killing both of them would be tricky." She smiled suddenly. "Fun, though."

"I don't want them killed," said Hardcastle flatly. "I want them kidnapped. They have interfered in my life far too often, and they're going to pay the price. They'll beg for death before I'm finished with them."

"I can't guarantee to take both of them alive," said Roxanne. "One perhaps, but not both."

"I thought you might say that," said Hardcastle, "So I've arranged some help for you." He tugged at the bell pull by his desk. There was a short, uncomfortable pause, and then the study door opened and Pike and Da Silva came in. Roxanne studied them warily from her chair.

Pike was tall and muscular, in his mid-twenties, with a clear open face and a nasty smile. He moved well, and carried his chain mail as though it were weightless. He was a familiar type; throw a stick in a gladiators' training school and you'd hit a dozen just like him. Da Silva was short and stocky, with a broad chest and a wrestler's overdeveloped arm muscles. He was a few years older than Pike, and looked it. His face was heavy and bony, and would have looked brutish even without the perpetual scowl that tugged at his features. As well as a sword, he carried a four-foot-long headbreaker of solid oak weighted with lead at both ends.

Independently they were proficient-enough mercenaries, but working together as a team they'd built a reputation for death and mayhem that almost rivalled Roxanne's. She glared at them both, and then switched her glare to Hardcastle.

"Why do you need them? You've got me."

"I want Hawk and Fisher taken alive," said Hardcastle. "The only way to do that without major casualties to my side is to make sure we have the advantage of overwhelming

numbers. Pike and Da Silva command a troop of fifty mercenaries. You will lead them against Adamant's people. Wulf
will supply magical protection. Is that clear?''

Roxanne shrugged. ''You're the boss, Hardcastle. What do
we do after we've taken Hawk and Fisher?''

''I've set aside a place for them. Pike and Da Silva have
the details. Adamant and his people should be hitting the
streets in about half an hour. Follow them, pick your spot,
and do the job. No excuses on this one; I want them alive. I
have plans for Hawk and Fisher.''

James Adamant led his people out into the High Steppes,
determined to make as many speeches as he could while the
polls were still open. None of his people said anything, but
it was clear to everyone that Adamant needed to reassure
himself of his popularity after so many things having gone
wrong. So with tired limbs and weary hearts they followed
him out onto the streets one last time. Adamant strode
ahead, out in front for all to see, with Dannielle at his side.
Hawk and Fisher followed close behind. Adamant's supporters had dispersed and gone home after the debacle of
the victory banquet, so only half a dozen mercenaries accompanied Adamant on his last excursion into the Steppes,
with Bearclaw and Kincaid bringing up the rear. It was a
far cry from the cheerful, confident host that had followed
him on his first outing, but a lot had happened since then.

Adamant hurried from street to street at a pace his retinue
was hard pressed to match, as though he was trying to leave
his most recent memories behind and be again the confident, unworried politician he had been at the start of the
day. Hawk and Fisher stretched their legs and kept up with
him. They walked with weapons drawn, just in case Hardcastle tried for a last-minute assassination. Hawk kept a
careful watch on Dannielle. He'd wanted to leave her behind, but she'd insisted on going with them. Trouble was,
she was right. Her presence was a vote winner, and her
absence would have raised questions Adamant couldn't afford to answer. She'd thrown the last of her dust on the fire
before she left. Adamant had just nodded stiffly, and turned

away. They were walking arm in arm and smiling at the crowds, but they hadn't exchanged five words since they left the house.

Hawk sighed quietly to himself. As if he didn't have enough things to worry about. Medley had disappeared, along with the notorious Roxanne, but it was too early to tell just how much information he'd betrayed to Hardcastle. Worst of all was the damage he'd done to Adamant's confidence. Adamant had trusted Stefan Medley implicitly, and allowed him to shape and plan his whole campaign. Now Medley was gone, and Adamant didn't know who or what he could rely on anymore.

On top of all that he'd found he couldn't rely on Mortice anymore either. Longarm and his men shouldn't have been able to break into his house at all, but the dead man's mind had been wandering again, and his wards had slipped. He'd promised it wouldn't happen again, and Adamant had pretended to believe him, but neither of them were fooled.

Adamant made another speech on yet another street corner, and as always a crowd gathered to listen. Even now, after all that had happened, Adamant could still sway a crowd with his voice. Perhaps because he still believed in his Cause, even if he was no longer sure of himself. The speech started off well enough. The crowd was responsive and enthusiastic, and cheered in all the right places. Bearclaw and Kincaid moved unobtrusively among them, making sure no one got out of hand. Hawk and Fisher leaned wearily against a wall, feeling unneeded. And then the crowd's cheers turned to screams as fifty mercenaries came pouring out of a side street with swords in their hands.

They cut their way through the scattering crowd, uncaring who they hurt. Bearclaw and Kincaid drew their swords and fought side by side as the tide of mercenaries hit them. Bearclaw swung his great sword two-handed, cutting down his attackers like a scythe slicing through overripe wheat. Kincaid leapt and danced, his blade cutting and thrusting in swift steel blurs. But there were only two of them, and the vast body of mercenaries swept past them without even slowing. The two warriors were quickly surrounded, and moved to stand back to back, still fighting. Adamant's mercenaries tried to make a stand, but there were only six of them and they were quickly overrun. Hawk and Fisher moved quickly forward and put themselves between Adamant and Dannielle and their attackers. They waited grimly, weapons at the ready.

The first mercenary to reach them went for Fisher, mistakenly supposing her to be the easier target. She parried his blow easily, cut his throat on the backswing, and was back on guard before the next mercenary could reach her. Hawk roared a Northern war cry and swung his axe in short, vicious arcs, scattering the mercenaries around him as one by one they fell before his unwavering attack. Soon the street was a boiling cauldron of milling men and flashing steel, and blood flew on the air. Adamant had drawn his sword and was keeping his attackers at bay, but he had trained as a duellist, not a street fighter, and it was all he could do to hold his ground. Dannielle cowered behind him, clutching a dagger he'd given her, hoping she'd find the strength to use it when the time came.

Hawk and Fisher fought side by side, and the mercenaries fell before them, unable to match their skill or their fury. Bearclaw and Kincaid fought alone, separated by the mercenaries, bleeding from a dozen wounds but refusing to fall. Dead men lay piled about them. And then Roxanne appeared out of nowhere, laughing aloud as her sword flashed out to slice through the meat of Kincaid's leg. His mouth gaped soundlessly as his leg crumpled beneath him, unable to bear his weight. He fell to one knee, still trying to swing his sword. Roxanne swept past him, grinning fiercely, heading for Hawk and Fisher. Pike and Da Silva came after her. Pike's sword lashed out to deflect a blow from Bearclaw, and Da Silva's heavy wooden staff swept across to slam into Bearclaw's side. Ribs broke under the impact. Bearclaw coughed blood, and fell forward onto his hands and knees. The mercenaries closed in around Bearclaw and Kincaid, and their swords rose and fell in steady butchery.

Roxanne burst through the milling crowd of fighters and threw herself at Fisher. Fisher tried to hold her ground and couldn't, forced back by the sudden strength and speed of the attack. Hawk tried to reach her, but Pike and Da Silva were quickly upon him, Pike engaging his axe while Da Silva circled patiently with his headbreaker, trying for a clear shot.

Roxanne thrust and parried, laughing breathlessly, and step by step Fisher was driven back, until her back was pressed up against a wall and there was nowhere else to go. Fisher was good with a sword, but Roxanne was an expert, inhumanly strong, and she never seemed to get tired.

For a moment, desperation gave Fisher new strength and she was able to beat aside Roxanne's attack long enough to cut through the mercenary's leathers and open a long, shallow wound along her ribs. Roxanne didn't even flinch, and her return attack drove Fisher back against the wall. Fisher's moment passed, and her strength faded away, replaced by the day's weariness. She struggled frantically to fend off Roxanne's sword, and then a mercenary stepped in from her blind side and clubbed her down with the hilt of his sword. Fisher dropped to one knee, still clinging to her sword. Blood spilled down her face from a torn scalp. Roxanne and the other mercenary hit her again with their sword hilts, and she fell blindly forward onto the bloody cobbles and lay still. Roxanne kicked her in the head.

Hawk saw Fisher fall, and screamed in fury that he couldn't get to her. He swung his axe savagely at Pike, and the mercenary was forced to retreat. The heavy axe blade smashed through Pike's defences and knocked him to the ground. Hawk stepped in for the kill, and Da Silva's headbreaker swung round in a tight arc, slamming into Hawk's side, knocking the breath out of him. Hawk staggered backwards, favouring his injured side, and snarled soundlessly at his opponents, daring them to come after him.

Adamant swept his sword back and forth, keeping the mercenaries at bay. For some reason they seemed more interested in keeping him occupied than in trying to kill him. Whatever the reason, it hadn't prevented them from whittling away at him like a carpenter with a block of wood. Blood ran freely from a dozen wounds, staining his fine clothes. Dannielle screamed behind him, and he spun round to see her struggling with a grinning mercenary. Adamant ran him through and turned quickly back to face his opponents. Their attitude changed immediately with the death of their companion, and for the first time they began to press their attack in earnest. Swords seemed to come at him from everywhere at once, and Adamant realised sickly that he couldn't keep off such an attack for more than a few moments. One of the mercenaries beat aside his sword and lunged forward. Dannielle screamed and threw herself in the blade's way. It plunged into her side. She grabbed the blade with both hands as she crumpled to the ground. Adamant screamed hoarsely, and ran the mercenary through. Two men stepped forward to take his place, their faces grim and determined. Adamant lifted his head and screamed at the dark sky above.

"Damn you, Mortice! You promised you'd protect her! Help us!"

The mercenaries froze in their attack, looked briefly startled, and then vomited blood explosively. They fell to the ground, kicking and shaking helplessly as blood poured from their mouths. Adamant looked round dazedly as one by one the attacking mercenaries dropped, coughing up their life's blood in harsh, painful spasms. In a matter of moments, Hawk and Adamant were the only ones left standing, surrounded by the dead and the dying. Adamant turned his back on them and knelt beside Dannielle, lying at his feet, curled around the bloody wound in her side. He took her hand, and she clutched it tightly. Her breathing was quick and ragged, and her face was covered with sweat.

"Screwed up again, didn't I?" she said breathlessly.

"Be quiet," said Adamant gently. "We've got to get you to a doctor."

Dannielle shook her head. "Bit late for that, James. I'm sorry."

"What for?"

"Everything."

"You've nothing to be sorry for, Danny. Nothing at all. Now, shut up and save your strength."

Dannielle gasped suddenly and clutched at her side. Adamant's heart missed a beat before he realised she was smiling in amazement.

"My side; it doesn't hurt any more. What's happening, James?"

Just doing my job, said Mortice's voice quietly in their minds. *The wound is healed. But you'd better get back to the house as fast as you can. You're right on the edge of my limits. I don't know how much longer I can protect you . . . .*

His voice faded away and was gone. Adamant helped Dannielle to her feet and looked around him. Hawk was checking quickly through the bodies.

"Where's Bearclaw and Kincaid?" said Adamant hoarsely.

"Dead," said Hawk.

"And Captain Fisher?"

"Taken. Roxanne and her two friends must have had their own magical protection."

Adamant rubbed tiredly at his aching head. "I'm sorry. So many dead, and all because of me."

Hawk turned and glared at him. "Stop talking nonsense. There's only one man responsible for all this, and that's Hardcastle. And Isobel isn't dead. She was alive when they took her. Now I'm going to get her back. Can you and Dannielle get home safely without me?"

"I think so. Mortice is back looking after us."

"Right. Go home and stay there until the result comes in. I'm going to find Isobel, and then I'm going to pay Hardcastle a visit. This has gone beyond politics now.

"This is personal."

Stefan Medley sat on the grimy bed in the dimly lit room, staring at nothing. He'd been sitting there ever since Roxanne left. He'd tried to work out what he was going to do next, but he couldn't seem to concentrate on anything. In the space of a few moments his whole world had collapsed, and he was left alone in a filthy little tavern he wouldn't have been seen dead in by daylight.

It hadn't seemed so bad when he was there with Roxanne. They only had eyes for each other, then. Now he could see how cheap and shabby it really was. Just like him. He rubbed tiredly at his aching temples, and tried to think. He wasn't safe as long as he stayed in Haven. Adamant would have no choice but to believe he'd defected to the other side. And Adamant was a first-class duellist. Even assuming Adamant wouldn't kill a man who'd once been his friend, there were certainly many in the Reform Cause with ready swords and no love for traitors.

Traitor. It was a harsh word, but the only one that fitted.

Hardcastle would be after him too, as soon as Roxanne revealed he wasn't going to defect. He'd insulted Hardcastle too many times, frustrated his plans too often. And Hardcastle was well-known as a man who bore grudges.

Medley frowned. With so many hands turned against him the odds were he wouldn't be able to get out of Haven at all. And when he got right down to it, Medley wasn't sure he wanted to leave Haven anyway. It was a cesspool of a city, no doubt of that, but Haven was his home and always had been. Everyone he knew, everything he cared for, was in Haven.

But all that was gone, now. He'd thrown it all away, all for the love of a woman who didn't love him. His friends would disown him, his career was over, his future. . . . Medley sighed quietly, and lowered his head into his hands. He would have liked to cry, but he was too numb for tears.

There hadn't been many women in his life. There had always been girls, part of the social whirl, but they never seemed to have time for a quiet young man whose only interest was politics, and the wrong kind of politics, at that. The bright young things, with their games and laughter and simple happy souls, went to other men, and Medley went on alone. There were a few women who saw him as a potential business partner. Marriage was still the best way to acquire wealth and social standing in Haven, and Medley's family had always been comfortably well-off. There were times when he was so lonely he was tempted to say yes, to one or other of the deals his family made for him, but somehow he never did. He had his pride. He couldn't give that up. It was all he had.

Roxanne had been different. No empty-headed, powdered and perfumed flower of the lesser aristocracy. None of the quiet calculation of a woman looking for a husband as an investment. Roxanne was bright and wild and funny and free, and just being with her had made him feel alive in a way he'd never known before. He could talk to her, tell her things he'd never told anyone else. He'd never been so happy as in the few precious moments he'd shared with her.

Looking back, he supposed he'd been a fool. He should have known a living legend like her couldn't really have seen anything in a nobody like him. Roxanne was beautiful and famous. She could have had anyone she wanted. Another hero or legend, like herself. Someone who mattered. Not just another minor politician, in a city full of them. How could he ever have believed that she cared for him?

No one had ever cared for him before. Not really. Not in the way of a man with a woman. He hadn't realised how bleak and lonely his life had been, until she was there to share it with him. She'd made him feel alive, for the first time in a long time.

And now she was gone, and he was alone again.

Alone. He'd never realised how final that word sounded. It seemed to echo on in his mind, as he saw his future spread out before him. His career was over. No one would ever trust him again, now that he'd betrayed his friend and colleague in the middle of an election. His friends would spurn him, and he'd gone against his family's wishes too often in the past to hope for any support from them.

There was no hope for him now. Hope was for men with a future before them.

But there was still one thing he could do. One last thing that might win him some rest, some peace. And perhaps then his friends would realise how much he regretted the harm he'd done them.

Medley drew the knife from his boot. It was a short knife, barely six inches long, but it had a good blade and a sharp edge. It would do the job. He sat on the edge of the bed for a long time, staring at the knife. He thought about what he was going to do very carefully. It was the last important thing he would ever do, and he didn't want to make a mess of it. He put the knife down beside him on the bed, and rolled up his sleeves. The flesh of his arms seemed very pale, and very vulnerable. He stared at his arms for a while. The long blue veins and the sprinkling of hairs fascinated him, as though he'd never seen them before. He picked up the knife and automatically stropped the blade against his trouser-leg to clean it. He realised what he was doing, and smiled. As if that mattered now.

He held the knife against his left wrist, and then had to stop, because his hands were shaking too much. He was breathing in great heaving gasps, and goose flesh had sprung up on his arms. He concentrated, summoning his courage, and his hands grew steady again. The blade shone dully in the lamplight. He pressed the knife into his flesh, and the skin parted easily under the blade. Blood welled up, and he bit his lip at the sharp pain. He gritted his teeth, and pulled the knife across his wrist. The pain was awful, and he groaned aloud. He could feel the tendons popping as they pulled apart under the blade. Blood spurted out into the air. He quickly grabbed the knife in his left hand, before the feeling could leave his fingers, and slashed at the veins in his right wrist. His aim wavered, and he had to cut twice more before he was sure he'd done a good enough job.

The knife slipped out of his fingers and fell to the floor. He was crying now. Tears and snot ran down his face as he struggled for breath amidst his tears. The blood pumped out surprisingly quickly, and he began to feel faint and dizzy. He lay back on the bed, squeezing his eyes shut against the horrid pain that burned all the way up his arms to his elbows. He hadn't thought it would hurt so much. He held his mouth firmly closed, despite the sobs that shook him. He couldn't afford to make any noise. Someone might hear him, and come to help.

He began to feel sick. He couldn't stop crying. This wasn't how he'd thought it would be. But he wasn't surprised; not really. He should have known he wouldn't even be allowed to leave his life with a little dignity. He could see his fingers flexing spasmodically, but he couldn't feel them any longer. The blood was still coming. It soaked the bedding around his arms. So much blood.

He looked up at the ceiling, and then closed his eyes, for the last time.

I loved you, Roxanne. I really loved you.

The darkness closed in around him.

8

Rescues

Roxanne was furious, and the mercenaries were keeping their distance. Pike and Da Silva had disappeared the moment they reached Hardcastle's safe house, ostensibly to lock Fisher safely away, but actually to get out of Roxanne's reach until she calmed down a little and took her hand away from her sword belt. The twenty mercenaries Hardcastle had detailed to guard the safe house weren't as quick-thinking, which meant they ended up taking the brunt of Roxanne's displeasure. They stayed as far away from her as they could, nodded or shook their heads whenever it seemed indicated; mostly they just tried to fade into the woodwork. Roxanne paced back and forth, growling and muttering to herself. She'd never felt so angry, and what made it worse was that she wasn't all that sure what she was so angry about.

Part of it came from losing so many men to Adamant's sorcerer. If she hadn't insisted on full magical protection from Wulf for herself and Pike and Da Silva, she and they would have died along with her men. Roxanne hated losing men. She took it personally.

Some of her anger came from not having taken Hawk as well as Fisher. She'd vowed to take them both, and she hated to fail at things she set her word to. Legends can't afford to fail; if they do, they stop being legends.

But most of her anger came from how they'd taken Fisher.

She'd been looking forward to crossing swords with the legendary Captain Fisher ever since she came to Haven, and in the end somebody had struck the Guard down from behind while she wasn't looking. That was no way to beat a legend. Winning that way made Roxanne feel cheap; like just another paid killer. And on top of all that, she hadn't even been allowed to kill Fisher cleanly. Hardcastle had specifically ordered that Fisher was to be kept alive for interrogation. Roxanne sniffed. She knew a euphemism for torture when she heard it.

She glared about her as she paced, and the mercenaries avoided her gaze. The safe house was a dump; a decaying firetrap in the middle of a row of low-rent tenements. Somehow that was typical of Hardcastle and his operations. Cheap and nasty. All in all, the whole operation had left a bad taste in Roxanne's mouth. She was a warrior, and this kind of dirty political fighting didn't sit well with her. She'd killed and tortured before, and delighted in the blood, but that was in the heat of battle, where courage and steel decided men's fates, not dirty little schemes and back-room politics. If anyone had ever accused Roxanne of being honourable, she'd have laughed in their faces, but this . . . this whole mess just stank to high heaven.

She wondered fleetingly what Medley would have thought of all this, and then pushed the thought firmly to one side.

She stopped pacing about, and took several deep breaths. It calmed her a little, and she took her hand away from her sword. The mercenaries began to breathe a little more easily, and stopped judging the distances to possible exits. Pike and Da Silva chose that moment to reappear. Roxanne glared at them.

"Well?" she said icily.

"Sleeping like a baby," said Pike. "But we've tied her hand and foot, just in case."

Roxanne nodded. "I'll take a quick look at her, and then I'd better report back to Hardcastle. He'll need to know what's happened. You two stay here."

Pike and Da Silva nodded quickly, and watched in silence as Roxanne disappeared into the adjoining room where they'd dumped Fisher. They waited until the door had swung shut behind her, and then looked at each other.

"She's getting out of control," said Da Silva quietly.

"If I didn't know better, I'd swear she was developing scruples," said Pike. "Still, Hardcastle knew there was a risk in using Roxanne for political work. Everyone knows Roxanne's crazy. It doesn't matter on a battlefield, but we can't have her running wild in Haven. She knows too much."

"So she's expendable?"

"Everyone's expendable in politics. Especially her. That's official, from Hardcastle."

"Which of us gets to kill her?"

Pike grinned. "I wasn't thinking of fighting a duel with her. I was thinking more along the lines of dosing her wine with a fast-acting poison, waiting until she'd collapsed, and then cutting her head off. There's a good price for her head in the Low Kingdoms."

"Sounds good to me," said Da Silva.

Roxanne stood just inside the doorway of the adjoining room, listening. She'd always had good hearing. It had kept her alive on battlefields more than once. She'd known Pike and Da Silva were up to something, but the casualness with which they discussed her death made her blood boil. The orders had to have come from Hardcastle; they wouldn't have dared make such a decision themselves. Hardcastle had sold her out to a couple of back-alley assassins. She wanted to just charge out into the next room, draw her sword, and cut them both down, but even she wasn't crazy enough to take on twenty-two armed men in a confined space. She hadn't made her reputation as a warrior by being stupid. She had to get out of there and think things over.

She threw the door open, stalked back into the main room, and pretended not to notice the sudden silence. "I'm going to see Hardcastle. Keep a close eye on Fisher, but don't damage her any further. Hardcastle's going to want that privilege for himself."

She nodded briskly to Pike and Da Silva, and headed for the door before they could come up with some excuse to stop her. Her back crawled in anticipation of an attack, her ears straining for any hint of steel being drawn from a scabbard, but nothing happened. She stepped out into the street, and slammed the door behind her, almost disappointed. She moved quickly off down the street to lose herself in the crowds.

She still wasn't sure what she was going to do next. She was damned if she'd go on working for Hardcastle, but she couldn't just walk out on him either. Deserting ship in mid-contract would ruin her name. Most of the time Roxanne didn't give a rat's arse what anyone thought of her, but her professional name was a different matter. If word got round she couldn't be trusted to complete her commissions, no one would hire her.

Most people were too frightened to approach her as it was.

But she couldn't let Hardcastle get away with threatening her, either. That would do her reputation even more damage. She scowled as she strode along, and people all around her hurried to get out of her way. All this thinking made her head hurt. She needed someone she could talk to, someone she could trust. But she'd never trusted anyone . . . except Stefan Medley.

The thought surprised her, as did the warmth of feeling that went through her at the thought of seeing him again. Stefan had been a good sort, for a politician. He understood things like honesty and honour. She'd go and see him. He was probably still mad at her, but they'd work something out. She headed back to the tavern where she'd left him. Someone there would be able to tell her where he'd gone.

The tavern was full of customers. Smoke hung heavily on the air, and the crowd round the bar were singing a Reform anthem, cheerfully if not too accurately. Roxanne made her way to the bar, elbowing people out of her way. She yelled for the bartender, but he was busy taking orders and pretended he hadn't heard her. Roxanne leaned across the bar, grabbed him by the shirtfront, and pulled his face close to hers. The bartender started to object, realised who she was, and went very pale.

"Stefan Medley," said Roxanne quietly, dangerously. "The man I came here with. Where did he go after he left here?"

"He didn't go anywhere," said the bartender. "He's still in his room."

Roxanne frowned, dropped the bartender and turned away. What the hell was Stefan doing, hanging around here? He must know the Reformers would already be hot on his trail, and it wouldn't take them long to find out about this place. Medley had always been very careful about their assignations here, but Roxanne had deliberately left clues all over the place. That had been part of her job, then. She shook her head. The sooner she talked to Stefan and got the hell out of here, the better. She hurried up the stairs behind the bar, taking the steps two at a time. Everything would be all right once she'd talked to Stefan. He'd know what to do. He always did.

The door to their room was locked. Roxanne looked quickly around, knocked twice and waited impatiently. There was no sound from inside the room. She knocked again, and called his name quietly. There was no answer. Roxanne frowned. He must be there; the door was still locked. Was he sulking? That wasn't like Stefan. Maybe he was asleep. She knocked again, and called his name as loudly as she dared, but there was no reply. Roxanne began to get a bad feeling about the room. Something was wrong. Maybe the Reformers had already caught up with him. . . .

She drew her sword, and kicked at the door savagely with the heel of her boot. The door shuddered, but held. Roxanne cursed it briefly and tried again. The crude lock broke, and the door swung inwards. The room beyond was dark and quiet. Roxanne moved quickly into the room and darted to one side so that she wouldn't be caught silhouetted against the light from the open door. She stood poised in the gloom, sword at the ready, but it only took her a few moments to realise there were no ambushers in the room. She put away her sword and lit one of the lamps.

Light filled the room, and for a moment all Roxanne could see was the blood. It covered the bedclothes, and had spilled down the sides to form pools on the floor. Some of it had already dried. Roxanne moved forward quietly and felt for a pulse on Medley's neck. It was still there, slow and feeble, but his skin was deathly cold. At first she thought the Reformers had got to him, and then she looked at his arms and saw the ugly black wounds at his wrists. Her breath caught in her throat as she realised what he'd done, and why. She turned and ran from the room.

She hurried back down the stairs and into the bar, fought her way through the crowd, and grabbed the bartender again. "I need a healer! Now!"

"There's a Northern witch on the first floor. Calls herself Vienna. She knows a few things. She's all there is, unless you want me to send out for someone. . . ."

"No! You don't talk to anyone about this. You do, and I'll gut you. Which room is she in?"

"Room Nine. Just round the corner from the stairs. You can't miss it."

Roxanne dropped the bartender, and ran back up the stairs. It didn't take her long to find Room Nine, but it seemed like ages. She hammered on the door with her fist until it opened a crack, and a suspicious eye looked out at her.

"Who is it? What do you want?"

"I need a healer."

"I don't do abortions."

Roxanne kicked the door in, grabbed a handful of the woman's gown, and slammed her up against the wall. She struggled feebly, her feet kicking helplessly several inches above the floor. She started to call out for help, and Roxanne thrust her face up close to the witch's. The witch went very quiet and stopped struggling.

"A friend of mine is hurt," said Roxanne. "Dying. Save his life or I'll kill you slowly. Now move it!"

She put Vienna down and hauled her up the stairs to the next floor and Medley's room. Vienna took one look at the blood and started to leave, then stopped as she met Roxanne's gaze. The witch was a tiny frail little thing, in a shabby green dress, and at any other time Roxanne might have felt guilty about bullying her, but this was different. All she could think of was Stefan, dying alone in a dirty tavern room, because of

her. She gestured curtly at Medley, and Vienna turned back
and examined his wrists.

"Nasty," said the witch quietly. "But you're in luck, warrior. He didn't make a very good job of it. He cut across the
veins instead of lengthwise. The blood's been able to clot and
close off the wounds. He's lost a lot of blood, though. . . ."

"Can you save him?" said Roxanne.

"I think so. A simple healing spell on the wrists, and another to speed up production of new blood . . ." She started
reciting a series of technicalities that Roxanne didn't understand, but she just let the witch babble on, unable to concentrate on anything but the great wave of relief surging through
her. He wasn't going to die. He wasn't going to die because
of her. She nodded harshly to Vienna, and the witch began
her magic. The rites were simple and rather unpleasant, but
very effective. The torn flesh at the wrists closed together and
fused, and faint tinges of color began to seep back into Medley's face. His breathing became steadier and deeper.

"That's all I can do," said Vienna finally. "Let him rest
for a couple of days, and he'll be as good as new. Keeping
him alive is your problem. Those cuts on his wrists were
deep. He meant business."

"Yes," said Roxanne. "I know." She untied the purse
from her belt and tossed it to Vienna, without checking to
see how much was in it. "Not a word to anyone," said Roxanne, still looking at Medley. The witch nodded, and left
quickly before Roxanne could change her mind.

Roxanne sat on the edge of the bed beside Medley, ignoring the blood that soaked into her trousers. He looked drawn
and tired, as though he'd been through a long fever. She let
her hand rest on his forehead for a moment. The flesh felt
cool and dry.

"What am I going to say to you, Stefan?" she said quietly.
"I never thought you'd do anything like this. You were just a
job to me, but . . . I liked you, Stefan. Why did you have to
do this?"

"Why not?" said Medley hoarsely. He licked his lips and
swallowed dryly. Roxanne poured him a glass of water from
the pitcher on the table, and held the glass to his mouth while

he drank. He managed a few swallows, and she put the glass down. Medley lifted his arms and looked at the healed wounds on his wrists. He smiled sourly, and let his arms fall back onto the bed. "You shouldn't have bothered, Roxanne. I'll only have to do it again."

"Don't you dare," said Roxanne. "I can't go through all this again. My nerves won't stand it. Why did you do it, Stefan?"

"It's not enough just to live," said Medley. "You have to have something to live for. Something, or someone. For a while I had politics, and when I grew tired of that, I found Adamant. He needed me, made me feel important and valued; made me his friend. But even at its best I was just living someone else's life, following someone else's lead.

"And then I met you, and you gave my life meaning. I was so happy with you. You were all the things that had been missing from my life. You made me feel that I mattered, that I was someone in my own right, not just someone else's shadow. And then you told me it was all a lie, and walked out of my life forever. I can't go back to being what I was, Roxanne. I'd rather die than do that. I love you, and if what we had was just a lie, then I prefer that lie to reality. Even if I have to die to keep it."

"No one ever felt that way for me before," said Roxanne slowly. "I'm going to have to think about that. But I promise you this, Stefan; I'll stay with you for as long as you need me. I'm not sure why, but you're important to me, too."

Medley looked at her for a long moment. "If this is . . . just another game you're playing, a way to get more information out of me, I don't mind. Just tell me what you want to know, and I'll tell you. But don't pretend you care for me if you don't. Please. I can't go through that again."

"Forget all that," said Roxanne. "Hardcastle can go stuff himself. Things will be different from now on."

"I love you," said Medley. "How do you feel about me?"

"Damned if I know," said Roxanne.

Hawk was tired, and his arm and back muscles ached from too much use and too little rest. During the past hour he'd been through half the dives in the Steppes, looking for a lead on Fisher. No one knew anything, no matter how forcefully he put the question. Eventually he came to the reluctant belief that they were telling the truth. And that only left one place to look. Brimstone Hall. Hardcastle's home.

He stood outside the great iron gates, and stared past the two nervous men-at-arms on duty. The old Hall looked quiet and almost deserted, with lights showing at only a few windows. Somewhere in there he'd find what he was looking for; someone or something that would put him on the right trail.

The two men-at-arms looked at each other uncertainly, but said nothing. They recognised Hawk, and knew what he was capable of. They hadn't missed the fresh blood dripping from the axe in his right hand. Hawk ignored them, concentrating on the Hall. Hardcastle and his people would be out on the streets now, so the chances were good he'd only have to face a skeleton staff. Maybe he'd get really lucky and find Isobel locked away in some cellar here. He remembered the way she'd looked as she'd been dragged away, bloody and unconscious, and the slow cold rage began to build in him again. He shifted his gaze to the two men-at-arms, and they stirred uneasily.

"Open the gates," said Hawk.

"Hardcastle isn't here," said one of the men. "Everyone's out."

"Somebody will talk to me."

"Not to you, Captain Hawk. We have our orders. You're not to be allowed entrance under any circumstances. As far as you're concerned, everyone's out and always will be."

"Open the gates," said Hawk.

"Get lost," said the other. "You've no business here."

Hawk hit him low, well below the belt. He doubled up and fell writhing to the ground. The other man-at-arms backed quickly away. Hawk pushed the gates open, stepped over the man on the ground, and entered the grounds of Brimstone Hall. The man-at-arms left standing took one look at Hawk's face and turned and ran for the Hall. Hawk went after him at a steady walk. No point in hurrying. No one was going anywhere.

He heard the approach of soft, padding feet, and looked round to see three huge dogs charging silently towards him. Hawk studied them carefully. Hardcastle's dogs were supposed to be man-killers and man-eaters, but they looked ordinary enough to Hawk. He took a bag of powder from his belt, opened it, held his breath, and threw the powder into the air right in front of the dogs. The dogs skidded to a halt, sniffed suspiciously at the air, and then sat down suddenly with big sloppy grins on their faces. Hawk waited a moment to be sure the dust had done its job, then walked cautiously past them. Two of the dogs ignored him completely, and the third rolled over on its back so that Hawk could rub its belly. Hawk smiled slightly, careful not to breathe till he was well past the dogs. He'd known the second bag of dust he'd found in Dannielle's room would come in handy.

He headed for the Hall. Everything seemed quiet. He'd almost reached the main door when it suddenly swung open before him, and five men-at-arms in full chain mail spilled out to block his path. Hawk smiled at them, and held his bloody axe so they could see it clearly.

"Where is she?" he said softly. "Where's Hardcastle keeping my wife?"

"I don't know what the hell you're talking about," said the foremost man-at-arms. "I'm Brond. I speak for Hardcastle in his absence, and he doesn't want to speak to you. You'd better leave now. You're already in a lot of trouble."

"Last chance," said Hawk. "Where's my wife?"

"Wouldn't you like to know," said Brond. He half-turned away and addressed the other men. "Throw him out. Don't be gentle about it. Show the man what happens when he messes with his betters."

Hawk slammed his axe into Brond's side. The heavy steel head punched clean through Brond's chain mail, and buried itself in his rib cage. Brond stood and stared at it for a moment, unable to believe what had happened, then fell to his knees, blood starting from his mouth. Hawk jerked his axe free, and the four remaining men-at-arms jumped him. The first to reach Hawk went down screaming in a flurry of blood and guts as Hawk's axe opened him up across the belly.

The other three tried to surround Hawk, but his axe swept back and forth, keeping them at arm's length. They surged around him, darting in and jumping back, like dogs trying to bring down a bear. Hawk smiled at them coldly, calculating the odds. The men-at-arms were good, but he was better. He could take them. It was only a matter of time. And then four more men-at-arms came running out of the main door, and Hawk knew he was in trouble. With Fisher to watch his back, he'd have taken them on without a second thought, but fighting on his own the odds were murder. Nevertheless he was damned if he'd back down. Fisher needed him. Besides, he'd faced worse odds in his time. He took a firm hold on his axe and threw himself at his nearest opponent.

And then suddenly there was another figure, fighting at his side; tall and lithe and very deadly. Two men-at-arms fell to the newcomer's blade in as many seconds. Hawk cut down a third, and suddenly the men-at-arms scattered and ran for their lives. Hawk slowly lowered his axe, and turned to face Roxanne. For a long moment they stood looking at each other, and then Roxanne lowered her sword.

"All right," said Hawk. "What's going on?"

"We've come to help," said Medley, approaching the two of them cautiously. "We know where your wife is. We can take you right to her."

"Why the hell should I trust you?" said Hawk. "You both work for Hardcastle."

"Not anymore," said Roxanne. "He broke his contract with me."

"And I never worked for him," said Medley flatly.

"Besides," said Roxanne, "Without our help you haven't a hope of finding and rescuing your wife."

Hawk smiled slightly. "That's a good reason."

He hesitated, and then put away his axe. Roxanne sheathed her sword, and the three of them walked back through the grounds to the main gates. They had to go slowly so that Medley could keep up with them. Hawk looked at him more closely.

"You don't look too good, Medley. Are you sure you're up to this?"

"He's been ill," said Roxanne quickly. "He's fine now."

Hawk looked at them both, and then let the matter drop. There was obviously a story there, but it could wait. "How did you find me?" he asked finally.

Medley smiled. "You seem to have spent the last hour or so cutting a path right through the seedier half of the High Steppes. All we had to do was follow the path of blood and bodies."

"You haven't said what you expect to get out of this," said Hawk.

"The dropping of any and all charges against us," said Medley. "A clean slate."

"All right," said Hawk. "You help me rescue Isobel, and I'll come through for you. But if I even suspect you're trying to set me up, I'll kill you both. Deal?"

"How could we refuse?" said Medley.

"Deal," said Roxanne.

Pike had been stuck in the safe house for over an hour, and the ale had run out. He couldn't send out for more because they weren't supposed to draw attention to themselves. He leaned his chair back against the wall and looked thoughtfully at the locked door that stood between him and Captain Isobel Fisher. The beautiful, arrogant Captain. Not so arrogant now, though. Pike smiled at the thought, and let his hand drop to the key ring at his belt. Hardcastle's orders had been quite specific about delivering her alive, but no one had said anything about intact. . . .

Pike looked around him. Six of his men were playing dice and arguing about the side bets. Two more were doing running repairs on their chain mail. The rest were scattered around the house, acting as lookouts. All in all, the house was thoroughly secure, and no one would miss him if he took a little break. He called quietly to Da Silva, and the mercenary left the dice game and came over to join him.

"This had better be good, Pike; I was winning."

"You can cheat at dice any time. I've got a more pleasurable game in mind."

Da Silva looked at the locked door, and frowned. "Wondered how long it would take for you to get the itch for her. Forget it, Pike. That's Captain Fisher in there. We can't afford to take any chances with her.''

"Come on," said Pike. "She's just a woman. We can handle her between us. Are you game?''

"I'm game if you are." Da Silva smiled suddenly. "Who gets first shot?''

"Toss you for it.''

"My coin or yours?''

"Mine.''

Pike took a silver mark from his purse, and handed it to Da Silva, who examined both sides carefully before returning it. Pike flipped the coin and caught it deftly before slapping it flat on his arm. Da Silva called *heads*, and then swore when Pike revealed the coin. Pike grinned and put it away. Da Silva glanced at the other mercenaries.

"What about the others?" he said quietly.

"What about them?" said Pike. "Let them find their own women.''

Da Silva looked at the locked door and licked his lips thoughtfully. "We're going to have to be very careful with her, Pike. If we give her a chance, she'll cut our throats with our own knives.''

"So we won't give her a chance. Will you stop worrying? First, she's already had a hell of a beating. That should have taken some of the starch out of her. And secondly, I tied her up hand and foot while she was unconscious, remember? She's in no position to give us any trouble. So, I untie her feet, and then you hold her steady while I give her a good time. Afterwards, we swop over. Right?''

"Right." Da Silva grinned broadly. "You always did know how to show your friends a good time, Pike.''

They walked purposefully towards the locked door. A few of the other mercenaries looked in their direction, but nobody said anything. Pike unlocked the door, and took a lamp off the wall. He grinned once at Da Silva, and then the two of them went in to see Captain Fisher.

The room had no windows or other light, and Fisher screwed up her eyes at the sudden glare. She'd been awake for some time, but alone in the dark she had no way of telling how much time had passed. Her head ached fiercely, and she knew she was lucky not to have a concussion. There were cramps in her arms from being tied behind her, and her hands were numb because the ropes at her wrists were too tight. Her ankles were hobbled and there was no sign of her sword. All in all, she'd been in better condition.

She struggled to sit upright, and looked at the two men standing by the door. They closed it carefully behind them, and from the way they looked at her, she had a good idea of what they had in mind. A sudden horror gripped her, and she had to grit her teeth to stop her mouth from trembling. She'd faced death before, been hurt so many times she'd lost count of the scars, but this was different. She'd thought about rape, she supposed every woman had, but she'd never really thought it would happen to her. Not to her, not to Captain of the Guard Fisher; the warrior. She was too strong, too good with a sword, too determined to protect herself for anything like that to happen to her. Only now her sword was gone, the strength had been knocked out of her, and determination on its own wasn't going to be enough to protect her. . . . She bit down firmly, on her growing panic. She had to keep her wits about her, and watch for a chance to thwart them. If all else failed, there was always revenge.

Pike put the lamp into a niche high up on the wall. He could feel Fisher watching him. He moved unhurriedly towards her. Her eyes were steady, but just a bit too wide. He grinned, knelt down beside her, and put one hand on her thigh. In spite of herself, Fisher shrank away from his touch.

"No need to worry, Captain," said Pike, giving her thigh a little squeeze, just hard enough to let her feel the strength in his hand. "My friend and I won't hurt you, as long as you behave yourself. No. You just be nice and cooperative and show us a nice time, and you don't have to get hurt at all. Of course, if you're determined to be unpleasant about it, my friend Da Silva here knows some real nasty tricks with a skinning knife. Isn't that right, Da Silva?"

"Right." Da Silva laughed as Fisher's eyes darted to him and then away again.

"I'm a Captain of the Guard," said Fisher. "If anything happens to me, you'll be in real trouble."

"That's out there," said Pike. "Things like that don't matter in here. In here, there's just you and us."

"My husband will track me down. You've heard of Hawk, haven't you?"

"Sure," said Pike. "We're waiting for him. He's good, but so are we. And there are a lot more of us than there is of him."

Fisher thought frantically. There was the sound of truth and confidence in his voice, and that frightened her more than anything. They didn't just want her, they wanted Hawk as well.

"All right," she said finally, her voice not quite as steady as she would have liked. "I won't fight you. Just . . . don't hurt me. Why not untie me? I could be more . . . cooperative then."

Pike's hand lashed out, slapping her viciously across the face. Her head rang from the force of the blow. She could feel blood running down her chin from her crushed mouth. She gritted her teeth against the pain and the dizziness. She'd been hurt worse in her time, but this kind of cold and casual violence was new to her, and all the more intimidating because of her utter helplessness.

"That's for thinking we're stupid," said Pike. "If I untie your hands, I'm a dead man. You're not going to get that chance, Captain."

He drew a knife from his boot, and Fisher tensed, but he only used it to cut the ropes binding her ankles together. Da Silva moved quickly in to hold her ankles while Pike put away his knife. Fisher's heart speeded up, and her breathing became ragged and uneven. Pike put a hand on her breast and pushed her so that she fell onto her back. He began to undo his trousers. Fisher struggled to sit upright again, as though that could somehow put off the inevitable. Pike laughed. He leaned forward and grabbed her hair, tilting her head back. He held her head steady as he put his face down to kiss her.

Fisher sank her teeth into his lower lip. Her teeth met, and she jerked her head back, taking most of Pike's lip with her.

Blood ran from his mouth, and for a moment the pain and shock held him rigid. Fisher spat out the lip and snapped her head forward in a savage butt to Pike's face. There was the flat, definitive sound of his nose breaking, and he fell backwards against Da Silva, sending him sprawling. Fisher scrambled to her feet while Da Silva pushed Pike aside and struggled up onto his knees. Fisher stepped forward and kicked Da Silva squarely in the groin, putting all her weight behind it. Da Silva's breath caught in his throat before he could scream, and he fell forward onto the floor, clutching at the awful pain between his legs. Pike was rolling back and forth on the floor with both his hands at his face, unable to think straight for the pain. Fisher kicked him solidly in the head until he stopped moving.

She heard movement behind her, and turned quickly to find Da Silva was back on his feet again. He was crouched around his pain, but he had a knife in his hand, and his eyes were cold and angry. Fisher backed away, and Da Silva went after her. He feinted at her with his knife, but she saw it for what it was, stepped quickly inside his reach while he was off balance, and kicked him in the knee. Da Silva fell forward as his leg collapsed under him, and Fisher's knee came up and caught him squarely on the chin. Da Silva's head snapped back, and he fell limply to the floor and lay still.

Fisher leaned back against the cold stone wall, shaking violently. Her head ached so badly she could barely think, but she knew she couldn't stop and rest. If the other mercenaries had heard anything of the fight, they might decide to see what was happening. And she was in no condition to take on anyone else. She took a deep breath and held it, and some of her shakes went away. She got down on her knees and groped around on the floor until she found the knife Da Silva had dropped. All she had to do now was cut the bonds at her wrists, which were knotted in the middle of her back where she couldn't see them, then work out a plan that would get her out of here without having to take on however many other mercenaries were waiting in the next room. Fisher smiled sourly, and concentrated on cutting the ropes and not her arms. One thing at a time.

• • •

The narrow street was almost completely dark, with only a single street lamp shedding pale golden light across the decaying, stunted houses. The parties and parades had passed them by, and nothing disturbed the street's sullen quiet. In the shadows, Hawk and Roxanne drew their weapons, while Medley kept a careful watch on the safe house. The shutters were all closed and there was no sign of any life. Hawk studied the house for some time, and scowled unhappily.

"Are you sure this is the right place? Where the hell are the lookouts?"

"There are spy-holes and concealed viewing slits all over the house," said Roxanne quietly. "Hardcastle's used this place before. There's at least twenty armed men inside that house, just waiting for you to try and rescue Captain Fisher."

"Maybe we should send to Adamant for reinforcements," said Medley.

"There isn't time," snapped Hawk. "Every minute Isobel's in there, she's in danger. I want her out *now*."

"All right," said Medley. "What's the plan?"

Roxanne smiled, a familiar darkness in her eyes. "Who needs a plan? We just storm the front door, cut down the guards, and kill anyone who gets between us and freeing Captain Fisher."

Hawk and Medley exchanged a glance. Roxanne had many qualities as a warrior, but subtlety wasn't one of them.

"We can't risk a straightforward assault," said Hawk carefully. "They might just kill Isobel at the first sign of a rescue attempt. We need some kind of diversion, something to distract their attention."

"I could set fire to something," said Roxanne.

"I'd rather you didn't," said Medley quickly. "This whole street's a firetrap. Start a blaze here and we'll lose half the Steppes."

"I've got a better idea," said Hawk. "Since they're going to see us approaching anyway, let's show them something they won't find threatening. We just walk up to the door with me unarmed, and Roxanne's sword at my back. Medley can carry my axe. They'll think you've captured me. Once inside, we study the situation and choose our moment. With any luck they'll want to lock me up with Fisher. So, we wait until they unlock the right door, then Medley passes me my axe and we kill everything that moves. Any questions?''

Roxanne looked at Hawk. "You're ready to trust me with a sword at your back?''

"Sure,'' said Hawk. "Because if you try anything, I'll take the sword away from you and make you eat it.''

Roxanne looked at Medley. "He just might.''

"Let's make a start,'' said Medley. "Before I get a rush of brains to the head and realise just how dangerous this is.''

Fisher shook the last of the rope bindings from her wrists and flapped her hands hard to try and get the blood moving again. There were angry red cuts on her arms and wrists from where the knife had cut her as well as the ropes, but she ignored them. Feeling began to come back into her hands, and she winced as pins and needles moved in her fingers. She padded silently over to the closed door and listened carefully. So far, no one seemed to have missed Pike and Da Silva, but she didn't know how long that would last. She went back to Pike and drew his sword from its scabbard. It was a good blade.

She looked at the two men lying bloody and unconscious on the floor. They would have raped her, abused her, and then handed her over to Hardcastle for a slow, painful death. Assuming she got out of this mess alive, she could have them both sent to the mines for the rest of their lives. No one messes with a Guard and gets away with it. But there was always the chance Hardcastle would buy the judge and Pike and Da Silva would go free. She couldn't allow that to happen. As long as they were free, she would never feel safe again.

She knelt beside Pike and put the edge of his sword against his throat. She could do it. No one would ever know. She knelt there for a long time, and then she took the sword away from his throat and stood up. She couldn't kill a helpless man in cold blood. Not even him. She was a Guard, and a Guard enforces the law; she doesn't take revenge.

She turned her back on Pike and Da Silva, moved over to the door and eased it open an inch. She didn't know how many mercenaries were out there, but from the muttered talk it sounded like quite a few. Her best bet would be to throw open the door and then make a mad dash for the main door. She might make it. If she was lucky. She eased the door open a little further, and then froze as there was a sudden pounding on the front door.

Hawk looked calmly about him, as though he couldn't feel the point of Roxanne's sword digging into his back. It occurred to him that if he'd misjudged the situation, he was in a whole lot of trouble. There were twelve mercenaries in the room, some carrying weapons, some not. According to Roxanne, there were more mercenaries on the next floor up. So, assume twenty men, all told. Ten to one odds. Hawk smiled. He'd faced worse in his time. One of the mercenaries walked over to him. Tall, muscular, chain mail. Wore a sword in a battered scabbard and looked like he knew how to use it. Regular issue mercenary. He nodded briefly to Roxanne, and looked Hawk up and down.

"So this is the famous Captain Hawk. Do come in, Captain. Don't stand on ceremony." He laughed softly. "You know, Captain, Hardcastle's just dying to see you. As for you, you're just dying."

"Where's my wife?" said Hawk.

The mercenary backhanded Hawk across the face. He saw it coming, but still couldn't ride much of the blow. His head rang, and he swayed unsteadily on his feet for a moment.

"You speak when you're spoken to, Captain. I can see we're going to have to teach you some manners before we let you meet Councillor Hardcastle. But don't worry about your wife. We haven't forgotten her. Even as we speak, she's being entertained by two of our men. I'm sure they're giving her a real good time."

He laughed, and Hawk kneed him in the groin. The mercenary bent forward around his pain, almost as though bowing to Hawk, and Hawk rabbit-punched him on the way to the floor. The other mercenaries jumped to their feet and grabbed for their weapons.

Hawk snatched his axe from Medley, yelled for Roxanne to guard his back, and started toward the first mercenary without looking to see if Roxanne was there. Hawk swung his axe up and then buried it almost to the hilt in the shoulder of the first mercenary, shearing through the chain mail. The force of the blow drove the mercenary to his knees. Hawk put his boot against the man's chest and pulled the blade free. Blood flew on the air as Hawk turned to face his next opponent. There was the clash of steel on steel as Roxanne struck down a second mercenary, and Hawk allowed himself a small smile of relief.

And then the door on the other side of the room burst open, and Fisher charged out, sword in hand. Hawk's smile widened. All this time he'd been worried about her, and here she was safe and sound. He should have known. She seemed a little startled to see Roxanne guarding his back, but she quickly set about carving a path through the mercenaries to reach him.

Hawk swung his axe double-handed, and blood splashed across the filthy floor. The heavy steel blade easily deflected the lighter swords, and punched through chain mail as though it wasn't there. Fisher fought at his side, her sword a steel blur as she cut and parried and thrust. Roxanne laughed and danced and cut her way through her fellow mercenaries with a deadly glee. Medley stayed out of the way. He knew his limitations.

A bearded mercenary duelled Hawk to a halt, his heavy long-sword almost a match for Hawk's axe. They locked blades, and stood face to face for a moment. Muscles bunched across the mercenary's shoulders, and Hawk quickly realised he couldn't hold the man back for long. So he spat in his eye. The mercenary jerked back his head instinctively and lost his balance. Hawk swept the sword aside and slammed the axe into the man's chest.

Fisher stood toe to toe with a tall, slender mercenary, trading blow for blow. She knew she daren't keep that up for long. He was bigger than her, and she was still weakened from what she'd been through. She locked eyes with him, stepped forward and brought her heel down hard on the instep of his right foot. She could feel bones crush and break in his foot. The sudden pain sucked the color from his face and the strength from his arms. Fisher beat aside his blade and cut his throat on the backswing. The mercenary dropped his sword and clutched at his throat with both hands, as though he could somehow hold the ghastly wound together. He was already sinking to his knees as Fisher turned to face her next opponent.

Roxanne swung her sword in wide, vicious arcs, and the mercenaries fell back before her. Her eyes were wide with uncomplicated delight, and she laughed breathlessly as her blade cut through their flesh. She was doing what she did best, what she was born to do. She moved among her former companions with neither mercy nor compassion, and none of them could stand against her. She killed them with professionalism and style, and the blood sang in her head.

Suddenly the mercenaries broke and ran, even though they still outnumbered their attackers. Pike and Da Silva might have been able to rally them, but without their leaders the mercenaries hadn't the nerve to face three living legends.

Hawk looked round the suddenly empty room, and lowered his axe. He was almost disappointed the fight was over so soon. He had a lot of pent-up anger to work off. He turned, smiling, to Fisher, and his anger turned suddenly cold and merciless as he saw what they'd done to her. Her mouth was bruised and swollen, and blood from a nasty cut on her scalp had spilled down one side of her face. He took her in his arms and held her tightly, and she hugged him back as if she would never let him go. Finally Medley coughed politely, and Hawk and Fisher broke apart. Fisher looked at Medley, and then at Roxanne.

"They're on our side," said Hawk. "Don't ask; it gets complicated."

Fisher shrugged. "That's politicians and mercenaries for you. Let's hope Adamant's the forgiving kind. There are two more mercenaries in the other room, out cold. We're taking them with us; I'll be pressing charges.''

Hawk caught some of the undertones in her voice. ''Are you all right, lass?''

''Sure,'' said Fisher. ''I'm fine now.''

9

Winners and Losers

The election was almost over, and Hardcastle was hosting a victory party in his ballroom. The faithful had come by the hundreds to share his hospitality and celebrate another Conservative victory in the Steppes. Hardcastle looked out over the milling crowd and smiled graciously at his favourites. People came to congratulate him, and politely remind him of all their labours on his behalf. Hardcastle had a smile and a nod for all of them, but his mind was elsewhere. The voting had to be nearly over by now, but so far he'd heard nothing about how the voting was going. None of his people had reported back, and Wulf had locked himself away in his room. Of course, he was bound to win. He always did. But the complete lack of news worried him.

There was no word on Hawk and Fisher, though they should have been captured or dead by now. There was no word at all from Pike or Da Silva. And Roxanne had disappeared. No one had seen or heard from her for hours. Hardcastle scowled. Something was wrong. He could feel it in his bones. But there was still one source of information open to him. He gestured to one of his servants and curtly ordered the man to fetch the sorcerer Wulf. The servant hesitated, but one look at Hardcastle's face convinced him there was no point in protesting. He bowed quickly and left the ballroom.

Hardcastle looked around him, and his scowl deepened.

The party seemed as loud and cheerful as ever, but somehow the mood didn't feel right. The laughter was too loud, the smiles too forced, and here and there, there were pockets of quiet, almost furtive talk. The musicians were playing sprightly music, but no one was dancing. Hardcastle frowned. He had to give them some positive news soon or their nerves would crack. Everywhere he looked he seemed to see worried faces with wide, desperate eyes. His guests looked more and more like wild animals gathered together, sensing a storm in the air.

Wulf entered the ballroom, and a sudden silence spread quickly across the guests. The musicians stopped playing. Wulf walked slowly forward, and the crowd drew back from him so that he walked alone. He wore his long black sorcerer's cloak wrapped tightly about his slender frame. The cowl had been pulled forward to hide his face. He came to a halt before Hardcastle, and the cowled head bowed slightly. A sudden chill swept through Hardcastle like an awful premonition, and he fought to keep it out of his face. He smiled at Wulf, and gestured for the musicians to begin playing again. They did so, and the party chatter slowly resumed.

Hardcastle glanced at his wife, standing silently beside him, as always. She was staring at the floor, her face calm and impassive. Hardcastle told her to move back a few paces, and she did so without looking up. Hardcastle fixed his gaze on Wulf. There were things he had to discuss with the sorcerer, and he didn't want any witnesses. Not even Jillian.

"All right, Wulf; what's going on? You've been cowering in your room ever since we got back from the Street of Gods. What's the matter with you?"

"It's the Being," said Wulf, his voice low and toneless. "The Abomination. The Lord of the Gulfs. I didn't understand. I couldn't understand what it was, what it meant. . . ."

"Pull yourself together, man," snapped Hardcastle. "I need information. I need to know what's happening in the city. What are the results? What's Adamant up to? Why haven't I heard from my people? Dammit, use your magic and tell me what's happening!"

"I daren't. He's too strong. I can feel him growing."

Hardcastle looked sharply at Wulf. "You told me you could control him. You told me that hosting that thing would make you so powerful no one could stand against us."

"You don't understand," said Wulf. "The Lord of the Gulfs isn't some demon or elemental, to be bent to my will by my magic. The Abomination is one of the Transient Beings; an aspect of reality given shape and form by man's perception. A single concept given flesh and blood and bone. It isn't real, as we understand the term. There are things that live outside the world, in the spaces between spaces, and they hunger for strange and awful things. I thought I could control it while it was still weak and confused from its long sleep, but it's so powerful . . . I can feel it in my mind, clawing at the wards I built to hold it. It's going to get out, Cameron. . . ."

"We can talk about this later," said Hardcastle. "Now get a hold of yourself. You're supposed to be a top rank sorcerer; act like one! I must have information, Wulf. I need to know what's happening out there on the streets. Use your magic to locate my people, and tell me what's happening in the election. That's an order!"

For a long moment Wulf just stood there, head bowed, and Hardcastle began to think the sorcerer was going to defy him. But finally Wulf nodded slightly and began to speak, his voice barely loud enough to be heard over the nervous chatter of the guests.

"The mercenaries you sent after Captains Hawk and Fisher are either dead or scattered. Their leaders, Pike and Da Silva, are under arrest. They have agreed to give evidence against you in return for lesser sentences. The voting is almost over. Adamant is winning."

Hardcastle stood very still. At first there was only disbelief and shock, but both gradually gave way to a cold and vicious anger. How dare they? How dare they turn against him and elect Adamant? They'd forgotten who was really in charge of the High Steppes, but he'd remind them. He'd teach the Reformers a lesson they'd never forget. He glared at Wulf, his voice slow and steady and very deadly.

"You are my man, Wulf; bound to me by vows sealed in blood."

"Yes, Cameron. I am yours to command."

"Then use this great power of yours. Go to Adamant's house and kill him. Kill him, and every other person there."

"That . . . may not be wise, Cameron. You need me here. Without my magic to augment and magnify your presence, you won't be able to control your followers with your speeches anymore."

"I was making speeches long before I had your magic to back me up. I can deal with my people. They'll do as they're told, as always. You have your orders, Wulf. Kill Adamant, and everyone with him. Obey me."

"Cameron . . . please. The Abomination . . ."

"Obey me!"

Wulf put back his head and screamed. The horrible piercing sound silenced the crowd in a moment. His cowl fell back, revealing what was left of his face. All the flesh was gone, devoured by some hideous internal hunger. There was only a grinning skull, barely covered by skin stretched tight across the bone like splitting parchment. His eyes were gone, the sockets raw and bloody. He rose up into the air, still screaming, his body twitching with awkward, ungainly movements that suggested the form inside the black robe was no longer entirely human.

He disappeared, and there was a small clap of thunder as air rushed in to fill the space where he had been. Someone in the crowd laughed uneasily, and slowly the babble of voices began again, as though if they could speak loud enough, they wouldn't have to think about what they had just seen. Hardcastle smiled. With Adamant and all his people dead there would have to be another election in the Steppes, but no one would dare stand against him. People would talk, but no one would be able to prove anything. He would be Councillor again. And then he'd make the scum in the streets pay for daring to defy him.

Medley hesitated outside the door to Adamant's study. He glanced at Roxanne, who nodded encouragingly. Hawk and

Fisher stood back a few paces, keeping a tactful distance. Medley was glad of their company, but if he was going to make his peace with Adamant, he had to do it on his own. He knocked on the door, and a familiar voice told him to enter. Opening the door and walking in was one of the hardest things Medley had ever done.

Adamant was sitting behind his desk, with Dannielle standing beside him. They both looked tired, and there were lines in their faces Medley had never seen before. Adamant gestured for Medley to sit down on the chair facing the desk. Roxanne leaned against the doorframe, her thumbs tucked into her sword belt, her eyes bright and watchful. Hawk and Fisher stayed in the doorway. Silence filled the room, an almost palpable presence filled with words no one wanted to say but that couldn't be ignored.

Finally Hawk coughed politely, and everyone looked at him. "With your permission, sir Adamant, Isobel and I will take a look around the house and make sure everything's secure."

"Of course, Captain. I'll call you if I need you."

Adamant's voice was as calm as ever, but his gaze never left Medley. Hawk and Fisher left the study, shutting the door quietly behind them.

"The house seems very quiet," said Medley finally. "What happened to the victory party?"

"I cancelled it," said Adamant. "It didn't seem right, with so many people dead."

Medley winced. "I should have known about Longarm's attack. My intelligence people provided enough hints. But I was too engrossed with Roxanne, and I didn't put the pieces together in time. I'm sorry, James. How many of our men-at-arms were hurt?"

"Twenty-seven dead, fourteen wounded. Luckily none of the guests got hurt." He looked at Roxanne. "So, this is your mysterious girlfriend."

"Yes," said Medley. "Isn't she splendid?"

Adamant's mouth quirked. "I suppose that's one way of describing her. The last time I saw her, she was cutting down my people and showing them no quarter."

Roxanne met his gaze calmly. "That's my job. I'm good at it."

"You killed Bearclaw and Kincaid. They were good men."

"They would have killed me, given the chance. That's how they play politics in this city. You know that."

"Yes," said Adamant. "Murder and betrayal have always been popular in Haven."

"For what it's worth, Stefan didn't betray you. Pumping him for information was part of my job, and he was so besotted with me he never even noticed. He told me all kinds of useful things without realising, and I passed them on to Hardcastle."

"Does he know you're here?" said Dannielle.

"No. I don't work for him anymore."

"Why not?"

"He broke our contract."

Dannielle looked from Roxanne to Medley and back again. "Is that the only reason? What about you and Stefan?"

Roxanne shrugged. "I don't know. We're just taking things one day at a time and seeing what happens."

Adamant leaned forward and fixed Medley with his gaze. "What are you doing here, Stefan? What do you want from me? Forgiveness? Your old job back?"

"Damned if I know," said Medley. "I'm sorry you were hurt, and I'm sorry people died, but I never meant for any of that to happen. I loved Roxanne, and nothing else seemed to matter."

"How do you feel about her now?" said Dannielle. "Knowing what she is. What she's done. Do you forgive her?"

"Of course," said Medley. "I love her, in spite of everything. Can't you understand that?"

Adamant looked at Dannielle, and put out a hand to hold hers. "Yes," he said finally. "I understand."

Hawk and Fisher prowled restlessly through the empty house. The rooms felt strange and deserted, and the quiet had a texture of its own. They went from room to room, but there was no sign of any life. Adamant's people were either dead or evacuated, and the guests had long gone home. Nothing remained to mark Longarm's assault save for a few patches of dried blood here and there, and the contents of the downstairs library.

Hawk found them, quite by accident. He pushed open the library door on his way back down the hall, and stopped dead in his tracks at the sight of the bodies. There were twenty-seven of them altogether. Hawk counted them twice, to make sure. All of Adamant's men who'd died at the hands of the militants. They'd been stacked together like bundles of kindling, face to face, arms and legs neatly arranged. Hawk felt strangely angry at the sight. These men had died for Adamant; they deserved a more dignified rest than this.

They'll get one, said Mortice's voice in his head. *But things have been rather rushed here of late. I did the best I could.*

Hawk looked at Fisher, and saw that she'd heard it too. "So you're still here, sorcerer."

Of course. Where else would I be?

"What happened to the bodies of the people who did this? Longarm and his militants?"

I disposed of them.

Hawk decided not to press the question any further. He didn't think he really wanted to know.

Get back to Adamant, said Mortice suddenly. *He's going to need you.*

Hawk and Fisher looked at each other. "Why?" said Fisher. "What's happening?"

Something's coming.

"What? What's coming?"

Something's coming.

Hawk drew his axe and Fisher drew her sword, and they ran back into the entry hall. They could see the study door standing open. Everything seemed quiet. Hawk yelled Mortice's name, but he didn't answer. Adamant came out of the study, his face grim.

"You heard him too?"

"Yeah," said Hawk. "I think we'd better get out of here, Adamant. I've got a bad feeling about this."

Adamant nodded quickly, and gestured for Dannielle to

come and join him. She did so, and Medley and Roxanne followed her out into the hall. Roxanne had her sword in her hand. She was smiling. Hawk looked away.

It's here.

Hawk moved quickly over to the front door, pulled it open, and looked out. In the last of the evening light, he could see a man in sorcerer's black walking through the grounds, heading for the house. As he passed, the things that lived in the ground writhed to the surface and died, the grass withered away, and the earth turned to sand and blew away. The sorcerer's power hung heavily on the evening air, like the tension before an approaching storm. Hawk eased the door shut, and turned to face the others.

"We're in trouble. Wulf's here, and he doesn't look friendly. Mortice, can you handle him? Mortice? Mortice!" There was no reply. Hawk cursed briefly. "That's it. We're getting out of here now. Isobel, take them out the back way. I'll follow as soon as I can."

"Why aren't you coming?" said Fisher.

"Someone's got to slow him down. Now, get moving. We haven't much time."

"I can't leave you," said Fisher.

"You have to. Our job is to keep Adamant alive, no matter what. We lost the last man we guarded. I won't let that happen again."

Fisher nodded, and led the others back down the hall. Hawk turned to the front door and slammed home the heavy bolts. He considered pushing furniture up against it as a barricade, but he had a strong feeling it wouldn't make any difference.

"Mortice? If you're listening, sorcerer, I can use all the help I can get."

There was a sharp cracking sound, and Hawk looked back at the door. It had split from top to bottom. As Hawk watched, the wood decayed and fell apart. The rotting fragments fell away from the rusting hinges, and there, in the open doorway, stood what remained of the sorcerer Wulf. Its face was little more than bone now, its grinning teeth yellowed with age. But still it moved and breathed and lived, and something else lived within it. Something hungry. Hawk gripped his axe tightly and backed away from the motionless figure. And then he heard raised voices and sounds of struggle behind him, and realised the others hadn't got very far. He risked a quick glance back over his shoulder, and his heart missed a beat as he saw the dead men filing out of the library.

Fisher had only just reached the end of the hall when the library door flew open and the first of the dead men lurched into the hall. It was one of Adamant's men-at-arms. No blood ran from the gaping wounds in the corpse, and its face was dull and empty. But its eyes saw, and it carried a sword in its hand. Another lich came out of the door after it, and another. Fisher and Roxanne stood between the dead men and the others, swords at the ready, backing slowly away to give themselves room to fight. And still the dead men came filing out of the library with weapons in their hands.

Roxanne stepped forward and brought her long sword across in a sharp vicious arc that cut clean through the first lich's neck. The head fell to the floor and rolled away, the mouth working soundlessly. The headless corpse moved relentlessly forward, sweeping its sword back and forth. Roxanne sidestepped and cut at the body, and it swayed under the force of the blow, but would not fall. Its sword arced out deceptively quickly, and Roxanne had to retreat a step. Fisher moved in beside her and cut at the lich's leg. It staggered and fell to one knee, but didn't release its hold on its sword. And then the rest of the liches were upon them, and there was nothing but flying steel and the growing army of the walking dead.

Hawk raised his axe to strike at the sorcerer, and an invisible force tore the axe from his hand. It spun clattering down the hall, and Hawk ran after it. He knew when he was outclassed. He snatched up his axe and waded into one of the liches from behind, severing its spine. It fell to the floor, and tried to crawl forward. Hawk jumped across it and moved among the dead with his axe, and they fell back from the sheer force of his attack. Medley seized the moment to move in beside Roxanne, his sword at the ready.

"You've got to get Adamant out of here," he said quickly.

"He's the important one. The Guards and I can hold these things off long enough to give you a good start."

"But what about you?" said Roxanne.

"I don't matter."

"You matter to me," said Roxanne, and kept on fighting.

Adamant had drawn his sword and Dannielle had her dagger, but even with their help, the little group was still driven back down the hall towards the waiting sorcerer. The dead men wouldn't stop, no matter how badly they were injured. They just kept pressing forward, swinging their swords, even if they had to crawl and drag themselves along the floor to do it. Adamant swung his sword in short, efficient arcs, even though he knew the faces that clustered before him. They had been his men, sworn to his service. Some of them had even been friends. They died because they sided with him, and now he had to kill them again.

Get ready, said Mortice suddenly in Hawk's mind. *I'm going to use my magic to cancel out Wulf's. When I give you the word, kill him. You'll have to be quick. He's become very powerful; I can't hold him more than a moment or two. If I wasn't already dead, I think I might be frightened. I never thought to see the Abomination rise again. Now, Hawk; do it now!*

Hawk drew back his arm and threw the axe with all his strength. It flew down the hall and buried itself in Wulf's skull. The sorcerer staggered back a pace under the impact, and then fell to one knee. His head slowly bowed, as though the weight of the axe was dragging it down. The liches froze in their tracks, and then slumped to the floor and didn't move again. Wulf fell forward and lay still.

Hawk hesitated a moment, unable to believe it was all over, and then walked forward to stand over the fallen sorcerer. He put his boot on the skull, reached down, and pulled the axe free. One look at the jagged wound was enough to convince him that the sorcerer was dead. No one could have survived a wound like that.

And then the body began to twitch. Hawk backed quickly away. Wulf's body shook and trembled and convulsed, the limp arms and legs flapping wildly. The black robe stretched and tore and the dead sorcerer's body split apart like some monstrous chrysalis. And out of the broken body blossomed the Abomination, drawing substance from the dead sorcerer to form a new body that was closer to its own nature. It filled the hall, its bony head brushing the ceiling. Its face was all mouth and teeth, and its muscles glistened wetly around its misshapen bones. Its twisted arms ended in foot-long claws. It stood like a man, but there was nothing human in it.

It was Hungry.

Free, said an awful voice. *Free* . . .

"I think we're in trouble," said Hawk.

"You might just be right," said Fisher. "Everyone start backing away. Maybe we can outrun the bastard."

"Stuff that," said Roxanne. "I'm going to kill it."

The Abomination surged forward, covering the space between them with impossible speed. The small group stood together and braced themselves to meet it. It burst among them with horrid strength, shrugging off their blows and scattering the group like so many skittles. The Abomination had got out, and there was nothing they could do to stop it.

In the laundry room, the trapdoor suddenly blew open, shattering its hinges and flinging the pieces aside. Down in the darkness of the cellar something stirred, and then slowly, one step at a time, the dead man came up the stairs and out into the light. Mortice was little more than a shrivelled husk by now, but his power was upon him, rippling the air around him like a heat haze. He moved purposefully towards the door, his cold body steaming in the warmth of the laundry room.

Hawk and Fisher fought side by side, keeping the Abomination at bay with the sheer energy of their attack. Their blades struck the Being again and again, but did it no harm, the steel ringing harmlessly from its hide as though it were armoured. Roxanne threw herself at the Abomination again and again, howling with fury and frustration. Adamant and Medley protected Dannielle as best they could, but all of them knew the Being was only toying with them. Soon it would grow tired of its game and let its hunger run free, and then all the steel in the world wouldn't be enough to save them. They fought on anyway. There was nothing else to do.

The Abomination spun round suddenly, ignoring its attackers to stare down the hall. Mortice grinned back at it, his skin cracking like brittle parchment. The Lord of the Gulfs cocked its awful head to one side, and a voice burned in all their minds like a red-hot iron sinking into flesh.

You cannot save them. I am free. I walk the world again. Neither the living nor the dead can stop me. This was promised me at my creation.

"I'm neither living nor dead," said Mortice. "I'm both. Goodbye, James."

He spoke a Word of Power, and an unnatural fire roared up around him, consuming him. The Abomination screamed and turned to flee. Mortice gestured sharply with one burning arm, and a fireball shot down the hall to engulf the Being. It fell to the floor, tearing at its own flesh as it strove to put out the flames. Mortice strode unsteadily down the hall, already half-consumed by the flames, and embraced the Being in his burning arms. There was a blinding flash of light and a fading scream, and then they were both gone, and the hall was still and quiet once again.

Hawk and Fisher looked at each other and put away their weapons. Adamant and Medley did the same. Roxanne padded down the hall, glaring about her, and only then reluctantly put away her sword. Adamant looked sombrely at the wide scorch mark on the floor that was all that remained to show where Mortice and the Abomination had been destroyed.

"Rest easy, my friend," he said quietly. "Maybe now you'll find some peace."

There was a polite cough from behind them, and they all spun round, weapons once more at the ready. The Council messenger standing in the open doorway looked at the levelled blades and swallowed hard. "I could always come back later. . . ."

"I'm sorry," said Adamant, lowering his sword. "We've had a rather trying day. What can I do for you?"

"I bear greetings and salutations from the Council," said the messenger, looking a little happier now that he was back on familiar ground. "The election's over. You won. Congratulations. Can I go now?"

Adamant smiled and nodded, and the messenger disappeared at speed. Adamant turned and looked at the others.

"I always thought it would mean more. I've paid a high price in friends and lives for this moment, and now I'm not even sure it's worth it."

"Of course it's worth it," said Medley. "You didn't fight this election for yourself; you fought it for the poor and the scared and the helpless, who couldn't fight for themselves. They believed in you. Are you going to let them down?"

Adamant shook his head slowly. "No. You're right, Stefan. The battle's over, but the war goes on."

Hawk and Fisher looked at each other. "I wonder if Hardcastle got a message too?" said Hawk.

Fisher grinned. "If he did, I hope the messenger's quick on his feet."

At Brimstone Hall, the silence was defeaning. The messenger had delivered the election results written down on a scroll, thus ensuring he had time to get away before the storm broke. Hardcastle looked disbelievingly at the parchment in his hands. He didn't need to read it out. His expression was enough. People put down their plates and glasses, and one by one they began to leave.

Hardcastle snapped out of his daze, stepped forward and began to speak in a loud, carrying voice. He would win them back. He always had. But this time the crowd reacted to his usual mixture of boasts and threats with sullen glances and open anger. Someone shouted an insult. Somebody else threw something. In moments the crowd became an angry mob, pushing and shoving. Fights broke out. Hardcastle was forgotten in the flurry of old grudges and recriminations. He stopped speaking and looked around him with something like horror. They weren't listening. He had lost the election, and as far as the Conservatives were concerned, that meant he wasn't anybody anymore.

He never heard the quiet scuff of steel on leather as Jillian drew the knife from its hidden sheath. The first he knew of it was when she plunged it into his back, again and again and again.

10

Making Deals

Adamant was throwing another victory party, and everyone who was anyone was there. He hadn't really felt like it, but his superiors had insisted. With Reform now holding the High Steppes, the Council was under Reform control for the first time in its history. As long as they were careful not to upset the independents.

The party filled the main dining hall, and spilled over into adjoining rooms. There was a huge buffet, and a dozen different kinds of highly alcoholic punch. The noise was deafening. All the movers and shakers from both the Reform and Conservative Causes had come to meet the new Councillor, and jockey for position. The Brotherhood of Steel had provided a small army of men-at-arms to ensure the party's security, for which Hawk and Fisher were grateful. It meant they could finally relax and get some serious drinking done. It had been a long day.

Adamant and Dannielle stood together, arm in arm, smiling at everyone. They seemed thoroughly reconciled, though whether that was just for public consumption was of course open to question. Personally, Hawk thought they'd make it. He hadn't missed the way Dannielle shielded Adamant with her own body when Roxanne led the attack against him. If it hadn't been for Mortice's magic she'd have died out there on the streets, and both of them knew it. Hawk smiled to himself. They'd make it.

Speaking of Roxanne . . . Hawk let his gaze wander across the crowd and there she was, towering over everyone, with an arm draped comfortably across Medley's shoulders. Everyone was giving her plenty of room, but she seemed to be behaving herself. Officially, Hawk was supposed to arrest her on sight, but he wasn't in the mood. Both she and Medley were leaving Haven first thing the next morning, and he'd settle for that. If his superiors didn't like it, they could go after her themselves. He'd send flowers to their funerals.

He looked at Fisher, standing beside him lost in her own thoughts, and smiled fondly. "Well, Isobel, what do you think of democracy in action, now that you've seen it up close?"

Fisher shrugged. "Looked much like any other form of politics to me; corruption and scandal and a sprinkling of honest men. I know what you want me to say, Hawk; you want me to get all excited because Reform won this one. But take a look around you; the big men from both sides are already getting together and making deals."

"Yes, Isobel, but the difference here is in what the Reformers are making deals about. The deals they make are for other people's benefit, not their own."

Fisher laughed, and put her arm through his. "Maybe. In the meantime, let's count our blessings. Adamant is still alive; so are we, and Haven got through the election without civil war breaking out."

"Yeah," said Hawk. "Not a bad day's work, all told."

They laughed and drank wine together, while all around them the chatter of guests filled the hall, deciding the future.

314